Mistress of London

Helen's Story

Helen's Story
Ladies of Independent Means Trilogy, Book 3

Evelyn Richardson

Kenmore, WA

A Camel Press book published by Epicenter Press

Epicenter Press
6524 NE 181st St.
Suite 2
Kenmore, WA 98028

For more information go to:
www.Camelpress.com
www.Coffeetownpress.com
www.Epicenterpress.com
www.evelynrichardson.net

All rights reserved. No part of this book may be reproduced or transmitted in any form or by any means, electronic or mechanical, including photocopying, recording, or any information storage and retrieval system, without permission in writing from the publisher.

This is a work of fiction. Names, characters, places, brands, media, and incidents are either the product of the author's imagination or are used fictitiously.

Cover design by Scott Book
Interior design by Melissa Vail Coffman

Mistress of London: Helen's Story
Copyright © 2022 by Evelyn Richardson

ISBN: 978-1-94207-894-4 (Trade Paper)
ISBN: 978-1-94207-895-1 (eBook)

Library of Congress Control Number: 2022935076

Printed in the United States of America

*To Carol Mahoney, the epitome of my heroine:
inspiring boss, devoted mentor, and generous friend
whose example led me to coin the phrase
"intimidation through fashion"*

Acknowledgments

No one could ask for a more generous and complete resource than all the dedicated authors of Regency Fiction Writers. Thank you.

Prologue

Julian was doing his best to hurry his niece and her mother through the press of people surging out of the theater towards their carriages and freedom from the mind-numbing social chatter of the two ladies. Yes, he had promised to foot the entire bill for Lady Charlotte's come-out, but he had not signed up to be a constant escort. Hiring a slim, elegant townhouse in Hill Street for the Season was something he could handle easily; not being thoroughly irritated by his companions was something else entirely, and far more difficult. *The Mountaineer*, an utterly unsurprising and uninspiring play, had been saved only by Kean's brilliant performance as Octavian which had been enough to keep him from utter boredom.

"Bracebridge . . . er, Lord Linton! How delightful to see you," a voice chirped directly behind him. Julian turned to find Lady Alicia Shelburne at his elbow, her smile wide and her eyes sparkling. "I must congratulate you on your recent elev . . ."

"Loss of my brother?" He did not bother to hide the sarcasm, obvious enough even for someone as determinedly cheerful as Alicia Shelburne.

"Well, yes, naturally, I do sympathi . . ."

"I beg your pardon, but if you will excuse me, I see our carriage, and my brother's wife and daughter are quite done in with the crowd." In fact, Charlotte and her mother were, if anything, energized by the entire spectacle, but Julian hurried them away before Alicia could discover that.

Once he would have given anything to have her smile at him the way she was now, to have the eyes light up when she saw him, but now he knew better. They were not lighting up for him, Julian Bracebridge, but for his new title, Earl of Linton.

He and Alicia had been childhood friends while growing up on neighboring estates, but Julian had quickly forgotten her when he had gone to school and he had avoided coming home to the grim reality of Linton Hall on holidays in favor of visiting friends whose fathers were not abusive wastrels. It had been a shock, therefore, to discover, when he had encountered her some years later, that his former playmate had turned into a beautiful young woman who infinitely preferred dancing to pony riding, and dance he would, partnering her as often as he could until she finally told him that it was doing her reputation no good to be seen so often with a penurious younger son with no prospects. This blunt announcement, however, was delivered, with such a provocative smile that instead of flinging away in a rage, he'd resolved to prove himself more than worthy of such a treasure.

Barely pausing to say farewell to his family, Julian had shipped off to India the next month in search of fame and fortune which soon were his after he convinced a local ruler to turn his swords into ploughshares, save the expense of war, and amass a fortune in agriculture, a proposition infinitely more profitable and comfortable than fighting with his neighbors. For his cleverness, Julian had been richly rewarded with both land and jewels that he immediately sent home to purchase a commodious house in Brighton where his mother could live out the rest of her days in comfort, free of her husband's excesses.

Julian had been planning to advance himself further in the ruler's service when word of his father's death had forced him to return home only to discover that his mother had passed away soon after her husband. It was then that he discovered that the name he had made for himself as a skilled diplomat and the fortune he had amassed were too tainted by trade ever to be attractive to a diamond like Lady Alicia Shelburne, too tainted, until his brother Richard, the new Earl of Linton, and equally as irresponsible as his father, had been killed in a hunting accident, leaving Julian with heavily mortgaged estates and a niece to launch into society, and now, apparently a willing prospect in Lady Alicia.

Julian's stomach turned at the thought as he loaded his niece and sister-in-law into their carriage and headed off toward the Strand in search of distraction, any distraction. Such was his anger and disgust that he did not slow down, much less become aware of his surroundings until he reached Pall Mall where, pausing his furious pace, to draw a ragged breath, he recalled his brother once waxing rhapsodic over London's most exclusive seraglio, a Mrs. Gerrard's in nearby St. James' Square. Julian would never have trusted Richard's judgment on anything else except beautiful women and a good time. On those two topics, the former Earl of Linton was a connoisseur. *Charming conversations, excellent suppers, and exquisite ladybirds* was how he had described the august establishment, and, at this moment, charming conversations with an honest woman, ladybird or not, was just the antidote he needed—an agreed-upon price for an agreed-upon diversion, no social maneuvering, no matrimonial aspirations hidden under a coquettish exterior, just an honest, straightforward exchange to the mutual benefit of both parties involved.

Chapter 1

"Lord Linton to see you, Madam." Fenwick barely had time to announce him before the earl strode into Helen Gerrard's office, his dark blue eyes blazing with anger.

Warned by the tiniest lift of her venerable butler's eyebrows, Helen had time to lay down her pen and glance up with studied coolness from the papers spread on the desk before her.

"You wished to consult with me on something, my lord?" She had recognized, when first introduced, that Julian Bracebridge, Lord Linton was very different from his brother Richard whose blond hair, flamboyant dress, ample form and ruddy features radiated bonhomie and dissipation. In fact, she had been somewhat surprised that the tall, soberly clad gentleman with a penetrating gaze and tanned angular features was patronizing her establishment in the first place. From the little she had heard about the new earl, he had seemed to be more interested in international commerce and diplomacy than the pleasures of the flesh to be found in her discreetly elegant establishment, but she had introduced him to Dora whose sunny personality and business acumen were likely to appeal to a man who was known in the City as being the one to consult on matters of trade with Indian rulers.

Something must have gone amiss in Helen's careful calculations—a highly unusual circumstance for one who kept herself better informed than Debrett's and the social columns of *The Morning Chronicle* on the comings and goings of the Upper Ten Thousand in order to ward off the very possibility of anything going amiss.

"No, I do not wish to consult you. I wish to tell you that it is unconscionable to keep the women here under your thumb as you do. Regardless of its exclusive location in St. James' Square, your establishment is little better than a prison for them."

Most people—men and women alike—would have been more likely to label her establishment heaven than a prison. Helen had certainly dedicated a good portion of her life to making it so. Not only did she know that, but its inhabitants did too and often thanked her for it. Her conviction of the truth of this was the only thing that kept her from throwing the gentleman out immediately. Instead, she gestured to the chair in front of her desk and inquired in a deceptively earnest tone, "Pray, tell me how you arrived at such a conclusion?"

Julian did not think he was one of those prigs who stood on ceremony—demanding the respect due to his station in life and all that, but he could not help being thoroughly irritated by the condescension of it all, being made to sit before her like some misbehaving schoolboy and questioned in a tone that implied that he was some overdramatic bounder.

It didn't help that the exquisitely dressed, coolly poised woman with inscrutable green eyes sitting across from him was stunningly beautiful and not at all like the greedy old crone one would expect to be running a place like this. "I offered Miss Barlow a townhouse in Marylebone, ample pin money and the management of all of it as my mistress and . . ." he paused, overcome with incredulity at the effrontery of it all, ". . . and she refused."

"She has a perfect right to you know." The conciliatory tone only infuriated him more.

"Only someone being held hostage by God-knows-what means would refuse such a flattering and generous offer."

That did it! Now Helen was thoroughly annoyed. "And why would she accept the use of a house in Marylebone from some man only for as long as she pleases him when she already owns one there herself?"

"What?"

There! That had shaken the self-righteous prig out of his self-congratulatory complacency.

"Yes, her own house."

"Then why? Then why . . ." All at sea, Julian hated himself for babbling like an idiot instead of the worldly businessman he was.

"Does she remain here? For the companionship and the remuneration. The inhabitants of my establishment earn more in one evening than most clergymen hope to earn in a year, and they are also provided with lodging." She gestured vaguely in the direction of the drawing room whose elegance far surpassed that of the house Julian had rented for his niece and her mother. "In addition to which we have set up an annuity for ourselves as well as a Beneficiary Society to provide for us in case of misfortune, not to mention the consols or canal shares in which so many of us have invested on our own. Now I suggest you look for companionship elsewhere, my lord. After all, to men of your type, one woman is so like another you will never notice the difference and we have no further wish for your company here."

There, that should silence his high-and-mightiness. And before he could annoy her further with his idiotic questions, Helen rose and rang for Fenwick who, bless his loyal heart and finely tuned instincts, was hovering right outside the door.

"Ah Fenwick, his lordship was just leaving. Please be so good as to show him out." With that, Helen returned to her papers, studying them intently until she heard the door close behind them.

Her eyes might have been focused on the work in front of her, but Helen's mind was not. Instead it was wondering what sort of person, despite his boorish articulation of it, noticed or cared about the welfare of women in a bawdy house?

Oh Mrs. Gerrard's was exclusive, its clients carefully scrutinized as much for their position in the *ton* as their ability to pay its exorbitant prices, but it still provided essentially the same services as any seraglio to be found in the stews around Covent Garden, even though its inhabitants were well-spoken, cultured, beautifully turned out, and exquisitely mannered. So why did a man availing himself of these services care so much that they were freely given, in a manner of speaking? While her customers were more likely to haunt her drawing room in search of companionship and charming conversation than those seeking the satisfaction of their baser desires in Covent Garden, they were still seeking distraction and the opportunity to forget the cares and responsibilities of the larger world; yet this man had thrown himself back into these cares by confronting her over Dora's wellbeing. Why?

Helen nibbled her pen thoughtfully as she tried to remember what little she knew of the Bracebridge family and the Earls of Linton. A gentle rap on the door interrupted these musings, and before she could answer, Dora's merry face peeked around it.

Dora! Just the person to cast more light on the situation. The most down-to-earth of all of Mrs. Gerrard's ladies, the former innkeeper's daughter had seen a larger slice of life than all of them and could be counted on to offer sage advice and penetrating remarks on anyone from any walk of life.

"I hope I am not interrupting but I thought you might have experienced a rather uncomfortable visit from Lord Linton."

"No more challenging than I could deal with."

Dora grinned. "I have no doubt about that, but I am sorry for having caused any unpleasantness, however unintended on my part. His lordship has been both entertaining and instructional. I had no idea that my refusal of his offer, graciously delivered though it was, would send him off in such a fit of pique.

There was no time to explain myself, which I certainly would have, if he had not stalked off in high dudgeon before I could open my mouth. I cannot imagine what set him off."

"He thinks, or he thought, for you can be sure I was quick to set him straight, that I am holding you captive here by some nefarious means." Helen's eyes glinted as she relived his lordship's brutal enlightenment. "He was somewhat surprised to discover that the promise the temporary use of a house in Marylebone held no allure for someone who owns one there."

Dora chuckled. "I imagine he was, though I am sorry he has been given his conge. I imagine you have sent him to the right about."

"I have. *No one* questions Mrs. Gerrard." The pride in Helen's voice was hard won. Upon the death of her father, she had been forced to earn her living as a governess where she was quickly cast off after having been raped by her employer, and she had fought her way back from being an unemployable governess to mistress of a highly respected, excruciatingly exclusive and lucrative establishment, and fierce protector of similarly preyed-upon young women who, in her care, won back their own measure of self-respect thanks to her encouragement and the offer of a better education than most men could hope to receive. In addition, there was the pay and the investment opportunities. Yes she was proud.

"You are quite right to dismiss him though I did find him most interesting."

"Interesting?" Helen's tone might be scornful, but this was the information she had been hoping for, much as she hated to admit it. The man presented a puzzle—rudeness in the service of compassion—and Helen, something of a connoisseur of human nature after years of experience could not help being intrigued even though she hated herself for being so.

"Yes. His tales of India are fascinating, dealing with warlike Zamindars and bickering rajahs, tales not told the way you might expect. He did not brag of covering himself with glory in daring exploits but of learning their language and customs so he could get them to trust one another, encouraging agriculture instead of war—so much better for everyone. He also introduced wider education and began working to improve their legal system. Not at all the sort of person you would expect to frequent our establishment, even as enlightened as we are. Now he is struggling to improve the cultivation on his own estates which, I gather, have been going to rack and ruin for some time. Now I gather he has come to London to launch his niece in her first Season not a task to his liking I can tell. Perhaps that is what put him in such a temper."

"It matters not what put him in a temper. We do not allow men like that here, having learned during our unfortunate incident with Basil Harcourt what trouble temper can cause."

Dora's sunny features clouded. "Yes, a thoroughly bad and brutal man,

Basil Harcourt, despite his being Viscount Wormleigh and our dear Freddy's future brother-in-law." Then she brightened. "However, if it hadn't been for that dreadful episode we would not have Freddy's brother conducting holy services here and matching wits with you at the card table or Tom Sandys as our second footman."

It took no special skills on Helen's part to see that the footman, former batman to Lord Adrian, Freddy's other brother rated very high indeed in Dora's estimation, or to hear the fondness in her voice when she spoke of the Claverton brothers: Freddy, Marquess of Wrothingham, the Reverend Lord John Claverton of St. George's Hanover Square, and Major Lord Adrian Claverton, late of His Majesty's Life Guards.

"Yes, well not all bad-tempered men are related, or about to be, to men as outstanding as the Clavertons. I believe we are well rid of Lord Linton, and the sooner we forget we ever knew him, the better. Now tell me, are the builders quite finished with your house in Marylebone, and have you found lodgers yet?"

Helen might have moved onto other topics, but Dora could see that Lord Linton's high-handed treatment still rankled. After all that Helen Gerrard had been through, she was not about to let anyone ruffle her composure; indeed she remained as coolly elegant and dispassionate as ever as she turned back to the papers in front of her, but Dora had seen the flash in those green eyes. Simple dismissal of the gentleman in question was not enough. Helen's pride was involved and apparently it was crucial to demonstrate to him just how very mistaken he had been. Dora hid a sly smile as she headed back to her bedchamber to pore over *The True State of the British Nation as to Trade, Commerce & etc.*, the book that had been recommended in a letter from Grace, Lady Maximilian Hawkesbury, now pursuing her musical career in Milan, as being something her husband thought Dora would find most enlightening.

Chapter 2

Ensconced in front of the fire in his chambers with a glass of port in his hand, Julian re-lived the scene in St. James' Square. The abrupt dismissal by a presumptuous abbess should not have rankled; after all Julian had never taken himself so seriously that he could not let slights and insults roll off his back without turning a hair. This sanguine attitude had, in a large part, been responsible for his success in both business and diplomatic endeavors. But this did rankle, mostly because he had been in the wrong, something that had been pointed out to him with brutal honesty. That he did not pre-judge people had also figured into his success, but again, in this instance, he had failed miserably by forgetting this, one of his cardinal rules, by prejudging Helen Gerrard. The intriguing woman behind the paper-laden desk had not in the least been what he had expected, and because of it, she had completely gotten the better of him.

Seeing a woman in the course of managing her business, as evidenced by the various account books and bills she was obviously laboring over, had been something of a shock and a revelation to Julian. Much as he hated to admit it, he had never imagined a woman as being interested or capable of such a thing, though, come to think of it, one of the very reasons he had enjoyed Dora's company so much was her genuine interest in the minutiae of his business affairs. Nor had he expected a woman to have the shelves full of mathematical treatises that had lined one wall of Helen Gerrard's office.

Then to discover that the woman behind the desk was young and stunningly beautiful had completed his defeat before he had even opened his mouth. He had met Mrs. Gerrard in the drawing room on first entering her establishment and she had introduced him to Dora. He had just never expected that the stylish sophisticated woman who had greeted him so graciously was actually the owner when, in truth, she looked more like one of her ladies than a successful businesswoman. It had not helped either that Julian found himself oddly drawn to her, with her understated elegance, enigmatic smile, and observant eyes. She exuded the subtle power of intelligence, knowledge, and confidence that drew him to her in the strangest way when they met and he had the oddest feeling that she reminded him of someone, though he could not for the life of him think who. But then the ebullient Dora with her ripe curves, ready smile and bouncing good humor had taken over and he had forgotten his mysterious hostess until he had found himself facing her over her desk, and not to his advantage.

Julian re-lived that meeting more than he cared to over the next several days, the image of the auburn-haired, emerald-eyed proprietress intruding at the most inopportune moments as he visited his newly docked ship to inspect its cargo or pored over dispatches from India at the Board of Control preparing to make recommendations to its members, should they need them.

And now he felt in need of greater distraction, any distraction, which meant that he was looking forward to the opening of Rossini's new opera that evening, *Il Barbiere di Seviglia*. Granted, he would have to put up with the company of his sister-in-law and his niece in order to enjoy it, but he was accustomed enough to blocking out their mindless chatter at the routs and balls to which they insisted he escort them that it was unlikely to bother him at the opera where he would sit back and enjoy the music as Maria and Charlotte sat at the front of their box commenting on the costumes and the conversations of the box-holders around them.

However, when Julian and the women arrived at their box that evening it was to discover it was already occupied by two women, elegantly, if quietly dressed, one in the somber hues of half mourning, and the other in the modest garb of a companion to the widow, The two women, who had been talking quietly when they entered look up in some surprise as Charlotte turned to her mother. "Mama, who are these . . ."

"Hush, Charlotte," her mother admonished in her most authoritative Countess of Linton tone, "your uncle will make inquiries."

"I beg your pardon, ladies." Ignoring his sister-in-law's clear expectation that he would eject the interlopers as swiftly and forcefully as possible, Julian smiled encouragingly, "Perhaps there has been some mistake?"

"Oh dear." The widow, a rather stunning raven-haired beauty of no more than thirty years, smiled apologetically. "In my eagerness to be here, I might have been a bit careless. Is this not Mrs. Fellowes' box? She is a distant cousin of my late lamented husband and she gave me use of her box because she knows I am particularly desirous of seeing this opera." A heavy jet bracelet slid up her gloved arm as she help up a ticket for Julian to examine.

"Ah no, Mrs . . . er"

"Ward," the widow supplied.

"Mrs. Ward, this ticket is for several boxes down. If you will permit me to escort you and . . . ," he glanced at her companion.

"Mrs. Taylor."

"I shall be happy to locate it for you."

"Really, Linton," his sister-in-law broke in, "the box-keeper can show them to their places. There is not the least need for you to trouble yourself."

"No need, perhaps, but I would be happy to." Julian held out one arm to the widow who rose, revealing a tall graceful figure, and the other to her companion. The widow smiled gratefully. . "I thank you, kind sir, and I apologize for intruding into your . . ."

"The Earl of Linton's box," the Countess supplied with a haughty swish of her skirts as she directed her daughter to her seat and then took her own.

"It is I who should apologize," Julian began *sotto voce* as they exited the box. "My sister-in-law does come across as a trifle severe when agitated or surprised."

"I see." The hint of a smile tugged at the corner of Mrs. Ward's mouth. "And here I thought it was my lack of a title."

He chuckled. "That too. But in her defense, Lady Linton is doing her best in a trying situation: her daughter's come-out and she is recently widowed.

"Ah, the Season, a time when every conversation, every encounter is fraught with social implications, and one is constantly posing oneself the question *Will it improve or will it ruin my daughter's chances of making a Catch?*

Julian grinned. "You are a marvel of perspicacity, and she may be given some excuse because she has not been much on the town so she worries a great deal over her lack of town bronze and social connections. But here we are," he led them the door of into the correct box. "I do hope the opera lives up to your expectations."

"Oh, I try never to have expectations, my lord. I find one can enjoy life much more that way. Come, Mrs. Taylor." And with that, the widow ducked into the box, leaving Julian to wonder if her smile were really that mischievous or if he had imagined it.

He was still pondering that, and Mrs. Ward in general, as the first strains of the overture floated over the general hum of conversation, but was soon caught up in the activity on stage. By the end of the first act, however he could not help wondering if the young composer's work held up to Mrs. Ward's expectations, even though she didn't deign to have them, and his focus shifted during the next act from the stage to her box where she watched with a concentration that set her apart from everyone else in the theater. What was her interest, for surely such an ingenious work, though delightful, was not the sort of thing to evoke the intensity reflected in her face or her posture?

Before Julian could even think up an excuse to seek out the answer to this question, his sister-in-law intervened. The curtain had not completely fallen between the opera and the ballet when she turned to him. "I see Lady Alicia over there nodding to us. Surely she wants us to visit her in her box, for there are far too many visitors there for her to leave them and come here." Giving Julian no time to reply, she rose and held out her arm.

There was nothing for it, but to endure Alicia's effusive, "My lord, how delightful to see you. I would never have guessed you to be a musical devotee, but perhaps it is just your kindness to my dearest Maria and Charlotte that brings you here." The arch smile accompanying this little speech made Julian want to do his former playmate a mischief, but he distracted himself by casting frantically about for an excuse, any excuse, to extricate himself.

"Ah, I see Canning over there. I must speak to him."

"Canning? But Charlotte and I have just . . ."

"It is about business at the Board of Control."

"Oh, business. Well then." The countess turned back to Lady Alicia. "Now tell me, do you go to Lady Cholmondeley's ball?"

Lady Alicia was forced to turn away from Julian to reply, and with a sigh of relief, he slipped out of the box and was soon being welcomed by Mr. Ward and her companion. "My lord, this is a delightful surprise!"

"I wanted to assure myself that you ladies are enjoying the opera."

"You are too kind. There was no need for you to desert your companions to inquire into the well-being of two dull matrons."

So she had been observing him as carefully as he had been observing her. How intriguing.

"But perhaps we are in the nature of an escape?"

There was no mistaking the mischievous twinkle in her eyes this time nor the provocative smile.

"Escape?"

"Come my lord, don't play the innocent with me. I am more than seven, you know, and I can tell a determined pursuit of a man by a women when I see one, even from across the theater. And," the smile faded, and he thought he detected just the faintest hint of sympathy, "a single man in possession of a title is constant prey, especially in London at the height of the Season. It is good of you to escort your sister-in-law and niece. Most men would not risk their peace of mind in such and endeavor."

"You are observant indeed, Mrs. Ward." Her tone might have been ironic, but Julian was strangely gratified by her remark. It was nice to be appreciated. "But tell me, how do you like the opera? You seemed to be enthralled."

"Did I now?" She tilted her head to give him an appraising look. "I suppose I was. In general, I find it amusing rather than enthralling, but I was much interested in how Madame Fodor performed *Un voce poco fa*.

"You were?"

"Yes. A dear friend asked me particularly to pay attention to it."

"She must be quite musical."

A wistful expression flitted across her features—gone in an instant. "That she is," she replied, almost as though she were speaking to herself.

Julian was silent for a moment. This woman had unusual depths. But before he could frame a suitable response, the orchestra struck up for the ballet. "Excuse me. I must return to my companions, but thank you for your conversation and the *escape!*"

Mrs. Ward regarded him speculatively, then, seeming to come to some sort of decision, dug in her reticule. "I too enjoyed the conversation. Should you wish to continue it, my lord, here is my direction. We are going directly home after the performance and would welcome further discussion of your impressions of the opera." This time there was no mistaking the smile; it was a promise.

Chapter 3

Julian was more than ready to take her up on that promise. There was something about the woman that drew him to her. Was it her close observation, her quick wit, or the depths of expression in those eyes that hinted she had seen a great deal too much of the world? Or it could it be that delicious mouth, the elegant figure, or the way she carried herself with grace and assurance. Whatever it was, he wanted to explore it further.

But not this evening, his good sense cautioned him. He had not dealt with power-hungry potentates and their devious underlings in India for nothing. It was all very well and good to pursue one's desires energetically, but not rashly. Caution never failed to triumph in the end.

It was not until later the next day, therefore, that he presented himself at the tidy house at 5 Wyndham place to be let in by a maid who seemed a good deal surprised to see him.

"Mrs. Ward? Er, yes, my lord, I shall just see if she is receiving visitors."

The girl reappeared some moments later and led him sedately, actually, rather slowly, he thought, to the drawing room.

"I hope I am not intruding."

"Not at all. I am delighted to see you."

There was nothing in the welcoming smile or the tidiness of the room to suggest he had caught its occupant unawares, despite the initial impression Julian had received from the maid. In fact he seemed to have disturbed nothing more exciting than reading, if the book on the table beside Mrs. Ward were any indication: *the Philosophy of Arithmetic exhibiting a Progressive View of the Theory and Practice of Calculation.*

Julian drew a sharp breath and stared into the emerald eyes fixed curiously on him. "I do believe that is the book that was sitting on your desk when I was so brutally dismissed from your establishment, Mrs. Gerrard. And I take it that now I am to admit that to men of my type *One woman is so like another* I *will never notice the difference.* To give you your due, Mrs. Gerrard, I did not notice ... until now."

His icy tone would have frozen the brashest of potentates, but Helen merely smiled up at him with that enigmatic smile as she pulled off the raven wig. "I see I have misjudged you, my lord. Oh, not about the one woman being so like another, but about your powers of perception. Dora warned me you were exceedingly clever. I should have paid more attention."

With which remark, Dora's voice floated up the stairs. "Good morning, Rose. Freddy and I have come so he can advise me as to the decorations. I ..."

"The house in Marylebone," Julian muttered, shaking his head in exasperation at his own stupidity.

"Precisely." Helen smirked and then turned to welcome her visitors. "Dora, Wrothingham."

Her visitors stopped dead in the doorway.

"Come in, come in. His lordship was just leaving."

"Lord Linton!" Dora's smile was as broad and genuine as ever, but he had not missed her furtive glance in her employer's direction. She turned to the man whose arm was linked with hers, "Lord Linton, may I present you to Lord Wrothingham who is being so kind as to share his considerable taste and expertise with me."

Freddy, Marquess of Wrothingham, acknowledged Julian with a friendly nod, but it was clear his attention was elsewhere as he examined the room. "Yes, the rose colored damask we looked at for the draperies will do very well, but you need something else to soften the light through the windows. Muslin, I would say. Ackermann suggests *white transparent voile* for that sort of thing. Filtered light is so much more flattering than the pitiless glare of broad daylight, don't you think?" He surveyed the group with a satisfied smile.

"And I know just where you can find some exquisite muslin."

Three sets of eyes swiveled towards Julian. There! That had caught their attention, though why he should be so eager to do so, he could not say. "Yes, my ship has just brought in a superb supply of muslin from India. Oh, I know Indian muslin is being discouraged in favor of our national supply, but I have some special contacts who do remarkable work for which they should be rewarded."

"Excellent! I should be delighted to take a look." Freddy's eyes brightened. "And what other treasures does your ship have in its hold, Linton?"

"Oh, teak, rosewood, mahogany—beautiful enough to make a cabinetmaker weep." It was a calculatedly offhand reply, but Julian knew he'd captured Wrothingham's' interest. From his intricately tied cravat to the exquisitely embroidered waistcoat, Freddy, Marquess of Wrothingham, practically shouted out connoisseur.

"His lordship is something of a cabinet-maker himself." Dora directed a teasing glance in Freddy's direction, "at least the design part of it. The looking glass he had made for Maison Juliette is absolutely splendid."

"Doing it much too brown," Freddy waved a dismissive hand, but his self-conscious blush betrayed his pleasure at the compliment. "But I should like to see the wood as well."

"As it happens, I am on my way to the warehouse now if you don't mind riding in my curricle." Julian had, had no such plans, but who was he to quibble when such and excellent means of escape from an awkward situation presented itself?

"I should be delighted, that is, if you two ladies would honor me by making used of my carriage to return to St. James' Square. No time like the present, eh, Linton?"

And with that, the two men were out the door, one with a sigh of relief, the other with the look of a hound with his nose to the ground in search of quarry.

"Well, did you ever?" Dora grinned as they heard the door below shut behind the men. "Didn't I tell you he was clever?"

"Awake on every suit." Helen shook her head ruefully as she deposited the wig on the offending book. "In my defense, he was completely taken by my subterfuge at the theater and it wasn't until he recognized Mr. Leslie's *Philosophy of Arithmetic* that he realized." She frowned. "Though he was cautious enough not to follow his baser instincts by visiting me last night—a man to be reckoned with, that is certain. He certainly took Freddy's measure immediately. The new Earl of Linton seems to have escaped the Bracebridge propensity for mind-numbing self- indulgence and drink. I do wonder how he and Freddy are enjoying the warehouse."

Helen had changed the subject deftly enough, but Dora was not fooled. What was it about the man that had made her go to such lengths to prove herself superior to him? Dora was not the only one asking this question. Helen herself wondered exactly the same thing. Why had this man made such an impression on her when no one else in all the years of seeing them pass through her drawing room had? Not only had he made an impression, he'd gotten under her skin enough to inspire her to enter into a ridiculous caper that was utterly beneath the queen of one of London's most select establishments.

Enjoying the warehouse was putting it mildly as Freddy examined the treasures laid out for him. "The muslin is just the thing, and you are entirely correct; it is far superior to English manufacture. But look at this brocade! It is exceedingly fine."

"Ah, well, Benares is noted for it. The . . ."

"And this shawl! Lady Adrian simply must visit—with your permission of course."

"Lady Adrian?"

"My sister-in-law, Lady Adrian Claverton, proprietress of Maison Juliette." Freddy shook his head in mock dismay at Julian's blank expression. "What? You have not heard of it? Have you no female relatives? It is quite simply the most sought-after modiste in all of London. One cannot hope to be *le dernier cri* unless one patronizes Maison Juliette, which never would have existed without Helen Gerrard."

Julian's blank expression morphed into bemused incomprehension.

"Mademoiselle Juliette Fanchon, actually Juliete de Flournoy, first got her start creating costumes for all of them at Mrs. Gerrard's—still does—until she met my brother Adrian. Now she is mostly at Ashbourne Hall with her son and husband while Alice runs the shop, but Lady Adrian does all the designs and selects the materials. She would be in transports over the lovely things you have here." Freddy sighed rapturously as he ran his fingers over the brocade. "How fortunate you are, sir, to seek out and procure such beauty." Then his eye caught the wood across the room and hurried over. "I don't believe I have ever seen mahogany so fine. Is it spoken for?"

"Julian shook his head.

"There is still much furniture needed at Wrothingham Abbey before it is habitable. I would dearly love to have my cabinet-maker use this piece to make some of it."

"It is yours, but surely it will take some time to turn it into furniture, and if you are hoping to live at . . ."

"No, there is all the time in the world. Lady Lavinia and I have been promised to one another since the cradle; no need to rush things," he explained so hastily that Julian arrived at his own conclusions about the nature of a betrothal which did not seem to be leading very swiftly to the desired event.

They eventually returned to the curricle and parted amicably as Julian dropped Freddy off at Claverton House after making plans for further negotiations on the mahogany.

Julian drove home in a thoughtful mood, its chief aspect being admiration for Helen Gerrard who, though she had not ultimately succeeded in deceiving him, had certainly proven her point. She had also proven her claims for providing for her employees exceedingly well. But it was more than money she supplied; that was clear to anyone who paid attention, and the Earl of Linton was definitely paying attention. It took more than money, it took confidence and inspiration to build a house in Marylebone or become a fashionable modiste in the capital of the *ton*. That was what Helen Gerrard gave her ladies—challenge and self-confidence. Julian had heard it in the pride in her voice and the assurance with which she had ordered him out of her establishment—an establishment he was now determined to visit again—not to take advantage of the entertainment offered, but to learn how she had done it.

Chapter 4

At the moment, Helen was not offering challenge and inspiration as much as much as she was escape as she welcomed her longtime friend and confidant, the well-known actress and singer, Olivia Childs. It was to Olivia that Juliette, now Lady Adrian Claverton, had fled when forced out on the street by her employer and Olivia's modiste, Madame Celeste. It was also Olivia who had rescued Grace, now Lady Maximilian Hawkesbury, when the owner of the theater where her father conducted the orchestra had forced himself on her and then cast her off when her father, whose employment she had guaranteed by her submission to Mr. Smedley, died. And now Olivia was here again with another tale of misery and abuse.

"This time I do not know what to do. Annie Bentley is no longer young, so she is not fit to be a maid or anything else in your establishment, and her spirit has been entirely destroyed by that vicious beast, her husband." Olivia stared down at her hands as she struggled to control herself. "I should have guessed he was a wife-beater. After all, I left the traveling theater company he managed in the Midlands because of his nasty temper. Why would I think that a man who visited such anger on me and others would not have also visited it on his wife? But she seemed to adore him so," the actress choked down a sob, "idolizing him as a dramatic genius and making excuses for him because of it. How could I have been so blind?"

Helen rose from her desk to take the chair opposite her friend, clasping her hands in a comforting grip. "If this happened before you came here to the Sans Pareil, it must have been many years ago. You were much younger then, intent on making a career for yourself and far too busy to see what was happening, and far too intent on defending yourself against this man, not to mention far too inexperienced to be able to deal with such a situation."

"I suppose so." Olivia sighed. "And Annie was older than I—so sophisticated, so beautiful, so successful that this man, her manager, fell in love with her, married her, and swore to take care of her which, to my naïve eyes, he did; buying her trinkets, praising her extravagantly, establishing her in a fine house with servants. I suppose the bruises I saw upon her arm one day did not come from tripping and falling into a chair, nor the dislocated shoulder from a riding accident. Now I know the bruises that I saw around her neck today bear the marks of his hand, as does the livid patch on her cheek."

"She is with you now?"

"Yes. I called my physician to attend her, but all he could do was apply poultices and prescribe rest." Olivia shook her head sadly. "All these years we have been writing one another and she never let on."

"Writing one another?" Helen rose and began to pace the room. "Then she has your direction . . . and so does her husband. You had best bring her here. We cannot have you risking this man's wrath and brutality by harboring his runaway wife."

Olivia's eyes shone with tears. "Thank you, Helen. You are right of course. I knew you would understand."

"Only too well after the tales my ladies have confided to me over the years."

"But Annie is not young or spirited like Juliette and Grace, nor is she very beautiful anymore—undoubtedly why her husband behaved so brutally this time that she felt she had to leave to save herself. She will never fit in here."

"It does not matter. For the moment she can stay in the spare maid's room next to Rose in the attic away from all the activity, where she can have peace and quiet and all the sympathy and understanding of the house's inhabitants when she feels well enough for company."

The actress rose, clasping her friend's hands once again. "Bless you, Helen, for your kindness to Annie . . . and so many others."

A dimple hovered at the corner of Helen's mouth. 'Your kindness too. If it hadn't been for you I would never have known Grace and Juliette, who in turn brought the Marquess of Wrothingham and his brothers, all of whom have brightened our lives."

And it was one of those brothers, the Reverend Lord John Claverton of St. George's Hanover Square, Helen planned to consult the minute her guest departed. As a man of the cloth for whom ministering others was his life's work, he might have some ideas of how to help Olivia's friend when she recovered. The reluctant rector of London's most fashionable parish, he longed for something more worthy of his energy and compassion than the privileged, the wealthy, and the bored who made up his congregation, which was why he had jumped at the chance to offer holy services and pastoral care to the inhabitants of London's most exclusive seraglio when Dora and Helen had suggested it.

"I do not know of any particular charities that minister to such unfortunate women." Lord John frowned into the cup of tea that Helen had just handed him as he sat in her office after presiding over their Sunday services. "It is a rather difficult situation, given the views on husbands' rights. I expect no one wants to challenge them for fear of being called to account on the subject. In fact," he looked up, his eyes deadly serious, "much as I applaud your generosity and your spirit, and as much as I encourage you to extend aid to the suffering, as you always do, I suggest you talk to someone who knows the law. Not," he held up a hand to forestall the inevitable retort, "that I am discouraging you in the least; I am merely encouraging you to be fully aware of what you are risking, especially since some people might see it as harboring a fugitive. Preparation is the essence of defense." He grinned. "As the best card player I have ever encountered, you know better than most that whoever can figure out the cards in one's opponent's hand is likely to win."

Helen nodded. "Much as I hate to admit it, you are right to suggest caution; however, my solicitor, clever as he is with contracts, leases, and other commercial documents, is not the sort of man to know about, or be interested in marital rights."

"I have a friend, a mathematician oddly enough, who I often see at the Mathematical Society. He was a Fellow in mathematics at Cambridge, but is now a barrister. I shall find out his direction, and perhaps he can advise you, or suggest someone who can."

"Thank you." Helen smiled gratefully, for really, she had been a little concerned herself, and if Lord John, compelled as he was to minister to those in need, was cautious, then she, a woman with no powerful family behind her, and a business to run, should be doubly so."

So it was that several days later, followed by Rose, she walked through the archway of 3 Essex Court and into the chambers of William Henry Maule, to whom she had written to request an appointment.

"Come in, come in," he greeted her in friendly fashion, pushing aside a pile of papers on his desk as he rose to greet her.

"I do appreciate your seeing me."

"Anyone recommended by Claverton is assured of being welcome here." He gestured to a chair in front of the desk as he returned to his seat and peered at her under shaggy brows. "But tell me, how may I be of assistance? You mentioned a delicate matter."

Helen gave a brief summary of Mrs. Bentley's unhappy story, what little she knew of it, as well as her own awareness of the risks she might be taking in helping the unfortunate woman.

Resting his chin on steepled hands, Maule listened intently, then leaned forward. "I am happy to advise you, but so far most of my experience has been involved with commercial questions. I do, however, know someone who might help, a fellow studying for the bar under me whose experience in trade has been most useful to me, but whose personal experience has made him passionately interested in just the sort of matter in which you are involved. An unfortunate family . . . well I will leave it to him to explain, but I think you will find him as knowledgeable as he is sympathetic, and as sympathetic as he is clever." The barrister rose and went to a door at the other side of the chamber. "Linton? There is a woman here who could benefit from your advice."

Helen's breath caught in her throat as a tall figure loomed in the doorway. It couldn't be . . .

"Mrs. Gerrard, may I present to you Lord Linton."

It was! Gathering her wits about her and keeping her face politely expressionless—she hoped—Helen rose to acknowledge him, waiting to see whether or not he would admit to any previous acquaintance.

"Mrs. Gerrard has a rather interesting situation which I shall leave her to discuss with you." And without further explanation, Mr. Maule retired to the room from which Julian had just emerged and shut the door.

"My lord," Helen sank back into the chair, but not before catching the twinkle of amusement in Julian's eyes, "I had thought you a man of business, yet I find you here."

Julian took the chair opposite her, the twinkle in his eyes now gone, his face deadly serious. "I had always meant to pursue the law. There were circumstances in my life that . . . well, let us just say, I saw situations in which wrongs cried out to be addressed, and the law seemed the only way to address them, so I took my degree in it at Oxford, only to realize that a fortune was also needed to redress those wrongs. I went to seek that in India. Now," he smiled bitterly, "I have the fortune, but the wrongs are not necessarily redressed, and thus, I have returned to the law."

Helen stared at him. I was not like her. She never let her ironic composure desert her, so she had never descended to something as stupid and inane as staring at someone, but this time she did. There were depths to this man, the man she had dismissed so summarily, that she had not known existed. Except that she had, or at least, on some level, she had guessed; hence, her elaborate charade at 5 Wyndham Place which had already proven to her how clever Julian Bracebridge, now Earl of Linton really was.

Chapter 5

"Mr. Maule says you have some expe... er, knowledge, of marital law."

"Experience is a more accurate word." There was a bitter edge to his voice, a darkness in his eyes, and a weariness in his face that told her his experience had been personal and hard won. He leaned forward to listen intently as she told him Annie's story.

"If Mrs. Bentley left her home to take shelter with someone not even related to her, the situation is dire indeed. My . . . er, no woman leaves her home in such a way unless her life is in danger, believe me. You are a good woman, Mrs. Gerrard, to offer her safety and sanctuary, but you are also wise to familiarize yourself with the law."

"I know nothing of the law, but enough of it to know that a woman ceases to exist once she marries." Helen's own voice took on an edge of its own, an ironic one. "In truth, I have more freedom, independence, and control over my life than the respectable matrons who refuse to acknowledge my existence."

"Better to be free than respectable, in my opinion, though I realize that as a man, it is easy enough for me to say that." Julian's grim smile reflected the truth of this statement. "You are entirely correct. To quote Blackstone, *By marriage, the husband and wife are one person in the law: that is, the very being or legal existence is suspended during the marriage.* He leaned forward, looking deep into her eyes. "Hurtful though it may be to you, I would prefer the independent legal existence you possess to the restricted *social* existence that people in the *ton* recognize."

There was a surprising depth of sympathy in the eyes fixed on her so intently, giving Helen the oddest feeling she had discovered a friend and ally in the most unexpected of places.

"You are, in effect, harboring someone else's property," he continued, "which could turn unpleasant for anyone who incurs a husband's wrath, but is doubly dangerous for you as the proprietress of an establishment whose impeccable reputation is much esteemed in the highest circles."

He chuckled at her surprise. "In addition to being an aspiring barrister, Mrs. Gerrard, I am a businessman. I do my research. Just as I am sure you know the family, titles, reputations, and bank accounts of your customers in minute detail, I learn the reputations and bank accounts of successful business enterprises I come across. Your friend, the Marquess of Wrothingham is a connoisseur of design and fashion, an admirer of the well-wrought snuff box, the exquisitely tied cravat, the beautifully designed interior, I am a connoisseur of a well-run enterprise, one with a carefully cultivated reputation and an enviable balance sheet. I am intrigued by how such an enterprise came to be and how it continues to grow simply because I enjoy learning such things. Yours is one of those enterprises, and I would not wish anything to stand in the way of its continued success. But I digress. You came to discover what you could do to help your unexpected guest."

"Yes," Helen nodded, but her mind was completely at sea; she was experiencing a situation and sensations entirely novel to her. This man admired her, not for her beauty, her wit, or her charm, not even for her skill at cards, but for the business she had created. And he was not praising Mrs. Gerrard's because it was London's most exclusive seraglio, but because it was a successful enterprise, much like the successful enterprise he had created. The tone of his voice, his posture as he leaned forward in his chair, elbows resting on his knees, hands clasped in front of him, told her he was speaking to her, not as a man to a woman, but as one businessperson to another. It was a heady feeling indeed, and one she must hang onto for dear life by gathering her wits together as swiftly as possible to frame a coherent response.

"I am concerned because it was well known in her husband's theater company that Annie and my friend, Olivia Childs, were friends and that they continued that friendship through correspondence. Someone determined to track down Annie Bentley could discover a connection between Olivia Childs and me. It may be a remote possibility, but a friend, a fellow mathematics enthusiast and card player, who suggested I consult Mr. Maule says it is always best to be prepared by understanding the cards in one's hand, or not," she finished ruefully. "This woman deserves to be free from harm, but how do I help her, other than offering a few days respite to recover from her injuries which, fortunately are not life-threatening?"

For a long time he was so lost in thought that Helen thought he was not going to reply, then he straightened with a start, as though summoning himself from far away to return to the matter at hand. "The ideal thing," he began, "and we must always presume that we can effect the ideal solution and then revise our approach, if necessary, would be if we could encourage Mr. Bentley to agree to a separation, which, depending again on *the ideal thing*, could bring her, her freedom and some alimony. Of course she could not remarry..."

Helen shuddered. "What woman, having endured that, would ever want to remarry?"

"Precisely. But however we pursue a separation, it will take some time and in the meantime, we do not want to endanger her or you by leaving her in a place where discovery is possible." Julian paused, again seeming to go to another place. "I might have a solution, if you would permit."

She gave a wry grimace. "Naturally, I infinitely prefer coming up with a clever solution of my own, but I have none, clever or otherwise."

"My mother's house sits virtually empty in Brighton. She died not long ago," a shadow crossed his face and was gone so quickly Helen was not even sure she had seen it at all, "and though there is a maid or two to take care of things, she never had a proper housekeeper, preferring to manage those things herself. I have no idea what skills Mrs. Bentley possesses, but presumably she knows how to manage a household. It is highly unlikely she would be traced to Brighton."

"And even if she were, it is highly unlikely that someone would risk displeasing an owner as important as the Earl of Linton."

Now it was his turn to grimace. "One of the few advantages to possessing a title."

"Not enough, I should venture to guess, to outweigh the burdens of owning an estate or successfully marrying off a niece."

Something akin to sympathy had prompted Helen to try to banish the darkness in his eyes, and his answering smile, reluctant though it was, told her she had succeeded—gratifying her all out of proportion to her effort. What was wrong with her? Why should she even notice if this man were happy or not, much less care? But the smile had transformed him, and she was struck with the realization that the Earl of Linton was a singularly attractive man. Why she should notice this in the midst of a serious discussion about a tragic woman's future was not something Helen wanted to contemplate, much less address, at this particular moment... or ever.

Gathering up her gloves, she rose. "I thank you for your counsel and your generous offer, but perhaps we had best wait to discuss anything further until Mrs. Bentley is well enough for me to bring her to your chambers. I shall say nothing to her of your most generous offer until you have had a chance to meet her and form your own opinion."

Drawing on her lemon kid gloves, she held out her hand. "Thank you again, my lord. It is rare one finds someone of such perspicacity..." and then, before she could render herself ridiculous by overwhelming him with gratitude, she hurried out the door, down the stairs, and through the archway, barely giving Rose a chance to catch up before climbing into the waiting carriage.

Immediately upon returning to St. James' Square, Helen hurried up to the tiny room under the eaves where Annie Bentley was recuperating. Much to Helen's gratification, she was up, dressed, and seated in a chair by the tiny window looking out on the roof.

"You are feeling better, I hope? You certainly look better." Indeed, marks around the woman's throat and the bruise on her cheek had turned from a bright angry red to a dull greenish purple, but the shoulders still drooped and the eyes were dark with despair.

"Thank you," she whispered. "I don't know why you are helping me, but thank you."

"I am helping because no man has a right to brutalize a woman, and all of us here have felt the pain and shame of that brutalization at one time or another."

"You?" The incredulity in Annie's voice betrayed how inconceivable it was that the self-possessed, fashionably attired woman standing in front of her had ever suffered the despair and helplessness of victimization.

"Yes. I have been where you are, oh, not a husband, but a man with power over my person and my destiny."

"But you did not choose to be with him." Tears of shame dripped down Annie's cheeks. "You did not excuse his brutality as the natural frustration of a brilliant mind forced to put up with mediocrity and stupidity. You did not allow yourself to be hoodwinked again and again by trinkets, you were not so weak and gullible as to believe one false promise after another."

No. Helen had not had a moment's hesitation in condemning the man who raped his daughters' governess as a lecher and a brute, but she might have remained silent to protect her livelihood if the man's wife, in a fit of jealous rage, had not cast her off without a reference. "No, I did not, but now you are no longer deceived. That woman is gone. The woman before me now is a woman who had the will and the courage to save herself, and that woman will find her own way it the world—with a little help. Now come, rest some more, and eat well. In a day or so I want to take you to meet someone who will help you to take that first step in regaining your life."

Chapter 6

As they climbed the stairs to Mr. Maule's chambers a few days later, Helen could not help reflecting on a notion she had seen proven and experienced herself times out of mid: the power of fashion to instill confidence. That morning, the ladies of her establishment had gathered for a critical dressing session as they sought the exact costume to set off Annie to her best advantage. The round dress of pink jaconet muslin, donated by Dora, enhanced the rich coloring, dark brown eyes, and curls so like Dora's, while the white braided lutestring spencer, belonging to the fair-haired Clarissa, made her appear fresh and youthful—a decided contrast to the gray, exhausted woman who had arrived in St. James' Square barely a week ago. The wide brim of the Leghorn bonnet, offered by Jane, obscured the slowly disappearing bruise on her cheek while the strangulation marks around her neck were completely obscured by a triple fall of lace at the throat.

Annie had not been able to believe the transformation. "Why I look . . . I look . . . I don't look at all like me," she exclaimed with a grateful smile to the assembled group. "I look like . . . like a fine lady."

"Because you are." Helen shook her head at the disbelief in Annie's voice. "And you will carry yourself the way your costume deserves. It is a very select few who have the privilege of wearing Maison Juliette's creations, but we who do carry ourselves proudly because we know we are in the first stare of fashion. I call it *intimidation through fashion*, and we take great advantage of that here. For those who do not have the interest or the concern to look below the surface to see the real people inside of us, a horrifyingly *a la mode* presence can make them question their own *a la modality*, which in turn makes them—since they lack true character themselves—prey to a great deal of self-doubt and social insecurity. Now come," she smiled, "prove me right."

Annie did prove her mentor right, greeting the Earl of Linton with a nice mixture of appreciation and quiet composure that made Helen give an inward sigh of relief. Gone was the timorous shrinking woman, replaced by one who listened intently, but with a quiet determination to all that Julian said.

"First of all," Julian gestured her to sit in a chair opposite the one he had taken, "you must not blame yourself for what has happened. This man is a scoundrel. No ordinary man would treat you so badly that you had to flee to save yourself. Nothing you could have done, no matter how unfortunate, could deserve such punishment as you have endured. You are only familiar with your own circumstances, but I know of many who suffered similarly, and it was not their fault either, so you must trust my experience on this. Not," he smiled ruefully, "that you are in any mood to trust any man about anything at this moment."

That drew the tiniest smile from Annie, and Helen began to relax as she saw some of the tension drain out of her friend.

"Now, in order to keep you safe, we need to move you somewhere your husband would never think of looking. It is too easy to connect you with Mrs. Childs and then to Mrs. Gerrard. Once you are safe, we can go about trying to convince him to agree to a separation. You would not be free to marry again, nor would he, but you would agree to live in separate households. Perhaps we might even get him to consent to some sort of support, but that is being extremely optimistic, and as yet I know very little of your husband. Is that agreeable to you?"

"Oh yes, she breathed. "To live quietly and unafraid, it would be heaven to me."

"And I take it you know how to run a household?"

Annie looked blank.

"You and your husband did live in your own house?"

"Oh yes. It was a beautiful one on the Square in Birmingham. My husband wanted a place worthy of his success where he could impress everyone with his hospitality and his elegant dinners. I did enjoy overseeing the menus and what not. Our cook was the envy of all who visited," she observed with a proud smile that left no doubt who was responsible for hiring and retaining such a treasure. "She used to say it was an honor to cook for someone who knew about food and appreciated it as much as she did." A shadow crossed her face. "But it was never enough. Nothing was ever good enough."

Annie fell silent, her hands twisting in her lap, and when she at last looked up, her eyes were full of tears. "And I left her. I left her with that beast. Though, when you think about it, a good cook is worth her weight in gold, while a wife

". . . .No one will hire a wife away, but a good cook will be gone in an instant. Mr. Bentley had better have care or he will find himself without Mrs. Soames as well as a wife."

Julian looked grim. "I am afraid you are entirely correct on that point. A wife is expendable while a good servant is a prize to be treasured. And your other servants?" he continued.

Annie looked up in surprise. "The usual: scullery maids and housemaids. Mr. Bentley insisted that I employ a ladies' maid to maintain the fashionable image of someone worthy to be his wife, but poor Bess, no matter what she did for me could not help me meet his standards, when I grew older that is."

"Though I imagine he blamed you rather than Bess."

"Well, yes," she admitted slowly, struck by the novelty of this viewpoint, "but I would not allow him to berate her for something that was my fault."

"In other words," he concluded in an encouraging tone, "you were a good mistress."

Annie did not answer, then a smile quivered on her lips, lighting the somberness of her face. "Yes. Yes, I was a good mistress."

Julian reached over to pat her hand. "And I am sure you were a good wife as well, except that you were no longer the tantalizing, hero-worshipping actress that first enchanted him. You had become a responsibility and therefore a burden. And he resented the fact that he was tied to you when there were so many eager young actresses begging to be admired."

She gazed at him as though he were a magician. "But how would you . . ."

"Believe me, I have seen it times out of mind. But now we must put the past behind you. First, I am in need of a housekeeper for my mother's house in Brighton. It is not a large establishment and has not had anyone in charge since my mother died. No one lives there now so not much work is demanded. At most my sister-in-law and her daughter may spend some time there at the end of the Season, but that is unlikely. Do you think you are capable of attending to that?"

"Oh, my lord," tears filled the large brown eyes turned worshipfully toward him, "I will do everything in my power to make it the best kept establishment in all of England, and I will be forever grateful to . . ." she broke off, her voice suspended by tears.

"Very good." Julian glanced over at Helen who nodded ever so slightly. "As to the other, the separation, seeking a judicial separation can be a lengthy process, but it can be done much more quickly if it is done privately, and if no children are involved."

"No, there are no children." The sadness in her face spoke volumes.

"Then, in that case, if you will give me your husband's direction, I will find an attorney who can draft an agreement." Seeing her look of alarm, he smiled reassuringly, "I do not do that sort of thing myself, but I can certainly share my knowledge and experience with someone who does. Besides, if you will be managing my household, we do not want your husband thinking of me as anything but your employer. Now, get some more rest, and I shall let you knew when I have made arrangements for you to go to Brighton. And bless the good fortune that gave you a friend like Mrs. Childs and a protectress like Mrs. Gerrard."

She gulped. 'I will. I do. Thank you, my lord."

"Come Annie," Helen held out her arm, "we have taken up enough of his lordship's time." She ushered her charge slowly towards the door, but turned and paused after Annie had passed through it to give Julian a fierce look. "I know I cannot to pay you, but I *will* repay you."

He could feel the force of her pledge in both look and words. What sort of woman spoke like that? A Joan of Arc or a Boadicea. Truly Helen Gerrard was a warrior queen for the mistreated women she took under her wing.

Helen did not look like a warrior queen, however, when, upon entering St. James' Square, she and Annie ran into Dora on the stairway.

"And was Mr. Maule able to offer some useful advice? That *is* the name of the barrister Lord John recommended, is it not?"

"Oh no, it was Lord Linton who was ever so kind, and he has even offered me a position as housekeeper at his mother's house in Brighton." Annie beamed.

They continued up the stairway, but not before Dora had caught a glimpse of the revealing patch of color in Helen's cheeks. Helen Gerrard blushing! In all her years at Mrs. Gerrard's, Dora had never seen such a thing, which was why, a few minutes later, she cornered her employer in her office.

"Out with it," she commanded with mock sternness. "The Earl of Linton?"

"I had no idea." The patches of color on each cheek spread into a delicate flush over Helen's entire face. 'Indeed, I went to Mr. Maule's chambers, and he told me that the man studying under him had a great deal of experience in matters of disturbing marital relationships, and the *man studying under him* turned out to be none other than the Earl of Linton."

"Did it now?" A sly smile crept across Dora's lips. "Didn't I tell you the man was clever?"

"You did." Tossing her bonnet and gloves into one chair, Helen sank into the chair behind her desk. "And I find it highly irritating that I am now in that man's debt. I feel compelled to repay that debt but how to do it without having anything more to do with him?"

If Dora wondered why the thought of having anything more to do with the Earl of Linton was distasteful to her friend and employer, she declined to comment, merely saying, "I am sure you will think of something," before she closed the office door and went back to discuss the latest wine order with Fenwick the butler, which she had been on her way to do when she ran into Annie and Helen on the stairs.

As she thought about it later, Dora realized that the distaste Helen expressed had to do with her refusal to acknowledge the superiority of any man until today. There had never been any question of her maintaining that cool, aloof, superiority that she wrapped around herself like a protective cloak. Until today, Helen had always been the rescuer. Now she was one of the rescued, in a roundabout way, and it did not sit well with her. Dora could see that Helen had been unnerved by this new view of Lord Linton as an authority in an area of great interest to her, and, given that her initial reaction him had already provoked her into a completely uncharacteristic charade which he had seen through, this was doubly threatening to Helen's equanimity. Dora didn't know whether to be sympathetic or intrigued by the recent turn of events, but she thought maybe it was the latter.

If Helen Gerrard had truly met her match, maybe she had finally met someone she could trust, respect, and rely on. Certainly, she respected Lord John's mathematical acuity, and she relied on her own passionate devotion to the poor unfortunates whose lives she tried to improve, and she relied explicitly on Freddy's exquisite taste, but there was a core of iron in Helen, forged by suffering and experience that was lacking in both John and Freddy, despite their devotion to their own particular pursuits. Dora was beginning to suspect that Lord Linton had an iron core and experience of his own that drew Helen to him in ways that she did not yet recognize.

Chapter 7

The ballroom was already crowded and a bit stuffy as Julian, his sister-in-law, and his niece slowly moved with the crowd up the marble staircase of the Cholmondeley mansion to greet their hostess, but the complaints he expected about the closeness and the heat did not come. All was happiness and excitement.

"What a sad crush!" Lady Charlotte exclaimed.

"Dreadful squeeze," her mother agreed, a beatific smile on his face.

Julian repressed a sigh. After years of freedom from family and the attendant responsibilities, he was paying his dues, but it couldn't end quickly enough. The sooner his niece attracted an eligible suitor, the better, but how was that ever to happen? Charlotte was only marginally attractive and not particularly stylish. Even Julian, uninterested as he was, and caring less about such things, recognized that, and despite the sizeable dowry he had conferred upon her, she was not particularly well-connected to the people who mattered in the *ton*.

They reached the top of the stairs, gratefully acknowledged their hostess and stepped into the ballroom, looking around with ruthlessly concealed unease.

"Linton. How delightful to see you here. Forgot to ask you about a number of things in your cargo the other day and now here you are. Frightfully convenient." A beaming Marquess of Wrothingham greeted him. "Oh, and yes, I must present you to my sister, Lady Georgiana." He turned to a tall blond woman standing next to him who rolled her eyes ever so slightly at her brother's single-mindedness, then smiled indulgently and added, "And this must be your sister-in-law and niece that Freddy mentioned."

Georgiana turned to the Countess and Charlotte. "And how are you enjoying the Season thus far?"

This could not be happening! To be acknowledged as friends by an arbiter of fashion like the Marquess of Wrothingham and his sister who, although no great beauty, had the presence and the subtle style of a woman who did not care, nor even wonder if she were part of the *haut ton*. It was a miracle, judging by the ecstatic expressions on the faces of Charlotte and her mother.

Then Julian remembered the intentness in Helen's eyes and the determination in her voice when he had last seen her. She was repaying her debt to him, and brilliantly too. What a magnificent woman she was.

"Yes," Freddy continued, I mentioned the Benares silk and shawls to Lady Adrian—and the muslin too, but I shall be wanting a good deal of that for the windows in the drawing room at Wyndam Place—and she was most interested. She wondered if it would be possible to look at them. You can be sure if Maison Juliette creates ensembles with your materials, they will become all the rage and you won't be able to import enough of them." He turned to Charlotte and her mother. "Don't know if you have heard of Maison Juliette—my sister-in-law—exquisite design."

The beatific smiles on both their faces said it all. Freddy beamed. "Why just look at what Maison Juliette has done for my sister here. She used to be nothing more than a *great, gawky girl* and now she's the picture of fashion."

"Well, not quite that, but Ju . . . Lady Adrian does know how to design things that not only flatter a person, but make one feel like oneself . . . if you know what I mean," Georgie trailed off with a desperate glance at her brother.

"Er, quite. I am sure my sister would be happy to mention your interest to Lady Adrian, that is if you are interested."

"Oh yes," Charlotte breathed, "most interested. Indeed, we would be most grateful, wouldn't we, Mama?"

"Most appreciative," the countess agreed.

Julian had not missed the look that passed between Lady Georgiana and Freddy. Yes, Helen was definitely repaying her debt . . . in spades.

"Wrothingham, I must have been mistaken. I had thought you otherwise engaged when I mentioned Lady Cholmondeley's ball to you the other day."

A voice that sent chills down Julian's spine broke into the conversation. He turned to find a hatchet-faced woman at his elbow and stepped aside to give her better access to her hapless quarry. She smiled in what a casual observer would deem friendly enough and laid a hand on what was obviously her fiancée's arm, but Julian sensed the icy resolve beneath it and saw the instinctive wince of his new-found friend, proving his original suspicion correct that the Marquess of Wrothingham was in no hurry to claim Lady Lavinia Harcourt, his betrothed since birth, as his loving wife.

"I beg you, Wrothingham, introduce me to this young lady," a silky voice spoke at Lavinia's elbow.

Julian turned slightly to see a rat-faced man staring fixedly at his niece. The Earl of Linton was not one to give in to flights of imagination, but there was a glint in the man's close-set eyes that made him distinctly uneasy.

"May I present Lady Lavinia Harcourt and her brother, Viscount Wormleigh, Lady Linton, Lady Charlotte Bracebridge." Freddy nodded vaguely in the direction of his future brother-in-law.

This time it was not a flight of imagination, it being perfectly clear to Julian that the Marquess of Wrothingham was not happy about the introduction, nor did he allude in any way to his relationship to Lady Lavinia or her brother Basil. In fact, to Julian's way of thinking, he rather pointedly ignored it.

"Delighted to make your acquaintance." Basil bowed to the ladies and then edged towards Charlotte. "Your first Season in London, I take it?"

Before Lady Charlotte could hide the expression of dismay at being so easily classified as being a mere green girl, Lady Georgiana came to her rescue. "Don't mind Basil," she turned to Julian with a resigned expression, "the man never had, had any manners." The triumphant look Georgie shot at Lady Lavinia did not escape Julian. There was no love lost there either; truly a fascinating situation.

"Then I shall make amends by asking you for this dance . . . with your permission of course." Basil bowed to Charlotte's mother who nodded blankly. Indeed, the orchestra was tuning up and couples were making their way to the floor where Basil lost no time leading his quarry to join them.

Seeing Lady Alicia eyeing him from across the room, Julian edged around Freddy to address his sister. "Thank you, Lady Georgiana. I am sure my niece is most grateful for your kindness. First Seasons can be very trying."

"I find any Season trying, my lord," she confessed with a wry grin. "Freddy will tell you I am a hopeless case, despite having a brother who is a veritable Tulip of the *Ton* to guide me, but we all have our duties to family." She glanced briefly between her brother and Lady Lavinia before adopting a more cheerful note. "But in the main your niece is enjoying herself?"

"I believe so." Now that he considered it, Julian did not have the least idea what Charlotte enjoyed; she never seemed to be doing anything in particular except pore over fashion magazines and dress to go out. "And thank you for agreeing to mention Lady Charlotte to your sister-in-law. I gather from my niece's reaction that fashions from Maison Juliette are highly sought after."

"Very definitely, and with good reason. My sister-in-law does not follow fashion; she creates it." The statement was proud and unequivocal. "And it is because she designs to suit the wearer that she leads the taste of the *ton*. For example, another modiste, whose name I shall not mention, insisted on forcing me into fussy, frilly gowns that were not only decidedly uncomfortable, they made me look ridiculous, yet she blamed *me* for being a *great gawky girl* which only made me more uncomfortable and ill-at-ease," Lady Georgiana finished with a dark look. "Juliette really sees the people she designs for, and she creates gowns that make them feel better about themselves rather than worse. She helps them recognize possibilities in themselves, no matter how tall or short or plain or ordinary. I beg your pardon," she caught herself, "I do go on sometimes, but" she raised her chin ever so slightly, "if we have to endure the marriage mart, we might as well be as comfortable in our clothes as possible while we do it."

"That is quite an endorsement." Julian smiled. He liked both the passion and forthrightness of Freddy's sister, who would surely one day be a force to be reckoned with, if she weren't already, and he felt slightly ashamed of himself for his original motivation for the conversation which was to avoid Lady Alicia. It seemed to have succeeded admirably, for she was no longer in sight. Julian wished he could ask Lady Georgiana about her prospective brother-in-law, but even someone as plain-spoken as she might take exception to such a personal question. He did know who he could ask, however. Helen Gerrard made it her business to know everything about everyone. She would tell him when he called on her to thank her for her *repayment*.

"Freddy says you lived in India and have seen many faraway places. It must be wonderful to experience so much that is unusual and exotic instead of this." Lady Georgiana waved a disparaging hand at the brilliant throng around them.

"You sound like someone who longs for a challenge."

"Yes." Her face lit up and Julian could feel a pent-up frustration that perfectly mirrored the way he'd felt when first encountering the world of the *ton* in spite of his initial fascination with Lady Alicia. He shuddered inwardly, recognizing now that what had seemed like misfortune at the time had indeed been a blessed escape. "I hope, then, that you find someone who enjoys a challenge as much as you do."

"So do I." Again the saucy grin. "At least Juliette let me help get her shop ready and she continues so successfully with her business that Mama and her mother, the Comtesse de Flournoy, daren't object to it, so perhaps I can also find something that engages me in the same sort of way."

There was a slight commotion as the dancers returned. "Thank you, my lord," Lady Charlotte smiled gratefully at Viscount Wormleigh as he restored her to her mama and uncle. But before Basil could press his advantage, his sister had taken his arm in a vicelike grip. "Come, Basil, I see the Duchess of Paxton beckoning us." And with the barest of nods to the rest of the group, she led him away with a determination that brooked no resistance.

"How remiss of us. Come, Georgie, let us introduce Linton and his family to some other interesting people they should know instead of keeping them all to ourselves. There is your particular friend, Lady Verena Carstairs and her mother." Freddy smiled at Charlotte, and then, extending one arm to Charlotte's mother and one to his sister, he headed out into the crowded ballroom leaving Julian and his niece to follow.

Chapter 8

While Helen had declared absolutely no interest whatsoever in whether or not her repayment to the Earl of Linton for his lawyerly advice succeeded, when she had described their consultation with him to Dora, much to her own disgust, she not only wondered if the repayment had occurred, but if it had worked. She would not, however, absolutely would not, wonder if the earl had recognized the repayment for what it was.

Fortunately, she did not have to torture herself with both the wondering and the self-disgust for long. The very day after Lady Cholmondeley's ball, Freddy, resplendent in a coat of dark blue Bath superfine and biscuit-colored pantaloons, tastefully embroidered waistcoat and exquisitely tied cravat, sought her out in her office.

There was a flat parcel wrapped in paper under his arm and an eager expression in his face. "I saw this and took the liberty of purchasing it for Wyndham Place . . . with Miss Dora's permission of course, but I wanted to consult with you first." He unwrapped the package to reveal a glowing watercolor of a harbor, a castle, and a monastery-crowned hill in the distance. "It's Mr. Turner's view of the quay in Naples, *Naples from the Mole* I believe he calls it. It is lovely, but more ordinary than what you might expect from Mr. Turner, which is why I think it might be perfect for Marylebone. On the other hand, I have seen brilliant works from his visit to the Rhine which I think would fit beautifully into your drawing room and stimulate conversation as well—not that any conversation needs stimulation in your drawing room, of course."

"Why thank you, Freddy." Helen was as touched by the compliment as by his continuing interest in her décor. "I think it an excellent idea. I shall leave it up to you, shall I?"

He beamed. "And as to the other thing I came for. Mrs. Cholmondeley's ball, it all went rather well I thought. Georgie and I were able to introduce the Countess of Linton and her daughter to several friends and they seemed to get on, though," the good humor faded from his face, "Basil did manage to lead Linton's niece to the floor before Georgie or I could think of any way to forestall him. Unfortunately," he shook his head, "Basil overheard Lady Charlotte's mother, who seemed to think it incumbent, upon her announcing how grateful she was to Lord Linton for settling such a large portion on her daughter—not in the best of taste, but no one seemed to notice, except Basil of course. At any rate, we did our best. The girl has been given an introduction to Maison Juliette as well as a number of our acquaintances so she should do well enough for herself now."

"Thank you, Freddy. You are such a dear."

The Marquess turned quite pink with pleasure. "Happy to be of service to the woman who has been such *a dear* to me as well. Must saunter on though. Rundell and Bridges has several new snuff boxes they want my opinion on."

And that answered that, but it didn't. What Helen really wanted to know was how it had all appeared to Lady Charlotte's uncle. Had it made his task of shepherding his niece into society any less onerous than it already was? Helen devoutly hoped so, but was at a loss as to how to find out. How provoking!

Fortunately for her peace of mind, the person in question had questions of his own, and it was only a few days later that Fenwick knocked on Helen's office door. "The Earl of Linton to see you ma'am."

"Send him in." Helen did her best to sound offhand as she hastily pulled a pile of accounts in front of her as though she had been working assiduously on them when, in reality, her mind had been wandering in the direction of the man now standing in her doorway.

"I know you have banished me from your premises, and I would never disrespect your wishes, but I am in dire need of your advice."

"My advice?" She was no proof against his hesitancy or his acknowledgement of her edict during their last encounter in that room, nor his disarming smile. And who could resist being sought out for advice? Dora was right. The Earl of Linton was a dangerously astute and intriguing man. "Do sit down." Helen hoped the smile she summoned to her lips was the epitome of graciousness. "How may I help you?"

"First, I want to thank you for Lady Cholmondeley's ball. My niece and her mother consider it a resounding success, thanks to the kindness of Lord Wrothingham and his sister."

So he had figured it out. Helen hated to admit how much she had hoped he would be clever enough to see her guiding hand behind the situations, but she was surprised at the gratification his acknowledgement gave her. There was nothing so satisfying as being appreciated by someone else who seemed to be awake on all suits. What she had not expected at all was the heat his look of admiration brought to her cheeks. In fact, she had never even known she could blush... until this moment.

"I am glad Freddy and Lady Georgiana were able to seek them out as it was expected to be a terrific crush."

"Which you knew because you make it your business to know everything that is going on in the *ton*."

She nodded. "I do."

"Then, perhaps you might enlighten me about the Viscount Wormleigh."

"He was there?"

"Ah, you answered part of my question already. Something of a loose screw is he? Someone not likely to attend such a tame but exclusive social function? A loose screw in spite of his relationship to the rigidly... er, proper Lady Lavinia whom I also had the dubious pleasure of meeting that evening."

"Very interesting. As you so correctly surmised, Basil usually prefers gambling dens to balls, and he generally avoids his sister's company almost as much much..."

"As Wrothingham appears to? I thought I sensed some reluctance there." Julian stroked his chin. "Poor fellow, he certainly seems to be in no hurry to be married."

Helen nodded. "Being the heir to a dukedom is not so fine as one would think, especially if it means longstanding agreements about marriage between families. But you ask about Basil with more than casual interest. I take it he showed your niece particular attention?"

The dark blue eyes fixed on her intently. "Yes. How did you guess?"

"Freddy mentioned your niece's dancing with him and also hinted at your sister-in-law's reference to the very generous portion you settled on your niece as being rather bad *ton*. Fortunately, Basil was the only other one who heard the remark." Helen leaned forward with her own intent look. "It is not just that he is a loose screw, or even a fortune hunter. Basil Harcourt, Viscount Wormleigh is a thoroughly bad man. Two years ago he ran into Lord Wrothingham and his brother, Lord Adrian, at Gunter's one day as they were conversing with Dora, Juliette, now Lady Adrian Claverton, and Grace, now Lady Maximilian Hawkesbury, and threatened to tell his sister that her fiancée was consorting with ladybirds unless Wrothingham brought him here. The moment the three men walked into the drawing room, I could see that Freddy was supremely uncomfortable, and I guessed that he had been blackmailed into bringing Basil because my establishment never grants admission to someone with as unsavory a reputation, not to mention the debts as his future brother-in-law. He was right, but I felt sorry for Freddy so I allowed Basil in. I did give him to Dora who, as you know, has her wits about her and is more than a match for a rag-mannered man." Helen shot him a teasing glance that made Julian feel as though he'd been invited to become a member of an exclusive club, a club of people whom Helen Gerrard trusted enough to share a private joke.

"Not five minutes later," she continued, her expression grim, "we heard a scream and a crash, and rushed to discover Wormleigh throttling the poor girl. Lord Adrian tore him off her, marched him downstairs, and dispatched him in our carriage to his chambers while the rest of us watched in horror. Poor Freddy was most upset, and naturally, Dora was dreadfully shaken, but fortunately, Freddy's other brother, Lord John Claverton, who was playing cards with me in the drawing room, was here to comfort her. And that is how we came to have Sunday services here."

"Sunday services?"

Helen laughed. "If you could see your face, my lord. Yes," she continued, still chuckling, for really he did look too funny, "Lord John is the rector of St. George's, Hanover Square, and once he is through with services to his bored, but fashionable parishioners there, he comes here to administer to the spiritual welfare of people who actually need his help."

"Truly an unusual establishment," Julian gasped as he tried to wrap his head around the rector of London's most exclusive church preaching to the denizens of London's most exclusive seraglio. It was so astounding that he lost the thread of the original conversation.

"But to continue with Basil—he doesn't deserve such an impressive appellation as Viscount Wormleigh, Lord Adrian was also certain he was behind the near accident to Juliette a little while later."

"Accident?"

"Narrowly averted. A carriage rounded the corner here too fast and would have run her down if Lord Adrian hadn't pulled her out of harm's way in the nick of time and in a very heroic manner. He maintained, and I tend to agree, that it was no accident, for no carriage would have been going at that speed in the square if the horses hadn't been whipped to a frenzy just before it entered it. We did discover later that one of the maids had been paid to tell a *very respectable gentleman* about Juliette's whereabouts, but when pressed, all Daisy could remember was that he was a *nice spoken* and *middling* everything—height, weight—well, it was useless. Our footman, Tom Sandys, Lord Adrian's former batman, trailed a likely looking suspect to a gambling hell, but before he could learn anything further, the porters became so suspicious that he had to leave. Out of sheer frustration, Lord Adrian confronted Basil in his chambers, but he insisted on his innocence, and then," Helen shrugged, "Waterloo happened and we forgot all about it."

"Except that there was that letter from the solicitor for the freehold," Dora's voice broke in. "I beg your pardon for interrupting, but I *did* knock—several times—and since on one answered, I thought you were elsewhere. I was just going to leave this on your desk." She waved a sheaf of papers.

Julian, suddenly alert, sat up. "The owner of the freehold? And what did he want?"

"It could have been a she," Dora rounded on him.

He held up a hand. "Touché, Miss Barlow. It could have been, but probably unlikely. So what did the owner of the freehold want?"

"The solicitor for the owner threatened eviction for certain *irregularities* in the lease," Helen bit out the words. "As if Samuel would not have noticed such a thing at the outset."

Julian made a mental note to find out more about this Samuel later.

"But as usual, the offer of a little extra blunt made all objections disappear," Dora waved an airy hand, but Julian could see the triumphant gleam in her eyes.

"Yes," Helen corroborated, "filthy lucre."

"But could it have been Basil?" Julian persisted.

"I doubt it." The women spoke in unison.

"Basil is too much the gambler, wasting all his time in the hells and stews, drowning his sorrows, for he nearly always loses, to be able to execute any sort of plan, especially to carry out something as risky as running down Juliette in front of her own home."

The word *home* was not lost on Julian who apologized again in his heart to this remarkable woman for ever having thought so critically of her.

"Besides, if Basil owned a freehold in St. James', he would have used it as collateral to pay off his debts instead of selling his soul to the cent-per-cents who now, it is said, will have nothing to do with him."

Dora nodded in agreement before whisking off to leave the two of them to what looked like a most interesting conversation.

"Samuel was a very successful man and he left me the leasehold for this place in his will," Helen smiled sadly, "because he was grateful for the companionship I offered, the chance to talk to someone who was actually interested in his business. His wife and children were ashamed of it, and of him because being connected with trade was bad *ton*. I was under the impression that the leasehold was owned by a business associate who needed the money and Samuel was doing him a favor. My solicitor looked it all over and nothing seemed amiss. All he could discover was that the name on the freehold was an L. Askew, and it never occurred to us to look further since I was in possession of the leasehold. Samuel was an extremely astute, not to mention cautious, businessman, and it would have been utterly inconceivable for him not to have examined everything most thoroughly, assessing all possible risks before committing to such a transaction. Surely he would have had nothing to do with, nor would he have trusted such a despicable character as Basil."

"That certainly answers my question about Viscount Wormleigh. I thank you for being so frank with me, Mrs. Gerrard, at some cost to yourself, I think. It cannot be pleasant dredging up such memories." As he smiled at her, Julian found himself wondering about those memories, and so many others that must have been equally unpleasant. Helen Gerrard did not look or act like the sort of woman who would have voluntarily chosen the uncertain and frowned-upon life of a mistress, even to someone apparently as honorable and appreciative as her Samuel. What unhappy circumstances had precipitated such a choice and would he ever learn what they were?

But now Julian realized he was in danger of overstaying his welcome, so having no other excuse to remain, he rose, extending his hand. "I am in your debt, and so is my niece, though she is unlikely ever to know it."

Helen took his hand, reveling in all that the gesture said about him—about them. He considered her his equal. He respected her judgment and her knowledge and was perfectly comfortable admitting that he needed it. Even more unusual, he was perfectly comfortable expressing his appreciation. His hand was strong, warm, and solid, just as the man was proving to be.

"In a few days I shall be going down to Brighton and I hope Mrs. Bentley will be ready to accompany me. I shall let you know for sure which day if you can confirm she is comfortable with the idea."

Helen retrieved her hand to ring for Fenwick, ruthlessly ignoring her reluctance to do so. "I am sure she is looking forward to it. She is fortunate indeed that you are so kind . . . as am I," she added softly, so softly that Julian was not even sure he had heard her say it, but then Fenwick was at the door, bowing him out, and there was nothing to do but follow.

Chapter 9

Helen climbed to Annie Bentley's attic room and knocked on the door. There was dead silence, then a rustle of what sounded like papers being thrust into something and then, at last, "Come in."

Annie sat in a chair by the window, colored papers in a basket beside her with a pair of scissors holding them down. "Oh, Mrs. Gerrard, it is you." The conscious look on her face did make Helen wonder what she was hiding.

"I came to tell you that Lord Linton is hoping to take you to Brighton quite soon in the next coming days. I hope you are still looking forward to being his housekeeper."

"Oh yes! Very much. It is so kind of him to take me without any references."

Annie's eager look allayed Helen's fears that for some unknown reason she might have thought better of the scheme.

Annie glanced at the basket as if reading Helen's mind. "I was going to surprise you and Miss Barlow by getting these framed to present to you for your kindness, but you have found me out." She lifted up the papers and pulled out what appeared to be two pieces of pasteboard, then turned them over.

Helen gasped. "But they are the spitting images of us! How did you, when did you do them?"

"Oh, I had a good deal of time, what with sitting here recovering," she smiled shyly, "and I had a little money to purchase the paper and pasteboard which Rose was so obliging to procure for me so I did not have to go out." The apprehension, quickly banished, that darkened her eyes showed how much, even if irrationally, she feared her husband's pursuit. "I wanted to do something, you see," her eyes filled with tears, "to show you how very grateful I am for . . . for . . ." her voice suspended in a sob before she gulped and carried on.

"I won't be a watering pot, I promise you, but I wanted you to know that I am eternally grateful—not so much for your very real support, but for your belief in me and my story, which means more than I can ever say."

Helen laid a hand on her shoulder. "There was no need. We have all been in your position. All we can hope is that someday you will be able to help someone just like you."

"Oh I will," Annie resolved. "Now please, take these as a token of my gratitude. I had hoped to get them framed, but then I decided not to, not knowing what you might want to do with them."

"Treasure them, is what we will do. But how did you ever come to learn your art?"

"When I was a girl, I excelled at drawing, and my father encouraged me, bought me everything I needed, but then he died and my mother married again. She and my stepfather started a new family which I was called upon to watch over. I could not carry paper, pencils or an easel as I minded the children, but I could manage paper and scissors, so I practiced making silhouettes of them. Mr. Bentley was a lodger in one of the houses my stepfather owned, and he would stop by and talk to me when he paid the rent or asked about a repair or two. It was he who encouraged me to go on the stage. I was good at it too, but then he began to be jealous of the attention I was attracting from the audience and the critics, not to mention the admirers, so he asked me to marry him.

"Of course I was extraordinarily flattered that he thought enough of me to ask me to be his wife, and to get out of the house, for I wanted little ones of my own, but they never came and Mr. Bentley would not allow me back on stage. We entertained his friends a great deal, but it was mostly men—his colleagues, or investors in the theater. I had no real friends of my own so I started working on my silhouettes again after the household chores were done." She paused, shaking her head sadly, "I had to leave all my silhouettes behind. I expect they've been discovered and destroyed by now, but," she squared her shoulders, "I will start again once I am settled, for which I have you to thank, and Lord Linton of course." A shy smile lit up her face.

"You certainly shall, and maybe we can find a place to sell them. The Marquess of Wrothingham has excellent taste and artistic connections of all sorts for he is a connoisseur of a great many things. I shall show these to him and see what he says."

"Oh, they are never good enough to sell!"

"We shall see. One never knows until one tries. Now, you set about getting yourself ready for the next chapter in your life." She patted Annie's shoulder again before leaving her to her artistic endeavors.

That evening in the drawing room Helen handed the silhouettes to Freddy who moved into the light of the sconces above the mantelpiece to get a better look. "Hmmm . . . .these are very good—untrained perhaps—but she knows how to capture a likeness. I occasionally frequented Mrs.Beetham's shop in Fleet Street before she died, and your friend's work is reminiscent of her early work though, of course, Mrs. Beetham did study portrait painting. Yes, all in all, I would say these are quite good."

"Good enough to sell?"

"Oh, most definitely. There are always silhouette stalls at fairs and markets, you know, not to mention Mr. Miers' shop in the Strand and several shops I know of in Bath."

"Then perhaps a silhouettist in Brighton . . ."

"The very place for that sort of thing," Freddy agreed enthusiastically.

"Thank you, Freddy. I do so rely on your advice."

Poor Freddy turned quite pink with pleasure. It was illuminating to see the heir to a powerful dukedom overset by such mild praise, which was sad, really, because, to Helen at least, it meant that praise had been a rare commodity in his life. Compared to Freddy, she, with a father who had recognized her intellect and her mathematical talents to which he dedicated his life encouraging, Halen had, had a fortunate childhood indeed. Yes, she had lost her mother at a young age, but she had been old enough to have felt the tenderness of a mother's unqualified affection, and to witness the very real love between her parents. Of course she had been too young at the time to recognize it for what it was, but now, as she thought back on it, she knew that her parents had adored one another. But unlike Grace's, whose father had destroyed himself with drink after the death of his beloved wife, Helen's father had thrown himself even more into his duties as a country vicar and his devotion to his daughter after his wife's death, until he too had died. Helen would not think about that though, or what had happened immediately afterwards.

"You are far too kind."

Helen came to with a start. "Never, Freddy. You know I am always brutally honest."

He chuckled. "Fearsomely so, which is why we all stand ready to cater to your every whim," he held up a hand to forestall the ironic rejoinder he knew was coming, "with great pleasure, mind you. No one deserves such obeisance more than you do."

It was Helen's turn to feel self-conscious, but unlike Freddy, she did not blush. Only one man had ever made Helen blush, and no, she was not going to think about that men . . . but she had to because in a matter of days he would be calling again in St. James' Square, this time to take Annie to her new position in Brighton, safe from the abusive husband who deserved to be made to suffer as much as he had made his wife suffer.

At that very moment, while it could not be said that George Bentley was actually suffering the physical abuse he had visited on his wife, he was being made to feel distinctly uncomfortable by the determined young man seated across the desk from him in George's office at the theater. "So you see, Mr. Bentley, it is to your advantage to let Mrs. Bentley lead her own separate life, supported by a small annuity from you, of course."

"No, I do *not* see." Mr. Bentley's once handsome, but dissipated face grew redder and puffier, and his chin, already thrust forward belligerently, projected even more alarmingly.

"If you separate from Mrs. Bentley and provide her with an annuity, a very small annuity, mind you, then you are free to enjoy all the lovely young actresses I am told you pursue without any objection from Mrs. Bentley."

Apoplectic now, the man across from the solicitor rose from his chair and leaned on the desk, his face inches from the young man's. "Now see here, Mr . . . ."

"Duncombe," his visitor replied calmly, "Henry Duncombe. And, as I said before," he continued patiently, "it is in your best interests to do so. A mutual agreement of separation can be easily accomplished. If, however, you wish to contest, we can pursue a judicial separation."

"Ha, you do not frighten me; you cannot prove any grounds for a separation."

"Actually, we can. Cruelty."

"Cruelty! I gave my wife everything she could want: a roof over her head—a fine one I might add, clothes, a carriage. Where is the cruelty in that?"

"In the welts on her cheek, the blackened eye, the defensive bruises on her arms. These are not the injuries of someone beaten with an implement *no bigger than a thumb* and they were all witnessed by the man who sent me here, a powerful man, Mr. Bentley, a wealthy man, an influential man who takes great exception to brutes like you. I suggest you consider this offer very carefully. Here is my direction. I expect to hear from you very soon. Now good day." Rising in one smooth motion, the solicitor laid his card on the desk and left without a backward glance.

"And I do think he will come 'round," Duncombe reported to Julian two days later. "Mr. Bentley is all bluster and no fight, hence his dreadful behavior towards a poor defenseless woman."

"Thank you, Henry. It was a lucky day I discovered a Kettering neighbor outside the court—a most fortuitous meeting for me."

"And for me, my lord. It is inspiring to discover the Earl of Linton devoting himself to the law."

"But not enough to his estate, eh? I know, I know, there is much to be done there. I wish your father were still alive to advise me about a steward. The one Richard employed was worse than useless. It was a good day for everyone when

I dismissed him; one less burden on the ridiculously low income derived from what should be a thriving property. You do not know anyone perchance?"

The young lawyer shook his head. "No. I have been gone too long."

But oddly enough, help in this matter came from an unexpected quarter.

Julian was waiting in St. James' Square for Annie to gather her meager possessions before departing for Brighton when he happened to mention the dereliction of his ancestral duties to Dora and Helen. "I know the estate could be far more productive with only a little more attention paid to it and a little decent management which it has not had since my grandfather's day. But where and how to find someone?"

"You did mention it was near Kettering, did you not?" Dora asked.

"No I not, but clearly someone did." He shot a challenging look at Helen, who had the grace to look conscious in the face of his raised eyebrow.

"Ah," Dora grinned at her employer, "the mistress of Debretts'. Well, at any rate I might be able to help you. Ned Stornaway, the squire's youngest son, was always far more clever and interested in their estate than his older brothers. He did not seek his fortune elsewhere because he loves the country, but he is a likeable fellow, awake on all suites, honest and diligent, paid his bills on time at the taproom in our inn—and what young man does not try to skip out on such obligations once in a while?" Dora's face clouded for a moment before resuming its usual sunny expression, leaving Julian, with the certainty of one familiar with sad stories to conclude that something terrible had happened at that inn.

"That is a recommendation indeed, Miss Dora, and coming from a hard-headed businesswoman such as yourself, one to be taken most seriously and gratefully. If you can give me his direction I shall pursue this immediately upon my return to London. But here is Mrs. Bentley and it is time to be on our way."

The goodbyes, expressions of gratitude and well-wishes were fervent, and then the travelers were off, leaving Helen and Dora alone in the hall, watching the coach as it rounded the corner of the square.

"Well, that ends most successfully, I would say. Now to the accounts." Helen metaphorically washed her hands of Annie Bentley's unhappy past and the Earl of Linton and headed upstairs to her office.

Except that it was not that simple. The realization hit her as she arrived on the landing in front of the drawing room before proceeding. She did not want it to end. Yes, she wanted to know how it turned out for Annie, but the thought that dropped like a lead ball in the pit of her stomach was that now there was no reason to expect to see Julian Bracebridge, Earl of Linton, ever again. And the emptiness that yawned before her at this discovery was not something she wanted to contemplate now, nor did she want to contemplate what it might mean to miss his company. Yes, she had mourned her father and mother when they had died, but they were with her always, and she knew what had become of them. Yes she missed Lady Adrian and Lady Maximilian, but she saw Lady Adrian whenever she was in town and she read the reviews of Lady Maximilian's triumphant progress as well as carrying on a regular correspondence with her and Lady Adrian. But Julian? Would she ever know if he became the barrister he aspired to be, if he was able to make his estates profitable again, recoup the family fortune and the family future? She would never know about the part of his past that brought the haunted look into his eyes and the note of determination into his voice.

No! Helen squared her shoulders, rounded the turn and climbed the next set of stairs. She did *not* care. She had her own affairs to handle. She was a successful business woman; Julian had said so.

Chapter 10

Annie Bentley could not believe she was to ride to Brighton in the Earl's private traveling carriage. "I could have taken the stagecoach and gotten there on my own once you had given me the direction," she protested as Tom Sandys handed her in the carriage in front of Mrs. Gerrard's.

"I am happy to take you, as I need to check on the property anyway and I wish to pay a visit to my mother's friend, Lady Standiford." Julian did not add that it would also provide him with the opportunity to become better acquainted with the woman he had just hired as a housekeeper. He was always one to help a fellow human being when he could, especially a woman who had been as badly treated as Annie had, as his mother . . . no he would not think of all that; it was still too painful and he had been too late to help in any meaningful way. Yes, he was always happy to help, but he was not a fool, and this time together in the carriage would allow him ample opportunity to take the full measure of the woman to whom he had made what might have been a rashly generous offer, though his instincts told him he had been right to do so.

"But tell me about the silhouettes. Helen, Mrs. Gerrard told me that Lord Wrothingham was most impressed."

Annie smiled and shook her head. "He is too kind. It is just something I did to pass the time when work was done. I did it for myself, really, to prove . . . to prove I could do something useful, something that was unique and mine . . . .I don't know why, really."

"But I do." His eyes were kind. "You did it because your husband had made you feel that you could not do anything, that you were worth nothing."

She stared at him. "Yes, I believe that was why. But how did you know?"

"Because I have seen such a thing happen to others, to . . ." he broke off to gaze blankly out the carriage window before collecting himself. "It is not only cruelty to wives like you, but servants whose very beings have been crushed by brutal masters. You will meet such a person at my mother's house, her maid Betty, who, along with one of Lady Standiford's servants, has been looking after the property. My mother came along her by the side of the road one day, starving and ill, running away from a dreadful master who had terrified her into being the maid of all work in an establishment far too large for one person to handle, but she had grown up in the house where her mother had been the cook until her death, and the poor girl knew nothing else. Mother took her in, nursed her back to health, and taught her everything she needed to know to make her a most valuable helper indeed."

"Your mother must have been a wonderful person. But should not this Betty be your housekeeper?"

He shook his head. She is loyal to a fault and hard-working as the day is long, but she is a simple lass and not capable of managing anyone. You, I think, can."

"I used to think so," Annie replied sadly, "but now I am not so sure. How could I have been so deluded by a handsome face, talent, and a clever mind that I did not see who he really was? How could I have been so blinded by his importance—owner and manager of the theater—and so flattered by his interest in me that I agreed to marry him after knowing him for so little time? Why did I not realize that someone as cruelly critical of others was not demonstrating superior taste, but meanness of spirit? When Olivia Childs became so disgusted by his treatment that she left, why did I not follow her? Why did I not suspect that his proposal of marriage the very next day was motivated by something other than passion for me? For now I see that he made me his wife to keep me cowed and quiet to stop me thinking and asking questions."

"You mustn't blame yourself," Julian reached over to pat her hand. "I am sure he was as brilliant and talented as you thought; after all, he made the theater successful. But such charismatic men can be ruthless, believe me. The ruler in India who paid me the first part of my fortune was just such a man. He never dared threaten me, as he did countless others, but I learned to recognize the danger of such people and to avoid them as much as possible. Now you will do the same." He gave her an encouraging smile. "Now, however, you must rest. You are looking rather fatigued, you know, and much work awaits you, I am sure." Julian leaned back and closed his eyes and so did she.

Annie found it difficult to credit that she had slept so soundly, through changes in horses and miles of road. When she awoke, it was to the sun sinking in the sky and the smell of sea air. Already she felt refreshed by it.

"How lovely!" she could not help exclaiming as they pulled up in front of a bow-windowed house in the middle of a crescent of similar houses with verandas on the first floor looking out to sea.

"My mother liked it, and her health improved after she moved here, just as Lady Standiford predicted it would."

A lad of indeterminate age ran down the steps to hold the horses, quickly followed by a woman a little older than Annie in a mob cap and simple print muslin dress. "Welcome to Brighton, Mrs. Bentley." The smile which lit up the plain, honest face, revealed a sunken cheek, testament to a blow that had landed more successfully than those delivered by Annie's own husband, and Annie felt an instant kinship. "Thank you, Mrs . . . ."

"Betty. Just call me Betty as her ladyship did. But here is John to help you with your things."

It hardly seemed possible that the old man, bent with age, who appeared behind Betty, would be as capable of carrying her things as Annie was, but he grabbed her satchel and headed upstairs with a surprisingly sprightly step.

Julian followed Annie into the black and white tiled entry and paused. "I must take my leave now as Lady Standiford is expecting me, and I imagine you would like to settle in and learn all about the place. Betty is a fount of information; my mother trusted her skill and knowledge implicitly, and I am sure you will too. I wish you every success, and look forward to visiting you again in the near future to see how you are coming along."

Tears stood in Annie's eyes and clogged her voice. "How can I ever thank you, my lord?"

"By taking care of this house and working with Betty to hire anyone else you require to do the work, especially someone who is in need of a position—qualified, mind you, but in need of a position, and I shall be back within the month to see how you are faring."

And with that, he was gone, leaving Annie and Betty to repair to the kitchen for a cup of tea and the conversation he hoped would lead to a formidable partnership.

"Hello, my darling boy," Lady Standiford welcomed Julian as he was ushered into the library of Standiford House an hour or so later. "Goodness, you resemble your dear mother more closely every day." She cocked her head, surveying Julian from head to foot and then the welcoming smile faded. 'But what is wrong? You look as though you've seen a ghost."

Indeed he had. It was Helen Gerrard standing before him. Well, Helen Gerrard in twenty years. The hair was a less brilliant red, the firm chin was softened, but the gaze was sharp and challenging—Helen Gerrard, just the same.

"Tell me, Aunt Honoria," Julian had no aunts, but Lady Standiford was as close, if not closer than a real one, "do you have any female relatives who take after you?"

She looked bewildered. "No, all my relatives are boys, or men, every one of them and they don't take after me in the least. Why?"

"I met someone who resembles you so closely she could be your twin." Of course Helen had looked familiar when he first met her. How could he not have recognized it before? How could he have been so obtuse? "Well, since she is a generation younger than you, not your twin, but your daughter."

The green eyes, so like Helen's, glinted with amusement. "Stop that you dreadful boy."

"What?"

"What you are thinking. I have been a faithful wife all my years of marriage—no by-blows of my doing, nor my brothers'. You know them, hopelessly dull and lacking in any sense of adventure, every one of them. Though . . ." she paused.

"Though?"

"Many years ago, my mother's nephew, Henry, the second son, was disinherited by his father, Lord Falkland for refusing not only to marry the bride of his father's choosing, but also for rejecting an army commission in favor of the church, and not a respectably wealthy parish in Surrey, but a needy one in Nottinghamshire where he married a young lady of excellent family who also cast her off for marrying a man with such modest expectations. My mother kept up with him to some degree, enough to know that they did have a daughter and that his wife died in childbirth when the daughter was still young. I gather he doted on the child, the way a scholar does, pouring his energies into her education, but then he died. It was said she became a governess to some local family and my mother lost all contact."

A scholar, Julian though, quite possibly one highly intrigued with mathematics, or if not mathematics, a highly appreciative father to a daughter who was. "Do you know where in Nottinghamshire?"

"No, though for some reason I connect it with coal. My mother referred to it as a very poor parish which would appeal to someone she described as *wanting to right the wrongs of mankind*." She shot a look at him. "You are very much taken with this woman, aren't you?"

"No." Julian felt the heat rise in his face and was grateful that years in the Indian sun had rendered him swarthy to such a degree that it could not be detected, even by his sharp-eyed Aunt Honoria. "I mean, it was just the uncanny similarity in looks that struck me and intrigued me, but now I can assume that this woman is the daughter of your mother's nephew and the question is resolved."

Not likely his aunt thought, not deceived for a moment by his sudden assumption of nonchalance. Lady Standiford had never known her *nephew* to evince the slightest interest in women, except for his ill-advised youthful infatuation with his former playmate, Lady Alicia, that social schemer who never encountered a fortune and a title she did not want to make her own, except that somehow, she had never managed to do so.

Privately, Aunt Honoria thought it would do Julian a world of good to find someone to distract him from the grim memories that still haunted him. All one had to do was look in his eyes to see that time had not softened them. 'But I keep you when you must be longing to wash off the dust of travel. We shall talk more at dinner and you can tell me what brings you to Brighton and brightens this old lady's day with your presence."

It did feel good to remove his traveling clothes, wash up, and relax with an excellent glass of port in front of the fire in his bedchamber, but Julian looked forward to dinner and conversation with one of the few good memories from his childhood, his Aunt Honoria's visits when he father had been attending to his parliamentary duties when his mother freed of that dictatorial presence was like a woman reborn—loving and laughing with the woman who had been her dearest friend from the moment they had met at school in Bath. And later, after his mother's death, it had been Aunt Honoria who kept her memory alive, who told him how his purchase of the Brighton house had given her friend a new beginning, brief though it had been, offering Julian consolation, albeit small, for his never having been a witness to her safe establishment in a place where she could live as she wished, where she could begin to enjoy life once again.

"But tell me, what brings you here, and how did the house look?"

"I came to bring Mrs. Bentley and introduce her to the household, what little there is. Things looked very good there. I thank you for lending us Jim. He is a likely looking lad and he ran out immediately to greet us and take care of the horses, though perhaps I should have asked him to carry up Mrs. Bentley's things as Roger is looking more grizzled than ever. He does move far more spryly than one would expect for a man of his years, though."

His hostess smiled reminiscently as she swirled her glass of claret. "Roger, another one of your mother's rescues. On her way from Linton Hall to her new home in Brighton, she saw him at a coaching inn begging for a few pennies to help in the stable."

"She helped a great many people that way over the years."

"And you helped her," Lady Standiford's eyes misted as she nodded fondly at him across the table, "never forget that."

"Not enough. If only I had made it home in time . . ."

"Purchasing that house for her gave her a longer and happier life than she ever could have had without it."

"But what if I had never gone to India, had become a barrister in London and looked after her as I should have instead of abandoning her in search of fame and fortune?"

And to escape the misery that was your family life Lady Standiford added mentally. She would not allow herself to think that he had also been inspired—hopelessly it had turned out since he'd had no title at the time—by that rapacious bloodsucker, Lady Alicia Shelburne. "I am not convinced you could have done more for your mother if you had remained. You didn't have the wherewithal for an establishment of your own where you could have taken her under your wing."

She rose and walked around the table to place her hands on his shoulders. "You did what you could. She adored you from the moment you were born and your letters home gave her so much joy, so full as they were of colorful and interesting detail and conveying your love and concern for her in every line. They were a lifeline. Then you bought her a house by the sea, a refuge where she could be free to relax, breathe the fresh air and be herself once again. It was short, but you gave life to her, and that is what you must remember."

Chapter 11

His Aunt Honoria's words were still ringing in Julian's ears and reverberating in his heart as he climbed into his carriage the next day and waved goodbye. In an odd way, even thought he'd grown up in a completely different part of the country, coming here to Standiford Hall felt like coming home—not that he had actually known what *coming home* felt like, at least not in the sense that most people spoke of it—and he liked it. He shook his head at his own naïve sentimentality. He wanted that peace, that sense of belonging that he had often scoffed at in others for himself. His rational, critical mind told him that such a thing did not truly exist; he was willing to wager that most of his clever friends did not actually believe in it themselves, and that supreme cynic and expert in human nature, Helen Gerrard, would laugh him out of the room if she knew he entertained such mawkish nonsense in his head, even for a moment.

Speaking of Helen Gerrard, well, thinking of Helen Gerrard, he could not wait to see her, but then what? Fortunately, he had the excuse of reporting on Annie's successful installation in Brighton as a reason to visit St. James' Square, but how was he to broach the topic of her parentage which was, in fact, none of his business? He wanted to make it his business, however. He wanted to know her story, to know what forces had shaped the poised, indomitable, highly successful, and generous person she had become. He wanted to know her. And why did he want to know her when most of his life he had avoided close friendships because bitter experience had taught him how fraught such relationships could be, how painful it was to long for the happiness of the person nearest and dearest to you? Why was he doing this? Because he cared, Julian finally admitted to himself. He admired Helen Gerrard and he had cared about her deeply from the moment she had ordered him out of her sight, the green flame of righteous anger burning in her eyes.

Julian vowed he would not fall prey to this irrational desire to see her again. He told himself that he would not rush right over to St. James' Square the moment he returned to London, but go calmly about his regular routine, spending much of the day in his chambers and then making the obligatory call in Hill Street to see his niece and sister-in-law.

That was a mistake. The Countess of Linton welcomed him in her usual colorless manner, but exhibited more enthusiasm when he asked after his niece. "Charlotte has gone for a ride in the park with Viscount Wormleigh," she announced proudly. "He has been most flatteringly attentive to her since meeting her at Lady Cholmondeley's ball."

"Flatteringly attentive to the settlement you told him I was providing her." Julian didn't try to hide his disgust. "Don't bother to assume that affronted air with me, Maria. All you had to do was look at Wormleigh to know he was a loose screw."

"Oh surely not! He comes from such a good family, and . . ."

"As did my brother, who had not a feather to fly with when he married you and then proceeded to make mice feet of your fortune in short order, not to mention behaving like a useless bounder the entire time right up until his death."

"Oh no, he was a most gen . . ."

"Cut line, Maria, I knew my brother, and I know what he put you through. You cannot want such a thing for your daughter."

"But his sister, Lady Lavinia, is the most proper person you can imagine. Surely she would not countenance bad behavior from her nearest and dearest, and surely she would not encourage such a match if . . ."

"Encouraging such a match? Things have moved swiftly, very swiftly indeed." He eyed her skeptically.

"She has been most kind, inviting Charlotte to drive with her in the park and inviting her to a concert at the Academy of Ancient Music."

"I see." He was right. Things had moved very swiftly, too swiftly. Julian drew a breath and forced his features into a more conciliatory expression. "I understand your desire to see Charlotte suitably settled, but do not allow that desire to cloud your discretion. Do not allow yourself, or her, to be rushed into matrimony simply because you wish her to be settled." He smiled and laid a comforting hand on her shoulder, "There is plenty of time. I know you are concerned, but believe me, I am here to see that you do not want for anything."

She sniffed as she hunted frantically for a handkerchief, then dabbed her eyes before straightening to look up at him. "It's just that you've been so kind and I . . ." She sighed.

"I know. You have had a difficult life, but that is over. I shall find a new steward and make the estate profitable again, but you must speak to Charlotte and warn her about Wormleigh."

She nodded, and he left, hoping that he had made his point. His sister-in-law was not a bad woman. She was not even a silly one; she had just been worn down by years of living in the shadow of a blackguard of a father-in-law and a weak, self-indulgent, spineless husband. If anyone knew how dispiriting that could be, Julian did. How to help his sister-in-law stave off Wormleigh gave him another topic of conversation to broach when he visited Helen Gerrard, which Julian did the very next day.

Helen refused to acknowledge the spark of—of something that she was not about to identify—that ran through her when Fenwick announced, "Lord Linton." She did not acknowledge it because she was concentrating too hard on maintaining her coolly disaffected exterior as she nodded at Julian and invited him with a wave of her hand to sit down.

"I trust you had a pleasant and successful journey, my lord?" There, not an ounce of eagerness in her voice to suggest how glad she was to see him or how relieved she was that he wanted to report all the particulars to her.

"Most successful . . . and pleasant too. Mrs. Bentley will do well, I believe, and she and my mother's devoted Betty seemed to take to one another instantly."

So, he had used the journey to learn more about Annie and her capabilities. As Dora said, the Earl of Linton was a clever man.

"And I could see the change in her the moment she saw the ocean and smelled the sea air. She said it made her feel better already, which is precisely what Lady Standiford said it did for my mother. The same shadow that Helen had seen before crossed his face. There was great sorrow there.

"Yes," he continued evenly as the shadow receded. "As my mother's oldest and most devoted friend from school days, Lady Standiford knew it would make her hap . . . er improve her health, which had been weak for some years. I learned from her when I visited her at Standiford Hall after depositing Mrs. Bentley that it did improve my mother's health. I also learned something else."

He paused, fixing her with a look that Helen, skilled as she was at reading people, was at a loss to interpret. "I learned that her mother was aunt to a rebellious younger son who was disinherited not only for choosing the clergy as a profession, but for insisting on ministering to a poor parish in Nottinghamshire, her nephew being the Honorable Henry Falkland."

Julian castigated himself for being an insensitive brute as he watched the color drain from her face, but there was no way to raise that topic that would not be a shock to her. He could not bear the desolation he read in her eyes, for the briefest of moments before she reassumed her customary cool composure. "Helen," he rose from his chair to come around the desk and kneel in front of her, clasping her icy hands in his. "Please, I did not mean to pry . . . well, I *am* prying, but I did not set out to do so. It's just that my *Aunt Honoria*, as I call Lady Standiford, has reminded me so strongly of you, I had to ask her about her family. When she mentioned the daughter of a disinherited son it made sense, and it also clarified the inexplicable sense I had when I first saw you that somehow we had met before. But I would not for the world distress you, and I give you my word that I did not say anything about you except that I had been introduced to someone who bore such a striking resemblance to Aunt Honoria that she must be a relative."

Her voice was devoid of all emotion, as was her expression, but she could not control the throbbing of the vein in her neck that tore at his heart. Julian drew a deep breath. It was now or never. He had to prove that he was her friend, that he could be trusted. "Whatever happened was dreadful, I know, and I would venture to guess that you have never confided to anyone what you suffered. Would you? Could you possibly do me the great honor of telling me how you survived?"

Helen closed her eyes. She'd been so sure no one would ever find out. No one would ever see Miss Helen Falkland, devoted, bookish vicar's daughter in the worldly cynical Mrs. Gerrard, queen of London's most exclusive seraglio. Now what was she to do? Tears pricked her eyelids.

"Helen," he whispered softly, "no one will ever know. I swear my life on it. In fact, I should never have mentioned it except that I want to help. I would do anything to help. Things left buried in the past, unacknowledged and unexplored, will continue to wound you until they are confronted." Just how ready was he, Julian Bracebridge to follow his own advice, he, whose tortured existence was proof of the truth of his words, he was not about to address.

Her hands clasped in the reassuring warmth of his, Helen felt his strength and conviction flowing into her, giving her the courage, not only to revisit the past, but to speak of it. The darkness in his eyes, and the painful twist of his lips told her that he knew full well what he was asking of her, giving her the strength to ask the same of him some day. But not today. Today was her moment to face, and as he rose, still holding one of her hands in one of his, and pulled his chair to sit next to her, she knew she could do it.

"I have told my story before, briefly, and with no names to Dora, Grace, and Juliette—anyone here who needed convincing that they too could do it, that they could survive and triumph and become independent, that it could be done because I had done it, but I never gave any details and never mentioned my previous life."

She drew a deep breath. "You are correct, my father was Henry Falkland, vicar of Eastwood, Nottinghamshire where he and my mother devoted themselves to serving the unfortunate in the parish. My mother died in childbirth, as did my baby brother, when I was ten, and after that, Papa concentrated all his energies on raising me like the son he never had, sparing no expense on my education."

"We were happy, Papa and I, as happy as we could be without Mama, until he caught a fever from a sick parishioner and died soon after. I had no family, nothing, but our carefully selected library, but Lady Fairleigh, wife of the most important landowner in the parish, offered me a position as governess in her cousin's family in King's Lynn."

"It wasn't until later I learned how desperate Lady Broughton was to hire a governess after five had quit in quick succession because of her husband. No self-respecting woman in the surrounding countryside would have been caught dead in the household of such a notorious lecher, but I was young and desperate, too innocent to recognize the threat in what I originally thought was simple kindness on his part. By the time I realized the danger, it was too late, besides which, I was no match for his brutish strength, even if he had not tried to lull me into passivity with his false overtures of solicitude. He took me one afternoon in the schoolroom, knowing I wouldn't dare scream or resist for fear of upsetting my pupils—two dear girls of eight and ten."

Tears welled up in Helen's eyes as she shook herself fiercely, willing them away. "To this day, I wonder how they have fared in such a household with such a father. Of course their mother, already on the alert after so many older, more experienced women with sterling recommendations from other employers in their possession had quit so abruptly, had watched her husband like a hawk, and the moment she caught him casting lustful looks in my direction, got rid of me immediately. Once again I was adrift with no money, no references, only this time, I was miles from my former home and anyone I knew."

She looked up at Julian with a bitter smile. "So I did what every dishonored young woman does, determined to try my fortunes in London. I could not afford to advertise my services in newspapers so I sold my books to pay for an outside seat on the coach, and upon arrival, sought out a register office, but the woman there quickly disabused me of the notion that all I needed was an extraordinary educational background. It was nothing without references. She was not unsympathetic, however, and introduced me to her friend, Mrs. Blackthorn, who owned a small discreet establishment in Marylebone that connected women with lonely men. It was through her that I met Samuel, Mr. Ward."

"He had started in life as a charcoal owner on the Weald. Naturally, he got to know owners of ironworks, and saw the potential of the industry so convinced wealthy landowners in the south to invest in manufacturing in the north. As coal took over from charcoal, he made more from arranging loans to manufacturers, and eventually, he became a banker in London where he lived in as great a style as any noble member of the *ton*, but his family, embarrassed by the source of their vast wealth, wanted nothing to do with his business, to the point that they ignored it entirely, and him with it. He became a stranger in a household obsessed with being part of the *ton*, all of them willing to shun him to advance their own social aspirations."

"My interest in his business enterprises was both a relief and a delight to him, a relief in having found someone to discuss it with, and delight in finding someone who was as eager to tackle problems and explore solutions as he was. Naturally, he was well enough acquainted with accounting principles and simple computations of interest, but when he saw the things I could accomplish with more sophisticated mathematics, he was enchanted. He set me up in a house in South Moulton Street and visited nearly every evening to share the particulars of his day with me." Her face softened at the memory of these spirited conversations, and Julian found himself envying the quiet evenings they must have spent together.

"I had no idea how much it meant to him until he died and left me the leasehold on all this," she waved her hand at the room around her, "and more money to live on than I could have ever dreamed of." Again there was a fond smile that pricked him ever so slightly with . . . could it be jealousy?

"And yet you felt compelled to go into business rather than enjoy the luxurious existence of a wealthy woman?"

The warmth of admiration in his eyes and in his voice flowed through her, filling Helen with something she had never known before. Was it recognition or appreciation? At any rate, it felt oddly like coming home. Yes, her father had loved her, had been proud of her brilliant intellect, and had done all he could to nurture it, but he had never been able to see or value her spirit.

"I am my father's daughter, despite my heathen interest in business, and I was determined to do good with my fortune. And," her smile was tinged with mischief, "I wanted not only to rescue women who had suffered as I had, but to pay men back for the liberties they had taken. To make them pay rather than the women."

Julian, glad to see the pain had receded from her eyes, could not help chuckling. "And pay they do, most extravagantly, but . . ." he held up a hand, "not at all unreasonably, for the companionship they find in this most elegant of establishments."

"Why thank you." She tilted her head, a roguish smile acknowledging the truth of his remarks.

Was she actually teasing him? Did that mean . . . ? Julian was transfixed by the sheer intimacy of the moment, an intimacy he had never shared with anyone else.

Chapter 12

A knock on the door broke the moment that transfixed them both, and Julian reluctantly released her hands.

"Come in." Helen did her best to assume her usual unflappable composure.

"A gentleman to see you ma'am; he was most importunate, I am afraid," Fenwick apologized. "A mister . . ."

"Constable Peabody." A corpulent man in a coat that was far too tight for him strode in behind the butler, barely giving him a moment to step aside.

Julian misliked the self-important demeanor of the man, but Helen, dismissing Fenwick with a conspiratorial wink, smiled at the visitor in a most welcoming fashion. "Hello, Constable, and what brings you to my doorstep?"

"Well, begging your pardon, ma'am" his self-important attitude evaporated with the butler's departure, "I hate to do this, you always being so kind to me and my men and all, but I have this." He handed her an official looking piece of paper.

Julian watched as Helen opened it. "A warrant against me for keeping a *disorderly house*?"

Something in the constable's face—a fleeting expression of discomfort—made Julian lean forward. "May I see it?"

Helen sighed. "Here, but I don't see what you . . ."

"Just let me look at it."

"Oh, very well."

Julian scanned the document. "Just as I thought."

"What/"

"There is no name attached to the complaint, nor is there a time limit." She raised a curious eyebrow.

"Without a date or a name, it is without merit and utterly useless. And, I would be willing to bet that the magistrate knows it. If he does not," he fixed Constable Peabody with a quelling look, "you undoubtedly do, as you probably also know that the sons of the Duke of Roxburgh, a very powerful man, politically speaking, are regular guests at this establishment. I ask you, sir, are the Marquess of Wrothingham and the Reverend Lord John Claverton of St. George's Hanover Square likely to frequent a *disorderly house*? I think not."

Constable Peabody stood silent, a silence Helen hastened to fill. "Lord Linton, in addition to his noble lineage, is also studying the law, so I expect he knows whereof he speaks. You can be sure he will follow up on this. Thank you, Constable, and I am sorry you were put in this uncomfortable situation."

"Thank you, ma'am." Somewhat abashed, the constable executed a hasty bow and departed as precipitately as he had come.

"I take it you *do* know what you are talking about and that it was not just lordly bluster." The green eyes twinkled.

"Mrs. Gerrard! You wound me to the heart!" Julian clutched his chest and Helen burst out laughing. "Of course I know what I am talking about." *But I have no idea what I am feeling at this moment*, the heart he was clutching responded. "If you ask me, which, I acknowledge, you have not, your Constable Peabody and his magistrate who wrote the warrant, received a complaint from someone too important to fob off, so they wrote up an incomplete and useless warrant to prove their diligence, but not necessarily their expertise. In other words, they are loath to further a complaint against such an august establishment which has been careful to cultivate Constable Peabody's good opinion."

"Which begs the question," Helen's brows drew together and her face darkened, "of who would wish to register such a complaint . . . and why?"

"Precisely. Now, if it is not too impertinent—you did involve me by conducting this business in front of me—I would like to see the letter Miss Barlow alluded to about the irregularity in the leasehold, the letter about a problem that an application of *filthy lucre* made disappear. And I would also like to see the document of the leasehold with the freeholder's name, the L Askew who is certainly not the titled aristocrat one would expect to own such a leasehold, much less the freehold that would have allowed him to sell the leasehold to your Mr. Ward's friend."

"I suppose I was remiss in not exploring it further at the time," Helen admitted as she dug through a drawer in her desk, "though I *did* show it to my solicitor who assured me that all was in order. But you are correct, no mere *mister* would own a freehold on St. James' Square. I do not like to think I have made such an enemy of someone that they would go to such lengths, but it does seem rather suspicious, does it not?"

"I shall be happy to look into it for you." Julian held up a hand as he saw the objections rising to her lips. "I know you are extraordinarily capable, not to mention forceful, as well as intelligent, but this is the field to which I am devoting myself. You do not insist on keeping your own livestock, though I know you patronize an excellent butcher, nor do you make your own gowns when you have Maison Juliette. Let me explore the legalities here for you."

The mulish look, for one could not call it anything else, remained, and once again Julian reached for hands that he could see she was fighting to hold still in her lap instead of twisting them in concern. "Helen," he looked deep into her troubled eyes, "I promise you, I will only investigate. I will *do* nothing. That is for you to decide. I am not trying to take control in an obnoxiously manly fashion; I am simply trying to help you make an informed conclusion."

Now it was his turn to look unsure of himself and Helen loved him for it. He truly did want to help her, and he truly did not want her to feel he was taking over. What other man, what other person had ever understood her so well? He not only understood, but he respected her wishes. She drew a deep breath and smiled. "Very well, but I want to know every detail, no matter how unpleasant—no protecting me from anything you think might discompose me."

"Discompose? You?" He grinned. "You have never been discomposed in your life, my girl." Then he grew serious. "You have so bravely and generously shared with me all that you have suffered and overcome that I have the utmost faith in your ability to tackle anything I might uncover." Knowing it was time for him to go before he found himself irritating her by offering her all the support and assistance he longed to offer, he gave her hands another reassuring squeeze, wishing he had another excuse to extend his visit, but there was none. Now, at least, he had another reason to call on her later.

Wrapped in a speculative fog over the implications of the incomplete warrant, Julian almost ran into the Marquess of Wrothingham striding along more purposefully than usual, a package clutched under his arm."

"Linton! This is a most fortuitous encounter. I have been meaning to ask you more about your cargo and if your ship will be returning to India for more. At the moment, I am on my way to show Mrs. Gerrard some furniture styles in the latest magazine from Mr. Oakley." He held up the package, "Now that we have done the drapes and the hangings in the drawing room, the furniture is looking a trifle demode. Perhaps we might meet here some evening? Tomorrow, possibly?" Freddy's chubby countenance flushed ever so slightly. "I realize it is a bit precipitate of me, but my fian . . . er Lady Lavinia, will be attending the Concert of Ancient Music, of which she is quite fond. In fact, if I recall, she has invited your niece and her mother, so I shall be quite free." The flush deepened and Julian saw it all. The Marquess of Wrothingham was the mildest, most amiable of creatures who would never court his fiancée's wrath by refusing to escort her somewhere, but pleading a prior engagement accomplished the same purpose and would deprive her of venting her displeasure on him. Come to think of it, Julian was delighted to be spared the outing as well. To top it all off, he would be able to spend the evening in Helen's company—not that she would have time for him, but just being near her made him feel more alive and hopeful about life.

Julian was entirely correct, Freddy's excuse of a meeting with a friend to discuss business was indisputable, but uncomfortable, nevertheless, when he broached the subject to his fiancée when he encountered her later at Claverton House.

"Business?" Lady Lavinia's thin eyebrows rose nearly to the top of her prominent forehead. "You have a business meeting? A Claverton in trade?" She snorted. "In the evening?"

"It is not a trade sort of thing," Freddy hastened to reassure her, "but Linton, you know, has ships that trade with India, and the wood they bring is exquisite . . . thinking of it for furniture at Wrothingham Abbey." He stammered to a halt under her basilisk stare.

"Really, Wrothingham, I shall be in my grave before Wrothingham Abbey is done to your satisfaction. Besides, the future Duchess of Roxburgh should be residing at Claverton with the current duke and duchess, not a paltry place in an obscure corner of Bedfordshire. The Countess of Linton does not object to this . . . this . . . *meeting*? I should have thought her brother-in-law would know his duty well enough to escort his niece to this concert. Well, what is done is done." And with a disdainful sniff, Lady Lavinia pulled on her gloves and marched down the stairs. It had been a thoroughly irritating day. The Duchess of Roxburgh and her daughter knew that Lady Lavinia usually called at this time, but it was typical of their ramshackle ways that they had completely forgotten this and gone for a ride in the park instead. When she, Lavinia, was Duchess of Roxburgh, she would run a much tighter ship, doing justice to the title at last and burnishing the image of the Claverton family to the brightness it deserved.

Chapter 13

"So kind of you to agree to our meeting here," Freddy greeted Julian as he entered the drawing room at St. James' Square the next evening. "My fiancée quite understood that a prior engagement . . . well," again the quick flush betrayed him. "At any rate, she could raise no reasonable objection, which, of course she would not because Lady Lavinia prides herself on being a supremely rational creature. So, it's a pleasure to see you. Do tell me, are you planning more cargo similar to what I saw in your warehouse?"

Lady Lavinia Harcourt might be a *supremely rational creature*, Julian reflected as he nodded pleasantly at the apologetic Freddy, who would not have looked so apologetic if his fiancée were truly as rational as he claimed. The example of a *supremely rational creature*, no, the epitome of a *supremely rational creature* was Helen Gerrard. She was more than rational—strategic even—and she imbued that rationality with an energy and magnetic self-possession that, from the little Julian had seen of Lady Lavinia, Freddy's fiancée lacked completely. In fact, Julian was willing to risk his last shilling that Lady Lavinia was less about rationality than the control of others—especially Freddy—while Helen Gerrard was all about another sort of control—self-control.

At the moment, Julian devoutly wished she had less of it. He wished she would look up from her card game, see him, lay down her cards, and hasten over to greet him. Instead, she surveyed her hand with a dispassion that verged on boredom as she lay down a card.

"Blast! Of course you would," the rakish looking fellow sitting next to Helen shook his head in admiration and frustration, while her partner, a soberly clad blond gentleman, regarded her serenely across the table. *That must be the legendary Lord John Claverton* thought Julian. There was a faint resemblance to

Freddy though his younger brother's blond hair and blue eyes were darker, his face more angular and his expression more serious. There was definitely a connection between Lord John and Helen that Julian envied. He could feel it, even though he could not describe it, and he desperately wanted such a connection for himself, only more so.

"My lord," Dora breezed in, brown eyes warm with welcome, hands extended. "Do sit down." She sank into a chair and patted the place next to her. "Freddy tells me you are here to talk to him about all the wonderful things your ships bring back from India, but we would like to know more about that exotic place itself and all the unusual customs and interesting things you have seen and learned on your travels, wouldn't we ladies?" She glanced around and Julian realized that not only Freddy had pulled up a chair, but so had several other exquisitely attired women whose faces were alight with curiosity as they looked at him expectantly. It was rather daunting to be the focus of such interest. Naturally, Julian had addressed members of the Rajah's court, members of the East India Company and the Board of Control, and barristers at Lincoln's Inn, but their motivations had always been relatively narrow and relatively clear. These were less so. These women were eager to learn and explore. Would he be able to live up to that expectation?

"Well," he began, "I went to India because I needed to earn a fortune." There was sympathetic recognition in the eyes regarding him. "But I found much more. Eventually I did earn a fortune, but I learned a great many things along the way, saw so many things differently than I had before I went." He drew a deep breath. "When I finally landed in Bombay, I was overwhelmed with the crowds and the color: streets filled with people, especially the women dressed in brocades and silks of all the hues of the rainbow, children running everywhere, and carts pulled by enormous bullocks." The mention of brocades and silks seemed to have struck a chord so he proceeded. "The women wear a short bodice with sleeves, and over that a long flowing sari wrapped around the waist, gathered in front and up across the shoulder, sometimes over the head. It is very graceful and allows for easy movement. The wealthy women are covered in bangles and jewels for they quite literally wear their riches on their person."

"I was welcomed most graciously into people's houses and fed meals of food so spicy it made my head swim."

"But how did you talk to them?" The blond with a pensive expression wondered.

"A great number speak English. They read widely and with great interest on a variety of topics." He went on to describe the ubiquitous palm trees that supplied a variety of useful products and the enormous sacred banyan trees whose fibers hung down from branches to take root in the earth below, as well as temples carved with such a panoply of gods and goddesses it was difficult to keep track of them all, and torch-lit processions fueled by the music of sitars and drums, and the snake charmers with their mysterious and sinister performers."

"I gather that most are of the Hindu religion?" Lord John, who had joined the group, asked.

"Yes, but there are also Parsees and Musselmans whose dress is so similar to the Hindu's that one is not immediately aware of the difference."

"I am most interested in the Hindu religion which I have read about enough to intrigue me with their concept of *atma*, which I gather is very much like our notion of a soul, and it is found in all living things?"

Julian nodded. As Steward says in his *Elements of the Philosophy of the Human Mind* that *in the superstitions of India no less than the lofty visions of Plato to recognize the existence of those moral ties which unite the heart of man to the Author of his being*, so, not so different from us in many ways." Julian could see from the expression in John's eyes that there would be more questions coming, but he turned back to his descriptions of the port of Bombay teeming with traders from all corners of the earth, selling mahogany and ebony from Bengal, silks from Benares, and cotton, rice, spices and jewels in exchange for iron goods and hardware brought from England on the East Indiamen like the one on which he had arrived twenty months after leaving England.

His audience grew quieter and quieter as he spoke until one could have heard a pin drop. Even the card players had ceased their game and he could see Helen, enigmatic as ever, at the far edge of the group clustered around him. At least she was interested in him enough to give up the card game, or it simply might have been that her partner wanted to know more about the Hindu religion-a lowering thought. But then as Julian looked up, he caught her eye and she nodded ever so slightly, and smiled, a special, secret smile, just for him that warmed his soul. For the first time in his life, Julian did not feel alone.

Julian was not the only one who saw that smile and guessed what it meant. The Reverend Lord John Calverton's parishioners might be far more interested in the comings and goings of the *ton* than in the Scripture, but they were human beings, nonetheless, and as their pastor, overlooked though he might be, John had grown adept at reading their expressions, to such a degree that he knew them more intimately than they could ever have guessed. Helen's smile, subtle though it might have been, told him far more than she would have wanted him to know. That someone as difficult to read as the unflappable Mrs. Gerrard, a woman who made it a point of pride to remain unaffected in the company of the most sophisticated and charming men of the Upper Ten Thousand, who frequented her establishment on a daily basis, smiled at a man as he related his adventures in India to a rapt audience said a great deal indeed. There was an intimacy, and approval in the smile that John had not seen in her, even when she was with her closest companions—Dora, Lady Adrian Claverton and Lady Maximilian Hawkesbury—and John wondered if even Helen were aware of all that it revealed.

This would bear some watching. John had wanted to question Linton further about his impressions of the Hindu religion; now he wanted to question him about his intentions toward Helen. He shook his head at his own foolishness, at the ludicrousness of being more protective toward the proprietress of a seraglio than he was of his own sister, but Helen was, in many ways, closer to him than Georgiana would ever be. She had immediately sensed his frustration with his own unsatisfying life, a life that most clergymen would have sold their souls to possess, but not John. He wanted to help people, to offer aid and comfort to the suffering, to bring them hope and meaning in their lives. Helen had given him that by inviting him to minister to her ladies, and the old gnawing dissatisfaction had lost its sharp bite. She had also challenged his mathematical proclivities to the utmost, showing a depth of knowledge and an innate sense for its complexities that left him in awe, and a little apologetic for his previous assumption of his own expertise. She had also, along with Lord Maximilian Hawkesbury, turned his mind to the practical applications of mathematics in establishing annuities and insurance for the women of Mrs. Gerrard's, fulfilling at the same time his preoccupation with numbers and with helping people.

John made sure he happened to be heading out as Julian bid farewell and promised his eager listeners to return with more tales of exotic climes, though, of course, John had checked to make sure he was not keeping Helen from saying a last word to Linton, but Helen had vanished, which was even more revealing.

He caught up with Julian in the entrance hall. "May I accompany you if we are going in the same direction? I do want to know more about your views of Hinduism."

"Certainly, though I must tell you that my feelings are mixed. Yes, there is a reverence for life, but there is also a rigid caste system which creates an existence of utter wretchedness for those at the bottom, more wretched even than our poor who at least have the hope, if not the reality of bettering their circumstances."

"Ah." John liked the earnestness of this man—not the sort to frequent Mrs. Gerrard's. "Then you will be returning to India on the ship that is to bring back Freddy's wood and silks?" He had overheard Freddy's requests for both as the two men had discussed Julian's ship's return to Bombay.

"No. Actually, I am returned to England for good. I am reading the law under William Maule, who kindly took me under his wing because of my experience in shipping and commerce."

"Maule, eh? It is too bad he gave up teaching for the law. The world lost a talented mathematician when he did."

"You are acquainted with him, then."

"I am. It was I who recommended to Mrs. Gerrard that she consult him about Mrs. Bentley's situation, and . . ." John raised a quizzical eyebrow, "I gather Maule felt you were more qualified than he to address the situation."

Julian could see that those serious blue eyes missed nothing, and the clever mind behind them saw a great deal, perhaps more than he was comfortable with, but he answered easily enough. "I do have some expe . . . an interest in such matters. Far too many women suffer the indignities that Annie Bentley has suffered."

And who was so near and dear to you that you were unable to help, for which you are suffering a lifetime of regret? John wondered, but he merely nodded as he replied, "A noble calling. You are to be commended."

They had come to a parting of the ways as they reached the entrance to Julian's chambers at Albany so John bid him good day, expressing the hope that they might speak in more depth about the Hindu religion. "Perhaps I shall see you again at Mrs. Gerrard's?" He said it more in passing than anything else, not giving his words a thought until he saw the uneasy expression—quickly hidden—on his companion's face. Hmmm. The situation did bear looking into; it was becoming more intriguing by the moment.

"I am not precisely welcome in St. James' Square. I was only there today at the request of your brother."

John's puzzlement grew.

"In point of fact, the first time I met her, Mrs. Gerrard threw me out."

"Gracious, that does not sound like her. A very subtle woman is Mrs. Gerrard, and not given to impulsive or dramatic action of any sort."

"I am afraid she was provoked," Julian admitted.

"Odder and odder."

"You see, I offered to set up Miss Barlow in a house in Marylebone. You smile, but I knew nothing of her investment at the time and I thought she was being held against her will, or, at the very least, under duress by Mrs. Gerrard so I naturally took exception to such treatment."

"Only to discover the truth." John laughed. "I am surprised you are alive to tell the tale."

Julian grinned. "I am too. And since then, I have been in awe of Mrs. Gerrard's prowess as a businesswoman and as one of the finest people it has been my privilege to meet. I only wish I could do something to help her."

"I thought you already had by offering your expert advice, not to mention refuge to Mrs. Bentley."

"I helped, but I want to do more, to help her, Mrs. Gerrard."

"That is a tall order indeed. I have found there is no one who needs help or desires it less than Helen Gerrard—a very proud and independent woman indeed."

But as he turned and headed toward Grosvenor Street, John wondered how such a serious and committed man had come to be at Mrs. Gerrard's in the first place.

Chapter 14

How could he help her? Julian had racked his brains. What could he offer someone so clever and self-sufficient as Helen Gerrard? He wanted to take her to meet what was left of her family, his Aunt Honoria, when he returned to Brighton to check on Annie at the end of the month, but that would be too interfering for his independent Helen to stomach. There was nothing he had to give that she could not get for herself . . . except perhaps, diversion, a chance to escape her myriad responsibilities and enjoy herself. But what could possibly divert someone whose establishment was the very essence of diversion?

"Lord Linton to see you, ma'am," Fenwick peaked around the open door into Helen's office.

Now what did the man want? Didn't he know he intruded into her thoughts far too much already without actually showing up on her doorstep? Helen hoped not. When she had seen Freddy enter the drawing room with him the previous evening, she'd kept her eyes firmly fixed on her cards with only the occasional surreptitious glance to read the faces of the other players, but when he'd begun speaking about his travels in India she could not help but listen. Fortunately, the other card players, who possessed only a small fraction of Helen's powers of concentration, except for Lord John of course, had quickly gravitated to the crowd surrounding Julian, leaving her with nothing to do, but follow.

She had been impressed by his tales, not so much with the exotic subject matter as with the nature of their telling which revealed the highly observant and sensitive nature of a man eager to learn about and understand the world around him. What had driven him to undertake such a perilously long journey away from family and friends? Surely it was not simply the need for a fortune.

The Julian Bracebridge she had come to know, and, she reluctantly admitted, admire did not seem the sort of person to do such a thing simply for *filthy lucre* or for a lark. Or would he? Never one to let a man off easy, she resolved to find out. After all, she had found herself confessing things to him she had never confessed to anyone, perhaps she might inspire him to do the same? It had felt good to see the understanding in his eyes, feel the sympathy in those strong hands that held hers so comfortingly. For one wretchedly weak moment she had wanted to collapse against that broad chest, lay her head on the firm, square shoulders, and give in to the cleansing tears of despair and anger she had never allowed herself to shed, but with a supreme effort of will she had resisted the impulse. Now she did not know if she were glad or sorry that she had.

"Why did you go to India?" she asked him baldly before Julian even got through the doorway. "I know you said it was to seek your fortune, but surely going into trade and becoming a barrister could have done that as well?"

Julian chuckled to himself. So she had been thinking about him, had she, and seriously too. Then he sobered as he took the chair, facing the desk between them, elbows on his knees as he began. "The story does not redound to my credit, but you certainly deserve to know since you have tumbled to some of it already." Good, he had surprised her. Julian admired Helen with all his heart and mind, but that did not mean he liked her having the advantage over him.

"When I was a young lad, the only person I knew close to my age was the girl whose father's estates joined ours, Lady Alicia Shelburne. She was something of a madcap, and we rode our ponies together all over the parish until I went to school. Years later I ran into her in London where I'd gone to read the law after graduating from Oxford and discovered that my former playmate had blossomed into the most beautiful, captivating . . . in short, I was besotted."

He paused, shaking his head at his own foolishness. "But she would have nothing to do with a penniless younger son. Oh she was friendly enough; after all, my father was an earl and many of my acquaintances from university were wealthy peers, sons who would inherit impressive titles. But I was determined to win her, and if a fortune would do it, a fortune I would make, and India was the place to do so. I made myself useful to a local rajah and did some good, I think, by convincing him to allow his soldiers to become farmers, bringing peace to his land." He could not help adding, with a touch of pride, "For that I was rewarded richly enough to purchase a ship and crew and engage in a most lucrative trading business. Having done so, I returned to London a wealthy man and threw myself at the feet of the exquisite Lady Alicia—still unmarried, remarkably enough—only to discover that a fortune was no use if it had been gained in trade. It was worse than no use, actually, it was a blot on my reputation. My eyes were opened then, as they probably would have been long before if I'd stayed in London long enough to discover her true nature."

"I am sorry." Helen frowned in sympathy. "But at least you were spared."

"Oh, but I wasn't. The moment my brother died and I inherited the title, I was re-born, all connections with trade forgotten. Now I was not only Earl of Linton, but unlike previous Earls of Linton, I was wealthy beyond belief. Suddenly I was Lady Alicia's *dearest Julian*."

"Ah, the woman pursuing you at the theater."

"Precisely." A grim smile twisted his lips. "Her pursuit was so determined even before what you witnessed that I was filled with disgust at her, at the idea of marriage, at the entire *polite world* which exists solely for seeking out and promoting precisely the advantageous matches she was angling for. So, I decided to find an honest woman and I came to Mrs. Gerrard's where one can find female companionship without putting one's entire life and soul at risk, where the price is clearly and decently stated at the outset."

"And yet you mistrusted me." Helen deliberately provoked him to drown out the joyous refrain that would keep ringing in her head: *I am an honest woman. He thinks I am an honest woman.* Who would have thought that a man like Julian Bracebridge, who clearly had strict standards of conduct where men and women were concerned, would think of an abbess like Helen Gerrard as *an honest woman*?

"It was simply because Dora was so adamant at not wanting to leave you which made me suspicious, as you know."

"Now, though," a slight flush tinged the high cheekbones, "I completely understand and sympathize with her wish to remain at Mrs. Gerrard's. I wouldn't want to leave you either, which brings me to my errand today."

The delicate eyebrows rose.

"You look at me skeptically, but as a connoisseur of business and good business management, I know that one can exhaust oneself by too much application." Realizing how patronizing, not to mention unflattering this sounded, he hastened to correct himself. "You do not look in the least exhausted, but someone as dedicated to your establishment as you are could use a little distraction now and then. I noticed that you appeared to be somewhat interested in my discussion of foreign culture and customs. The British Museum offers Hamilton's exquisite collection of Greek vases, sculptures from the Parthenon, artifacts brought back from the Polynesian islands by Captain Cook and a host of other treasures, if you are free on a Monday, Wednesday or a Friday between 10 and 4."

Her first instinct was to refuse. Helen Gerrard did not seek diversion, especially with a man, but as the word *No* hovered on her lips, she realized that this man was not offering to escort her to the opera or Vauxhall, or even a ride in the park where she could be shown off like a prize horse or any other accoutrement that a man might acquire to impress the world. No, he had selected a distraction that he thought might interest her, Helen Gerrard. He was hoping to gratify her intellect and nothing else. Not only that, but, judging from his wary expression, he was not at all certain that his invitation would be appreciated. He was watching her as uneasily as one would watch one of those cobras he had mentioned the previous evening.

"Hmmm." She appeared to give the proposal some thought, deriving a certain delight in making a worldly man of business nervous, then, taking pity on he, she smiled. "I might quite enjoy that, you know."

The happiness that lit up his swarthy features bowled her over. She couldn't remember making someone happy. Her father had been proud, Samuel had been content, many others had desired her, but no one had been simply happy at the thought of being in her company. It was a novel sensation and one that she hoped she did not come to regret.

It did not seem that she would when Julian called for her several days later at a most inelegantly early hour in the morning, selected expressly for its unfashionability. "So we can enjoy all the treasures that are on offer as free as possible from the intrusion of others. I prefer my experiences to be mine alone and not part of society's," he explained, reminding Helen of those long ago carefree days when all she did was live and explore without the least concern for what others thought of her.

The past, both her own, and the heroic past surged over Helen as she admired the exquisitely carved metopes. "The battle of the Lapiths and the Centaurs, how Papa would have loved to see his classical studies come to life. He longed to go to Greece, but his family would not afford a grand tour for the second son, the one who would have really appreciated it."

"Your father was a classical scholar? I thought he was interested in mathematics."

"No, I was the one interested in mathematics. I wanted to figure things out; I could have cared less about dead people."

Julian burst out laughing. She sounded more like a willful five-year-old than an exquisitely beautiful, terrifyingly intelligent woman. He should not think that way, he should resist comparing her to the goddess whose birth was depicted on a frieze before him—madness lay there. She was Athena herself, bold, beautiful, and undaunted, and he wanted her so desperately in so many ways. Ruthlessly he crushed the longings that were the antithesis of what he wanted to give her today—a moment free of men with their desires and needs that dominated her establishment.

"I was much like you, uninterested in people, but I found solace in roaming the fields and forests around my home." Anything to get away from a drunken brute of a father, an equally irresponsible brother, and a mother who cowered from them both.

Again, Helen saw the shadow flit across his face. The story of the quest for a fortune rang true, judging from the behavior she had witnessed in Lady Alicia, but it wasn't the whole truth. Something else, something darker and more desperate had driven Julian Bracebridge halfway across the world from his home.

Helen looked up at him. "If you are interested in natural history, then we should proceed to the upper floors where we can see animal specimens: snakes, worms, fish, stuffed birds, and quadrupeds, even a live tortoise brought from America, but that was in 1765 so it is probably stuffed by now as well regardless of their renowned longevity."

"I see you have been reading up on the museum like the consummate businesswoman you are. Never do anything without being fully informed," Julian teased, but he was touched that she had gone to the trouble to learn about the collections, and even more touched that she was as invested in his enjoyment of their excursion as he was in hers. When had anyone ever cared about what he wanted, except perhaps Lady Standiford? He rather liked the feeling, transitory as it was likely to be with a woman determined to forge her own way in the world without assistance from anyone, even someone who cared as deeply about her as he now admitted to himself he did.

Chapter 15

Dora was so immersed in *True State of the British Nation as to Trade Commerce & c* that she didn't hear the first knock on her door. Dear Max, even though he was no longer in London to teach them about annuities and insurance, he was still educating her and encouraging her aptitude for business from afar by recommending this book, Turin to be exact, where he was enjoying his position as British Resident.

"Miss Dora?" Tom Sandys, all burly six and some feet of him, resplendent in his footman's uniform, stood in her doorway. Goodness, he was a fine figure of a man with a square jaw, strong nose, and bright blue eyes set off by skin tanned from his years in the Peninsula as Lord Adrian's batman.

"Yes?"

"A gentleman to see you, a Lord Linton."

What could Julian possibly want after Helen had so unequivocally rejected his offer to set up Dora as his mistress? Besides, Dora had seen the way he and Helen looked at one another. Oh it was only a quick glance here, a secret smile there, but there had been a mutual respect, a shared understanding, you could call it, that Dora hoped would grow into something more. After all the fierce support and the caring Helen had lavished on all of them, the ladies of Mrs. Gerrard's, she deserved a little care and support of her own.

"Thank you, Tom. And I have told you to call me Dora, you know. I shall see him in the drawing room. And Tom," she cocked her head as he remained in the doorway, an uncharacteristically hesitant expression softening his bold features, "is something amiss?"

"Not amiss exactly, certainly not for you," he paused a moment, then drew a breath and plunged on, "but I hear tell that you've bought your own establishment in Marylebone." His voice held a wealth of admiration.

"That I have." A proud smile told the footman more than any words what it meant to her.

"Then you'll be leaving us, I suppose." Only someone as quick as Dora would have noticed the slight slump to the broad shoulders.

"Oh no. I like it here." Her wide smile included him in its expansiveness. "The house in Marylebone is purely a business proposition. Until of course," again she favored him with a saucy smile, "I can buy an inn of my own, like the one my father lost to that cheating scoundrel."

"An inn? That is a great deal for any one person to take on, even for you Miss . . . er, Dora." He moved so he could look directly into her eyes. "I would think you would need a dependable partner for that, someone with his wits about him, who can handle whatever situation is thrown his way, even in a foreign land."

The adoration in his eyes was what undid her. No one had ever looked at bouncy, ready-with-a-saucy-retort Dora Barlow like that. Certainly the men at Mrs. Gerrard's had lavished her with appreciative glances, but those had all been for her luscious curves, ripe red lip, and glossy brown curls that would escape the pins and tumble down her back no matter what she did, but they did not look at her with the respect, the admiration that this man did. "That I might, Tom. "I just very well might." She planted a kiss on the astonished footman's cheek and bounced out of the room, leaving him rooted to the floor, the bemused expression on his face slowly metamorphosing into a broad grin.

"My lord," Dora greeted Julian with a playful smile as he bowed over her hand, "this is an unexpected pleasure."

"Especially when I have been forbidden your company," he could not help smiling in return, "but I am sure you and Mrs. Gerrard have discussed that at length. What I am here for today is to ask you more about the young man you mentioned previously, the one with an aptitude for estate management. And, by the way, Mrs. Gerrard has given me her permission to speak to you."

"Ned Stornaway?"

"Yes, Mr. Stornaway. The time has come for me to take the estate's affairs in hand so I am off to Northamptonshire to do so. It has been badly neglected and mismanaged by both my brother and my father so it will be rough going. If you think he is up to it, what can you tell me about him that will help me convince him to take the job?"

Half an hour later, Julian was entirely satisfied that Ned Stornaway was just the man he needed to turn things around at Linton Hall. "Thank you ever so much. If all goes as you think it will, I shall be forever in your debt. Ah, I see from the speculative gleam in your eye that you are ready to ask for payment for this information up front, astute businesswoman that you are, Miss Barlow. And what would that payment be?"

"That you go to Helen's office and bid her a proper farewell." Behind the teasing reply was a wealth of meaning that not even the dullest could miss. Julian felt the heat rising in his face and prayed that the tan from the Indian sun would completely obscure it. "That I shall, directly . . . and thank you, Miss Barlow."

And that should take care of that, Dora told herself with smug self-congratulation as she headed back to her chamber and her book.

A successful approach to Helen in her office required a more formidable assistant than Tom Sandys. Julian sought out the support of the venerable Fenwick, whose devotion to Helen and her privacy was legendary, but Julian thought he had detected a softening toward Julian after he had routed Constable Peabody, and, more recently, when he had managed to mention their excursion to the British Museum within the butler's earshot.

"Mrs. Gerrard? Very good, my lord. I shall see if she is in and is free." Fenwick bowed and headed off to deliver the message, but with a softened gravity that left Julian feeling optimistic.

Helen was, in fact, quite free, freer than she would have liked after she had caught sight of Julian and Dora in the drawing room, a sight that had rendered her incapable of dealing with the accounts she had been buried in before going down to consult with Cook, thus walking past the open door to the drawing room. Julian had gotten her permission to speak with Dora, and the two of them were in a very public room with the door open; Helen should have taken some comfort from that, but she didn't.

This morning she had thrown herself into the accounts precisely to keep herself from thinking of Julian and the unexpected pleasure that their trip to the museum had brought her. Of course she had been struck by the beauty of the Greek vases and sculptures and awed by the zoological curiosities on the upper floors, but what had struck her most was the simple joy of being comfortable with another person, of sharing discovery with another person, something she had not had time or opportunity for since childhood. For a short while that lost innocence was re-captured, making her feel cleansed somehow, all of which she owed to the man who had been in deep conversation with Dora Barlow in the drawing room. Helen didn't begrudge them the conversation, but . . .

"Lord Linton to see you, ma'am." Fenwick stood impassive before her, the picture of the rigidly perfect butler.

"To see me?"

The dignified features softened a little. "Yes to see you, ma'am."

She drew a deep, steadying breath. "Send him in."

What was she doing? She had just witnessed how deeply this man could affect her and yet she was inviting him into her inner sanctum . . . again, the place where Helen Gerrard was utterly certain of herself, her value, and her right to be there. She was inviting him in when she should be sending him away, never to see him again.

The expression, almost apologetic, on Julian's face as he entered seemed as though he half expected her to do just that.

"Oh, do sit down, will you?" The frustration in Helen's voice was as much for her own weakness as for his hesitancy.

Julian grinned. So she was just as uneasy and anxious about how to proceed as he was. That was promising. "I wanted to thank you for joining me at the museum the other day and to say that I would very much like it if we could do it again some time except that I shall be leaving town for a bit."

If he expected her to betray any sort of response, even by so much as the flicker of an eyelash, he was fair and far out. Helen had herself well in hand by now.

"It's time that I attend to my inherited duties. I have neglected the estate too long, an estate that was already brought to rack and ruin by my predecessors." His voice was as cold and dismissive as though the predecessors were no relation to him at all, rather than being his father and his brother. "So I am off, I hope, to hire a new steward. Miss Barlow has been so kind as to vouch for the Squire's younger son, Ned Stornaway, and a recommendation from such a hard-headed critic of the human race in general gives me reason to hope that he can help me bring it back to health and productivity."

So it hadn't been an excuse for an assignation after all, just a business conversation. Helen was disgusted with herself. She should have had the sense to know that, and she would have trusted both Julian and Dora if she hadn't cared so much. *Cared so much*? She was all about in her head. It did not matter in the least what Lord Linton did, or who he saw, not in the least!

"But I do very much hope we can have another excursion when I return, perhaps study the Rosetta Stone or even compare the stuffed quadrupeds at the Egyptian Hall to those we saw the other day." His teasing smile was hard to resist.

"Perhaps." Then seeing the hope in his eyes, she relented. "Yes, my lord, I would like that. I very much enjoyed our outing." Helen was grateful that Dora or Grace or Juliette was not around to hear such a craven, not to mention awkward, admission. They would have thought she had taken leave of her senses.

It was way past time to end an interview that was deteriorating by the minute. Helen rose and held out her hand. "I wish you great success, my lord. Like you, I trust that anyone recommended by Dora would be just the sort of person you need for the job."

"Thank you. I hope to call on you upon my return." Julian rose and bowed over her hand. Then, before she knew what he was about he pressed his lips against it and left before she had a moment to react.

Even when Helen did have a moment, she was too astonished to think. She just felt: the firmness of his lips, a caress and a promise at the same time that did strange things to her breathing and her chest (she wouldn't call it a heart because she had none) as a warm, tingly sensation sparked across her skin. She grasped the desk and struggled to restore her breathing to a calm in-and-out, in-and-out, before snatching up her gloves and bonnet and ringing for Rose.

It was useless to try and work, not that she'd been working anyway, so she might as well distract herself with a brisk walk and the latest books to be had.

"Yes ma'am?" Rose peeked around the office door.

"Get your bonnet; we're going to Hatchard's."

"Yes, ma'am." Rose hurried off to do her bidding, her mind awhirl. Something was up with her mistress who never spoke in such a peremptory fashion, but that observation was no help in figuring anything out for Helen Gerrard kept her feelings, like her cards, close to her chest.

Rose seated herself on the bench outside the store with the other maids soaking up the warm spring sunshine while Helen went in to peruse the shelves, stopping first to place an order for *Essays on the Combinatorial Analysis showing its application to the most useful and interesting Problems of Algebra in the Multiplication, Division, Extraction of Roots &c* Once she had read that, she dared Lord John Claverton to expound on the topic!

As she headed to the shelves after giving the clerk the particulars of her order, she found herself face-to-face with a fellow customer, a coldly handsome woman with a high-bridged nose and rather closely set dark eyes that raked Helen over with a basilisk stare. The sheer effrontery of it took Helen aback, but she calmly brushed past the woman, refusing to be affected by what was clearly meant to be an unnerving examination. The woman gave a haughty sniff before sailing over to the clerk to demand the identity of his previous customer.

"Er, well," the clerk began uneasily, "that would be Mrs. Gerrard, my lady."

Another disdainful sniff. "Mrs. Gerrard? I am surprised that such a venerable institution as Hatchard's would allow a woman of her reputation to darken its doors."

"Well it *is* unusual for a woman to be known as such a connoisseur of mathematics, but a number of people consider her to be quite a discriminating reader and follow her taste in mathematical texts, Lord John Claverton, for one. And we have a standing order from Lord Maximilian Hawkesbury in Turin to send him whatever Lord John Claverton and Mrs. Gerrard are reading."

"One wonders what this world is coming to." The haughty lady turned on her heel and marched out of the store, leaving the astounded clerk to stare after her.

"My goodness! A woman of very strong opinions, I gather." Helen smiled sympathetically at the shaken clerk.

"Yes, Lady Lavinia Harcourt is a woman who knows her own mind without a doubt." The young man shook his head ruefully, then composed himself to ask if she needed any assistance.

"Thank you, no. You have been a great help, as always."

Poor Freddy was all Helen could think the entire way back to St. James' Square. Grace and Dora had seen Lady Lavinia at the opera, and Lady Adrian, no matter how much her future sister-in-law tried to avoid her, had actually met her. All of them agreed that it didn't bear thinking of that the kind-hearted Freddy was tied to the starched-up nasty piece of work that was Lady Lavinia Harcourt.

No, it didn't bear thinking of. No wonder he spent so much time in the cheerful company he found in St. James' Square. No wonder he was never satisfied that Wrothingham Abbey was fit to welcome its mistress. Surely something could be done, must be done, to rescue him from a life of misery, but Helen knew that longstanding, generational agreements between families such as the one between the Harcourts and the Clavertons were inviolable, and it made her appreciate the life she had. People might question Helen Gerrard's respectability, but they could not question her freedom, her independence, or the control she exerted over her own life.

Chapter 16

The reaction in Hill Street to Julian's imminent departure was far less restrained than the supportive one he'd received in St. James' Square. "Going to Linton Hall? At this time of year? Deserting us in the middle of the Season?" The Countess of Linton's voice rose with each question.

"It will only be a quick trip, but I have been given a recommendation for someone who can possibly serve as my steward, and it is high time to make the estate productive." If the Countess noticed that he did not say *productive again*, she did not comment. As far back as she could remember, the estate had not only been not productive, it had been a very considerable drain on her generous dowry.

"At the very least, I would like to restore to you some of the fortune brought to a place where it was so recklessly squandered."

"Oh, that," the Countess was somewhat mollified.

"Don't worry, I shan't be more than a week, certainly back in time to escort you and Julia to the Duchess of Thornton's ball."

If she was surprised he remembered the ball, Julian's sister-in-law gave no indication, moaning instead, "But Almack's . . ."

"I am sure you are now acquainted with enough members of the *ton* that you will be tolerably amused, Maria." And with that, he was off to make arrangements for the journey.

As it turned out, neither Julian nor Lady Linton needed to worry about Almack's—not that Julian did. Someone else was watching out for the Earl of Linton's interests and those of his family, someone who observed to Helen in her drawing room that evening as he sat listening to Clarissa play the new music he had brought her from Chappell's, "She is doing quite well on the pianoforte, is she not? Of course she is not Grace—no one ever will be—but she has improved a great deal under Lord Farnsworth's tutelage, wouldn't you agree? Freddy nodded happily as he leaned forward to catch the last notes of the piece.

Helen could not help noting the irony of Clarissa's being tutored by the very man whose uncle had been bound and determined his nephew, Randall would have nothing to do with the sort of women who inhabited this establishment where he was now a general favorite, as much for his musical abilities as for his sweetly innocent view of life.

"Yes, she has made remarkable progress, as has Lord Farnsworth. Your brother John tells me that Randall now plays regularly for holy services at St. George's, though I am not at all certain that such success pleases his parents." Freddy could not conceal his sympathetic sigh for another heir constrained by the prospect of inheriting a title which abolished all hopes of being able to follow his own particular passion.

Poor Freddy. Helen read it all in his puckered brow. He was blessed with unexplored artistic talents and sensibilities, but saddled with not only the responsibilities of the heir to a dukedom, but a harpy of a fiancée as well. It didn't bear thinking of. Pushing it out of her mind, she proceeded with the matter at hand. "Dear Freddy, I know I have imposed on your good nature before . . ."

"Never, my dear."

"And you were so generous in introducing Lady Linton and her daughter around, but . . ."

"I am yours to command." Freddy's normal sunny expression returned

"Lord Linton has taken Dora's advice as to a young man who might serve as steward for his estate so he has gone to Northamptonshire to see to it, leaving his sister-in-law and niece without his escort. If, perchance, you happen to see them at Almack's or elsewhere, could you ensure that they are not completely ignored?"

"But of course." Freddy beamed. "Anything I can do. And if Georgie or my mother is about, utterly bored as they both are by Almack's, I am sure they can be counted on as well."

The smile tore at Helen's heart—not that she had one, of course. Poor Freddy, so unappreciated for his many talents—exquisite manners, impeccable style, inordinate kindness—that when someone did appreciate them, he was pathetically grateful. Someday, Helen would repay him for all he had done for her and her ladies, even if she had to murder Lady Lavinia Harcourt herself. "Thank you, Freddy. You are such a dear." As the color rose in his cheeks she patted him lightly on the shoulder, then turned and headed back to the card table where Freddy's brother was waiting for his partner.

That was all Helen could do make Julian's life easier while he was trying to help his family, though why she should want to do so, she refused to consider.

Perhaps it was because she was still grateful to him for the care and concern he had shown toward Annie Bentley and her unhappy situation, not to mention his very real assistance in turning the poor woman's life around. Or, devil take it, perhaps she just liked the man in spite of herself, and doing something, even a little thing like this made her miss him less. And yes, she did wonder how he was doing, blast it!

Julian was doing very well indeed. Surveying young Mr. Stornaway across the desk from him in the library at Linton Hall, he liked what he saw. It was a frank, open face with earnest brown eyes set wide apart in strong square features. These eyes looked directly back at him with a calmness that showed a young man who was comfortable with himself and others, a man who would be trusted on first sight by tenants, servants, shopkeepers, and the local gentry.

"Thank you for agreeing to meet with me. As I mentioned in my letter, you have a most excellent reference from a very critical source.

"Miss Dora." Ned smiled. "She is a clever one all right. Always was bright as a penny, even as a young girl, and she stepped right up to help at the inn when her mother died, took over all the accounts, paid the tradesmens' bills, but try as she did, she couldn't keep her father from that bloodsucker."

"Ah. I gather there was an unfortunate story."

"Yes, a fire in the stables caused by a careless ostler with a lamp. Old Barlow didn't have the blunt to repair the damage, so when his neighbor, Mr. Crowle, a wealthy merchant, offered to lend him the money to do so, he accepted, not knowing what a scoundrel he was. Crowle kept raising the rate until Barlow, could not afford it, and then took him to court to claim the inn. It destroyed Barlow. He died soon after and Dora disappeared." He paused, frowning fiercely. "Everyone assumed she'd gone to live with family, but there never had been any mention of relations before. I always suspected that there was some further nastiness, but, well, I had no idea what, and she was gone before anyone could ask or help. But you know her from London. I do hope that means she landed on her feet."

"Most definitely." Julian chuckled. "She is now the proprietress of an excellent property in Marylebone which she intends to let for a handsome sum, as well as being heavily invested in the consols and a lucrative annuity-all toward her main goal of owning her own inn someday."

Ned laughed. "That sounds like our Miss Dora, a hard worker and a fighter if there ever was one. Never did let even the rudest customers get the better of her. I am grateful she remembered me. I do hope I may be of service to you. I admit that seeing after an estate such as this," he glanced out the window towards the land beyond, "fallow though it may be at the moment, is a sight more to my liking than working as a clerk in the bank, no matter how bright my prospects."

"I need someone with that sort of passion. As you so obviously noted, the estate needs that passion. I will convey your thanks to Miss Barlow. And Crowle? Did he make a success of the inn, then?"

"No," Ned replied with some satisfaction. "He had not the least idea how to manage it, and of course no one hereabouts would frequent the tavern after learning how Barlow had been done out of it, so he was forced to sell. Then, a few years ago, a maid found him unconscious on the floor in his office with a bruised jaw, as though someone had planted him a facer. The man hasn't been the same since. Naturally he's gotten older, but all the bluster is gone. You must be sure to tell that to Miss Dora when you see her."

"I shall. Now let us walk the property and discover the worst of it." Julian rose and the two men headed out.

As they walked and talked, Julian found himself relaxing. He had always loathed Linton Hall once the boyhood charm of roaming the fields and pastures had worn off and he had realized he was imprisoned in the gray stone *Tudor pile* as his drunken father had called it, a place as grim and gray as the loveless family that inhabited it. Now, hearing Ned expound on the fineness, albeit deteriorated, of the building, and the potential of the fields, pastures, and woods he had explored as a child, Julian began to feel hopeful. Maybe it could be made into a productive estate again. Maybe the house could be emptied of the detritus of the ages and repaired into a place that welcomed visitors from all over as the aged butler had told him it had in his great grandfather's time.

Unbidden, his thoughts turned to Helen. The place needed a mistress, not his washed-out sister-in-law, but a brilliant, strong-minded woman with the backbone to refurbish and manage such a place, and the taste, *savoir-faire*, charm, and dignity to draw people from far and near. What was wrong with him? He was all about in the head. He didn't want to live here. He had never wanted to live here, but suddenly Ned was making him see the place's potential, and as a good businessman, Julian knew that no one could help such a place realize that potential like Helen Gerrard. But that would mean the place needed a mistress, and he didn't want to marry to give Linton Hall a mistress. Marriage trapped people into misery, robbing them of their souls and their energy. He knew that. He had seen what it had done to his mother.

No, let Ned bring the estate back to the way it should be while Julian escaped back to his law books, back to London where he was involved in things that inspired him rather than being buried in an ancient pile in the middle of the country that only reminded him how lonely and empty life was.

Escape back to London he would, well satisfied that Ned's easy, knowledgeable manner and his connections with everyone in the surrounding countryside was winning him support among the staff—what was left of it. Julian bade

Ned goodbye several days later. "Mrs. Farnham is an excellent housekeeper, given the proper resources. Please encourage her to hire anyone she needs, especially if they are in want of work. Just tell her to do as my mother would have. She will know what that means, and now that people know you are in charge, they will not be so reluctant to work here."

Julian heaved a sigh of relief as he leaned back against the squabs of the carriage. His own instincts, as well as Dora's recommendation, had told him that young Stornaway would be good for the place, but when both Mrs. Farnham and Lawton, the aged butler, had voiced their cautious approval, he knew things were looking up at Linton Hall. Now, if nothing had deteriorated in Hill Street during his absence, the trip would have been successful indeed.

Things had not deteriorated in Hill Street, the Countess was happy to report. Not only was Julia at that very moment with Lady Georgiana Claverton at her sister-in-law's fashionable establishment, she was in alt over the first gown purchased at Maison Juliette which she had worn to great effect at Almack's.

"So you did go to Almack's." Julian saw that he was expected to give further opportunity to elaborate.

"Yes, we did," Lady Linton announced triumphantly, "in the Duke of Roxburgh's carriage, Lady Georgiana and her mother, and her brother being so kind as to invite us to join them."

Julian suspected that *kind* had nothing to do with it, for no matter how well-born Lady Linton and her daughter were, they were both rather colorless and boring, not to put to fine a point on it. If Freddy were involved, then it was very probable, that kind though he was, the idea had been planted by that clever strategist, Helen Gerrard.

He would have to call on her to thank her, as well as to report to Dora not only on Ned Stornaway but also on the unfortunate decline of Mr. Crowle.

Chapter 17

But the next day Julian appeared in St. James' Square with something a great deal more concerning than a successful evening at Almack's and news of Ned Stornaway on his mind. "It's Charlotte," he replied to Helen's unspoken question when she saw the tension in his face and shoulders. He sank in the chair in Helen's office having been hastily conducted there by Fenwick who knew a man in need of consultation when he saw one. Drawing a deep breath, he continued. "Her mother sent me a note a little over an hour ago demanding my immediate presence. Apparently Charlotte went driving in the park with," he ground his teeth in frustration, "Viscount Wormleigh, in his curricle. Why? I will never know. After all I said. You would think that going for a drive at such an unfashionably early hour would have given her mother pause. Well, that's neither here nor there, but her mother excused it as being perfectly unexceptionable because her maid was with her. Except that her maid was *not* with her. Yes, she had sat on the groom's seat until they reached the park, but then Charlotte suddenly remembered an errand she needed done for her at Yardley's and gave the maid a note to give to her mother, the note informing Lady Linton that her daughter and Viscount Wormleigh were on their way to be married. Can you credit the naivete, the sheer stupidity?"

"And the maid had no inkling? She packed no bags, no."

"None of that. Before I set people making inquiries at the stable of every inn on the Great North Road, I sent Griggs to Cavendish Square, but Harcourt's valet was as mystified as the rest of us, and the curricle has not been returned. No man is going to abandon his prime cattle and his curricle to the tender mercies of ostlers at some inn. If not Gretna, then where have they gone?"

"Hmmm." Helen rose and, turning to the bookshelves behind her, pulled down a well-worn volume, opened it, flipped through it, ran a finger down one of the pages, and paused. "Possibly to Wormleigh Manor? It's not far, near Harrow, not beyond the reach of a curricle."

His eyes caught the title as she closed the cover and shelved it. "The *Annual Register*. Why didn't I think of that? That's it! I *knew* you would know the answer! A special license. He's convinced the silly chit that he has a special license, and then he is going to use that to insure she brings him the dowry I promised to settle on her. Well," Julian smiled grimly, "he'll catch cold at that. I am going to stop them."

He rose, then paused, the expression on his face betraying an inward struggle. "You wouldn't . . ." he broke off and turned toward the door."

"Yes I would," she responded smoothly. "Just let me get my bonnet, pelisse, and gloves and give word to Fenwick."

"You are an angel! A clever angel. My niece will very likely ignore anything her old uncle has to say, but she might listen to you, another woman." Julian raised both her hands to his lips, then headed for the door.

"A witch or a sorceress perhaps," she laughed. "I have been called both, but angel? No."

"You're in the right of it," he agreed, smiling. "Far too awake on all suits to be an angel."

"I shall be back immediately with the carriage." He was gone, dashing down the stairs two at a time.

An angel. Helen's lips curved into a smile as she adjusted her bonnet in the looking glass. How sweet—deluded, but sweet. Far more rewarding, however, was the fact that he had come directly to her for advice when he was confused, and most rewarding of all was the grateful, knowing look as he cried *That's it! I knew you would know the answer*. Men had whispered many times that she was lovely, an angel even, and some had gone so far as to call her clever. Samuel had consulted her for her knowledge of mathematics and thus accounting but no one had ever relied on her for her cleverness, and no one she knew, except for Julian Bracebridge, Earl of Linton would ever have admitted such a thing. It took a strong man to do that.

Julian was back within the hour. He handed Helen into his traveling carriage, remarking, "At least we are only two hours behind them, three at best, so if all goes well, we ought to be able to retrieve her and head back before it gets very dark."

If Helen, whose life had never gone according to plan, thought this a trifle optimistic, she held her tongue.

"If nothing else," Julian settled back against the squabs, "it is a beautiful spring day. Let us make the best of it and enjoy our jaunt into the country."

"It *has* been a long time since I have been out of London," she acknowledged, and fell silent as the carriage rolled past Paddington Green and on to the Harrow Road. How long had it been since she'd walked on country roads, and paths through pastures and forests? In those days she had barely noticed them; they were just part of life in the country. Now they seemed like an incredible luxury.

Helen caught Julian examining her, not in an intrusive fashion, but with curiosity. It was a measure of how much she trusted him that she'd let her guard down enough to reveal anything in her expression, but clearly she had something that piqued his interest.

She shook her head, laughing at herself. "I can see you are dying to say *a penny for your thoughts.*"

It was his turn to laugh. "Once again proving that you are a witch or a mind-reading sorceress, but yes *a penny for your thoughts.*"

"I was thinking of what a stay in the country did for Grace. It seemed to give her back her youth. Of course she was looking after two young girls as their governess and music teacher while she was there, but still . . . ," she paused before admitting, "and it made me remember growing up in the countryside. Is it the fields and hedgerows, the birds and rabbits I miss, or the innocence of youth which, of course, I chafed at then."

"You craved the excitement of the city?"

"Not that so much as to travel, to study, to learn, to see what I had read about in books."

"Did you long to go to school the way my mother did?"

"Not that sort of school." She clapped a hand to her mouth. "I beg your pardon; that sounded dreadfully rude. What I mean is that I wanted to go to a school where I would learn more than globes, French, and the pianoforte, where I could learn all that I was fortunate enough to be taught by my father—Latin, Greek, algebra, the natural sciences—but surrounded by other students and friends. I never did learn the pianoforte," she added with a dismissive shake of her head. "If the truth be told, I longed to go to school the way you did."

Helen half-expected him to laugh at her.

"It saved my life," he responded, without bitterness, in a matter-of-fact way that made it all the more appalling. "And now, in turn, you want to say *a penny for your thoughts.*"

"Well?" She cocked her head.

"Fair is fair. Let us just say that I do not miss the innocence of my youth." The same dark shadow she had seen before was quickly banished as he leaned forward. "But tell me, what do you and Lord John Claverton find so enthralling about your mathematical discussions?" He was not, he told himself, trying to discover exactly what Lord John meant to her, or how much he meant to her; he was genuinely curious. As he listened, watching her eyes light up, her brow furrow as she tried to convey her fascination with the field, Julian found himself caught up in her enthusiasm.

He followed her explanation with his own tales of life in India, the machinations it required to convince the local lords to stop warring and start cultivating the land.

It seemed like no time at all, instead of the hours they had been on the road, when they saw the spire of St Mary's church in the distance and they paused long enough for the groom to ask a farm laborer the way to Wormleigh Manor. "I am avoiding requesting such information at an inn or from anyone who might remember us as being interested in the doings at Wormleigh Manor," Julian explained.

Silence fell as they both anticipated the confrontation that awaited them. Julian was a strong, clever man, with a wide experience of the world, but Helen knew that even a spineless wastrel like Basil could exhibit a scoundrel's ruthlessness when challenged and backed into a corner, and challenged he would be if the grim expression on her companion's face was anything to go by.

They pulled into a rutted drive flanked by beech trees, arriving at an equally unkempt sweep in front of a rambling Jacobean brick manor house that, to Julian's eyes, appeared more neglected than Linton Hall, if such a thing were possible.

The place looked deserted, the entrance barely visible between the two bays on either side of it, and no one came down the narrow stone steps to greet them. Julian climbed down from the carriage and was about to knock on the door when the barking of a dog from what must have been stables behind, roused an ancient servant who swung open the battered oak door and peered out. "Yes?"

"Lord Wormleigh."

"Er, he isn . . ."

"Go away, you fool," came an angry voice from the background, but since this seemed directed at the servant rather than him, Julian stood his ground.

"What the blazes are you doing here?" Basil strode forward, his chest thrust out pugnaciously.

"I've come to collect my niece," Julian responded calmly. Looking back over his shoulder, he nodded to the groom who had come around to help in the absence of other servants one might have expected at such an establishment.

"And what is *she* doing here?" If Basil's face had been twisted in anger before, it was livid with fury now.

"She has come to explain to Lady Charlotte just exactly the sort of brute you really are."

"You brought a *whore* to lecture my wife about me?"

"I doubt she is your wife yet, nor is she likely to be." Julian spoke as though he were quieting a restive horse. "Now I suggest we go inside instead of airing our differences on the doorstep like a couple of fishwives, but to answer your question, yes, I brought the owner of an establishment that was far too exclusive to let you enter its portals except that you were with the Marquess of Wrothingham. Mrs. Gerrard, who only welcomes the most sophisticated, well-connected, visitors with the most impeccable of reputations, both social and pecuniary, will be happy to explain precisely why a man she would ordinarily never have admitted into her establishment should not be my niece's husband."

Charlotte's face appeared, hovering anxiously at Basil's shoulder.

"Go back to your chamber!" He turned, pointing to the stairs.

"Exactly the sort of loutish behavior you were concerned about, I believe." Helen nodded at Julian as she took her place at his side.

"Oh very well." Basil led them into a dim, musty drawing room whose dirty windows did little to lighten the gloom, which was probably a good thing, Helen reflected, as Julian seated her in a chair on one side of the cold, empty fireplace.

"As I said, I am come to take my niece home before her reputation can be utterly ruined."

"But we are to be married!" Charlotte protested, having disregarded her supposed husband's orders to go to her room.

"Not married," Julian smiled grimly, "just as I suspected. And have you even seen this special license he told you he had procured?"

"No, but . . ."

"Then I should like to see it." He turned to Basil who was practically dancing with rage. "He may or may not actually have one, so we shall just see how big a scoundrel he turns out to be."

Basil stomped over to a desk by the window, opened a drawer, pulled out an official looking paper and thrust it into Julian's outstretched had with a smug smile. "There, you see."

Julian examined it carefully. "But I do *not* see. This is a license you had made up should you be questioned, but it is lacking the proper authority." Julian snorted as he tossed the offending paper on the floor. "Not that a man in your dire financial straits would want to lay out the blunt or the time necessary to procure the real thing. You did not think he was marrying you for love, did you?" Julian turned to his niece. "An honest man would have approached me, but he knew what I was likely to say, and so he devised a scheme to insure that the dowry I am bestowing on you would be his."

Julian favored Basil with a mocking smile. "You forget my legal training which ensures that I would guarantee my niece's protection in any marriage settlement, and that I would leave things in trust so that scoundrels like you are not able to pillage what she brings to the marriage as my brother did to her mother."

"Now, Charlotte, gather your pelisse, gloves, and bonnet which is, what your maid assures me, all you brought with you, and we shall be on our way."

"You have no . . ." Basil lunged forward, but Julian forestalled him, "I have every right. And if you make any sort of resistance, I shall see that you are charged with kidnapping."

"But I went with him willingly." Charlotte paused in the doorway as she went to do her uncle's bidding.

"Under false pretenses, for which he intended to demand ransom," Julian snapped, "the ransom of your dowry. There, look at his face. You can see it all writ large. Now get ready so that we can leave as quickly as possible."

Chapter 18

It did not take long for Charlotte to gather herself together and climb sullenly into the carriage after Basil had stormed off in a rage, and, the horses having been fed and watered during the confrontation, they were soon on their way back to London.

For quite some time silence reigned as they rolled past green fields and blossoming fruit trees, but finally Julian took the conversational plunge. "I do believe, despite the needless uncomfortable drama, that I am doing what is best for you."

"But he loves me, and he will be the next Earl of Harcourt," Charlotte sniffed, rubbing her eyes.

"I already told you that he proposed because he is in desperate financial straits and needed your dowry to stave off his creditors. It was love of his own skin, not love of you that drove him to this." Julian saw that she remained unconvinced. "Think of your mother and father. Do you wish to live the way they did? What is the point of being the wife of an earl if you are trapped on an estate in the country that is falling into disrepair with no funds to improve it? If that does not give you pause, then listen to what Mrs. Gerrard has to say about the sort of person he is."

Helen drew a deep breath. This was not going to be easy. The girl had a mulish look on features that were so unremarkable she had need of a generous dowry. "You would not want to live with a man who hurt you, I trust? Ah, I see you do not think Viscount Wormleigh capable of such a thing. I might not have either except that I saw him strangling my friend Dora with such fury that it took a battle-hardened soldier to pull him off, and she bore the marks of his hands around her neck for weeks. Now," she held up a hand, "you will say that she must have provoked him, but they had not been together long enough to do much to make him turn so violent; therefore, I say, he has a dangerously quick temper, not a good thing in a husband."

"But he would not lose it with me. I am a lady. I am respectable. You and..."

"Mrs. Gerrard is every bit as much a lady as you are!" Julian's voice cut through the pregnant silence like a whip. "She too is the granddaughter of an earl."

So I am. How odd, I had forgotten that after all these years. Helen could not help remarking to herself. "It does not take much for a *lady* to fall on hard times, to find herself without protection and at the mercy of the world. The daughter of one of the noblest soldiers and one of the most ancient titles in France, a daughter whose well-born mother threw her out when her stepfather became infatuated with her. I do not say such a thing could happen to you, I simply say that being a *lady*, or even being *respectable*," Helen could not banish the ironic note from her voice, "is no defense against misfortune, nor is it any protection against those who would do one harm."

Charlotte remained defiantly mute until her uncle, drawing his own deep breath, played his last card. "Charlotte, do you remember your grandmother, Marina?"

"Nnno," she shook her head slowly, "just that she was sickly and then she moved to Brighton for her health, and then she died not long after."

"She was sickly because your grandfather made her so, and not because he imbibed too freely, which he did, but because he beat her." He paused as she gasped. "Yes, he beat her regularly, so she was often confined to her bed for days at a time. She too thought she was making a good marriage ... to an earl," he smiled grimly, "an earl with uncontrollable temper who wanted her to suffer whenever anything went wrong in his life, which it frequently did because he was foxed most of the time. I should have known ... should have seen ..."

And now Helen knew where that shadow came from –the horror that had been Julian Bracebridge's childhood.

"When one is a child, one is too caught up in one's own childish problems to think of one's parents. And then, just as I began to wonder about Mama and her strange illnesses, I was sent away to school. I was happier away, away from my father with his cold threatening silences and angry outbursts, away from someone who told me I was stupid and doing everything wrong. I stayed away, spending school holidays with friends because anything was better than going home. It was not until I came home briefly from university to answer to my father as to what I was going to do with the rest of my life that I discovered the truth.

"I heard him yelling at her in the drawing room, then a crash and silence, and a little while later I heard him galloping down the drive at breakneck speed, which is what he often did when he was in a temper."

"I found my mother unconscious on the floor in the drawing room, a gash on her forehead where she had hit a table when falling, and bruises on her wrists from trying to fight him off."

"When I called the footmen to help me carry her to her room, I could see from the speed and smoothness with which they accomplished their task and the resignation on their faces that this was not the first time they had been called upon to do this."

"When my mother came to, I was sitting at her bedside. She tried to excuse him, to explain it away, but she could see I was having none of it, and she finally confessed. He had always been a tyrant and frequently hit her, but she had managed to keep it from your father and me. By that time, your father had married and was living with you and your mother at Bracebridge Manor. With your father and me gone, it was just the two of them, and his attacks grew more frequent and more violent."

"I had no money of my own to take her away and take care of her, but I did arrange for her to go on an extended visit to her school friend, Lady Standiford on her estate near Brighton. Once she was safe, I left for India to seek my fortune in the hopes that I could save her."

Julian drew a weary hand across his eyes. "Which I did, make my fortune, I mean. I was able to buy her house in Brighton, and I had studied enough law at Oxford to convince my father that it was in his best interest to agree to a separation. He did, and died soon after, but Mama never truly recovered. My father had broken her ribs at some point, and, she, too ashamed to consult a physician, had not healed well so her lungs were affected. I planned to come home once I had purchased my ship and established my trading business, and then, when I was headed home, Mama died too."

The suspicious sheen of the haunted eyes fixed on Charlotte tore at Helen's heart. She had suspected; no, she had *known* with the certainty of one who had also suffered, that there was a great sadness in him, a sadness that drove him to defend women with an intensity that was palpable. Now she knew why. The championing of Dora, the rescuing of Annie Bentley, even his respect for what she had accomplished spoke volumes about the man, a man strong enough to acknowledge the misery he had witnessed as well as the despair and quiet helplessness he had suffered himself, a man driven to right the wrongs he had seen, and dedicate himself to trying to prevent them from occurring in the future.

Silence fell once again in the carriage. Everything to say had been said. With a glance between them, Helen and Julian agreed that it was best to say no more, but to let it all sink in. If it did not, there was nothing either of them could do.

But as he watched Charlotte's expression fade from mulish to thoughtful, to miserable, Julian took pity on her. "There is no need for you to marry, you know. Don't look so horrified. What I mean is that you need not accept an offer simply because you think you must be married. The money set aside for your dowry is in a trust for you which you will be able to access when you are twenty-five, should you not be married, and earlier if you are, but it is in trust so it cannot be spent as your mother's was. I also intend to refurbish Linton Hall and make it profitable again, and you and your mother are welcome to live there, in more comfort than before, for as long as you wish."

"Thank you." It was barely audible, but it was an acknowledgement. Maybe there was hope for the girl after all, Helen reflected as she smiled at Julian.

The smile was a ray of sunlight in the gloom of the carriage, and it warmed his heart. Perhaps he had accomplished something after all. He hadn't been around to save Helen Gerrard—oh how he wished he had been—but maybe he'd saved his niece.

Julian had seen the tightening of her jaw and a flash of pain, quickly banished, in Helen's eyes at the word *respectable*. Only the most acute observer, only someone who cared for her the way he did would have seen it, but it was there. How odd, and how telling, that *I am a lady* had not affected her in the least, but *I am respectable* still had the power to hurt her after all these years. Someday, he promised himself, he would wipe away that hurt. He did not know how or when, but he would do it.

The sky had deepened from pink to the soft blue of evening when they pulled up in front of the house in Hill Street. Julian descended, handed his niece down and allowed the waiting footman to accompany her inside as he gave instructions to the coachman to deliver Mrs. Gerrard to St. James' Square.

Then he leaned in to take both Helen's hands in his as he looked up at her, his eyes dark with emotion. "I can't thank . . ." his voice suspended a moment, "I can't thank you enough, not only for your invaluable assistance in figuring out where they had gone, but for coming with me. I know it helped, not the least because it put Wormleigh in such a temper that Charlotte was able to get some inkling of what sort of man he is. But mostly . . . mostly, I thank you for being there for me when I needed you. No one, but *no one* in my life has ever done that. Bless you." He turned to go, but stopped to look back at her with an impish grin. "To quote a clever friend of mine, *I know I cannot pay you, but I will repay you*," and then he shut the door to the carriage, tapped on the side, and they pulled away as he climbed the steps to deal with whatever awaited him. Helen hoped it was heartfelt thanks.

It was not thanks so much as heartfelt relief, awkwardly expressed by a woman well aware that she should have taken her brother-in-law's advice more seriously. "I have sent her upstairs with her maid for a bath and supper in her bed chamber. "Charlotte's mother greeted Julian as he was ushered into the drawing room. "She said no one saw her, other than the woman who accompanied you."

Julian ground his teeth. "That woman was the one who figured out where she had been taken. Make no mistake about it, it was a kidnapping to force me to agree to the marriage and the dowry. There was no special license; it was a forgery, and not a good one."

"Good heavens," the countess clasped her hands to her breast. "But no one saw you? No one else knew?"

"No, I used the utmost care. It was all very discreet." How like Maria to be more concerned about her daughter's reputation than her actual safety, he thought in disgust and then, vowing to put it out of his mind with a good glass of port and the perusal of legal cases in front of his own fire, Julian headed down Hill Street toward Berkeley Square, Piccadilly, and home.

Chapter 19

Helen would have preferred to have supper on a tray quietly in her bed chamber where she could sit in front of the fire and reflect on all she had learned from Julian's recital of his mother's history, but there could be no such luxury for the proprietress of Mrs. Gerrard', so she allowed Rose to dress her as usual and descended to the drawing room, ruthlessly thrusting the day's events to the back of her mind as she mingled among the guests. Only Dora, observing her employer with senses sharpened by years of friendship, noticed the quietness about her, the softening of the sharp wit, the blunting of the tart rejoinders, smoothing the ironic lift of the brow. Lord John, too, felt the preoccupation in his partner—not enough to be noticeable to the other card players, but revealing to someone who was used to brilliance when mere excellence was being manifested this evening, and he resolved to get to the bottom of it. It must be something of importance for nothing and no one put Helen Gerrard even slightly off her game.

Some hours later, seeing the card players well absorbed in their games and the others in intimate conversations with their companions, Helen quitted the room and headed upstairs to bed, once again unnoticed by anyone except Dora and John who glanced at on another across the room in silent reaffirmation of their mutual concern.

Helen might have retired early, but it was not to sleep. How horrible for a son to suffer such an agony of worry and distress over his mother, and be so powerless to help her for so many years. How he must have loathed his father and scorned his brother for remaining so oblivious or unconcerned. Compared to the mental and physical anguish the Countess of Linton had suffered, Helen's life had been one of relative comfort and ease, if not of *respectability*. She smiled cynically to herself as she thought of the life of misery Charlotte had courted, all in the name of *respectability*. Give her control rather than respectability any day, Helen vowed as she thanked her lucky stars she had learned from male brutality early enough in her life never to be victim of it again, and to be given the rare privilege of helping others like her achieve the same state.

But Helen revised that self-congratulatory thought the very next day when Basil Harcourt stormed into her office. She rose to face him, wishing she had, had time to grab the poker by the fireplace, her hand surreptitiously moving towards the pile of books on her desk.

"You miserable bitch! This is the last time you will thrust your interfering nose into my business!" Face twisted with rage, he lunged at her, hands raised to throttle her neck as Helen's book slammed him in the forehead, throwing him off balance. "You whore!" He struggled to regain his footing. This is the end of you."

"I think not." Julian planted a right hook on the reeling viscount, landing him semi-conscious in a chair, then turned to Helen. Grasping her shoulders he anxiously examined her face for any signs of distress. There were none—just disgust, but he clung to her anyway. "You are not hurt?"

"No," she snapped, "merely irritated. She gave him her ironic half-smile as she retrieved the book from the floor. "I am sure Mr. Nicholson never dreamed his *Essays on Combinatorial Analysis* would be used to such stunning effect."

Julian laughed. "It was a superb hit, I do admit, but please," he studied her intently, "tell me that this . . . this filth has done you no harm."

"I am quite alright, my lord. I learned long ago not to pay the least mind to such *filth*, as you call it."

"And you," Julian turned back to Basil who was slowly recovering his sense and nursing his jaw, "will remain here in this chair reflecting on your miserable soul until Tom Sandys and Syed Muhammad escort you back to your lodgings.

When Julian had arrived in St. James' Square a quarter of an hour earlier, he had been met by a distraught Fenwick. "Oh my lord, I am that concerned. Viscount Wormleigh asked for Mrs. Gerrard and when I told him I would inform her of his presence, he just pushed me aside and stomped upstairs. Pushed me aside! And Mr. Sandys is on an errand for Miss Barlow. I . . . oh what am I to do?"

"I shall take care of it," Julian reassured the shaken butler. "Just tell Mr. Sandys when he returns to go to my lodgings at Albany and ask Mr. Syed Muhammad to accompany him back here. Now I must stop that scoundrel," he tossed over his shoulder as he mounted the steps two at a time heading towards Helen's office.

Now you will go quietly with these gentlemen," Julian stood aside as the two burly men helped a scowling Basil struggle to his feet, "because I am sure you don't want us to have to enlist the services of Constable Peabody. After all, we wouldn't want anyone accusing Mrs. Gerrard of running a *disorderly house*." The words had no effect; Basil's scowl remained, and, stealing a glance at Helen, Julian could see that she too was thinking that the lack of response meant that Basil was completely ignorant of the latest accusations against her establishment.

I should also caution you against appearing in the vicinity of Mrs. Gerrard's again—or of anyone connected to it. Syed Muhammad is not called the *Shadow of Bengal* for nothing. You will never see him, but his eyes will always be on you."

Basil looked almost like a child in between the two enormous men as they led him to the door, but there was nothing childish in the venom in his voice as he glared at Helen. "You think you are so high and mighty, but you are nothing but a whore. You may own the leasehold here, but you do not own the freehold. You had best take care, you trollop or you will find yourself out on the street."

"I don't think so," Julian replied grimly. "As someone who has just been called to the bar, not to mention being involved in business, I know when a legal document is solid, unlike your *special license*."

But Helen could not help frowning after the door shut. "Do you think he knows something we do not?"

"I am sure of it, which is why I am grateful that in his anger he forgot himself enough to reveal something he probably should not have."

"Oh." She could think of nothing else to say. In truth, now that the nasty little scene was concluded, Helen was feeling rather weak in the knees. She sank back into the chair behind her desk while Julian rang the bell for a servant.

"It's just me, ma'am, as Mr. Sandys has gone with . . . oh, hello, my lord." Mary, the newest maid at Mrs. Gerrard's, dropped a curtsey.

"I believe your mistress could do with a strong cup of tea," Julian smiled, "as could I."

"Very good, my lord." Filled with importance that such a task had fallen to her, the girl went off determined to accomplish it as expeditiously as possible.

"I am so sorry," Julian rounded the desk to take Helen's hands in his as the door closed. "This is all my fault. If I had not begged for your assistance with my niece, he never would have taken his anger out on you. But never fear, Syed Muhammad may in fact be here in England to assist scholars at Oxford with the translation of Asian manuscripts, Persian to be exact, and to teach Persian to those intending to work with the Mughal Empire, but for many years he was employed by, and even fought for the East India Company and therefore knows how to handle himself in a fight. I believe he is considered quite a fearsome ally by those in the Company who have fought alongside him."

His hands were so warm and strong that Helen could not help giving herself up to the pleasure of their reassuring clasp. They made her want to cling to him, lay her head on his broad shoulder, close her eyes and, just for a moment—only a moment—give up the weight of the world that lay on her own shoulders, but . . .

The door opened and Mary entered, bearing a tray laden not only with tea, but a wide array of cakes. Had it been that long Helen had sat there bemused and dreaming? She shook her head to snap out of it. What was she thinking? Yes, the weight of the world and her responsibilities lay on her shoulders, but she had chosen that; she also had control over it. Only she could decide how to handle it. She squared her shoulders, retrieved her hands, and began to pour the tea.

"Congratulations on being called to the bar." She grabbed the first topic of conversation she could think of, any topic to retrieve her composure.

She might have appeared calm and self-possessed to anyone else, but Julian was not just anyone. In addition to his well-developed powers of observation, his heart was involved. He saw the struggle in the shadows in those deep green eyes. Yes, he admitted it. He cared for Helen Gerrard, and if he had not known it before, he did now after the red mist of rage and protectiveness had nearly blinded him at the sight of her facing Basil. It was not a case of a helpless woman and a brutal man bringing back his own terrible memories for Helen was defending herself furiously and effectively. It was the thought of what she meant to him, how lost he would be without her in his life that had driven Julian's fist into that miserable cur's jaw, and he would have kept driving it again and again if he had not, in a supreme act of self-control, stopped himself from beating the man to a pulp.

"I am so glad," Helen continued, "that we have another champion in our world—not that you weren't a champion before—but now you have the legal power to bring brutes to justice, *to make bad men afraid* as Juliette wished to do when she convinced Lord Adrian and Lord John to teach us to box, but in addition to *making bad men afraid*, you, and only you, can make an example of them by punishing them in ways that will make those who would imitate them think twice before doing so."

His heart filled at her quick understanding of all he wished to accomplish, and her calm assumption that he would do so. "Thank you," he whispered.

Helen saw the glow her words brought into his eyes, and it gave her a joy she had never felt, even when helping women like Juliette and Grace. Yes, she had rescued them from poverty and helped them reclaim their lives, but looking in Julian's at this moment, she knew she had rescued his soul. Now what was she to do with it? And why did the thought of it scare her so much?

His eyes fixed on her face, Julian emptied his cup as he tried desperately to figure out what she was thinking now. It was something so complicated that even he could not decipher it. Setting down the cup, he rose. "I must be going." His lips twitched into a lopsided grin. "Now that you have mapped out my future for me, I must get on with it, and I need to get to work on repaying you."

She rose too. "You already have, abundantly." She eyed his knuckles which betrayed their contact with Basil's jaw.

"Nonsense. You rescued yourself. I will be the one who decides when you are repaid because only I know how much you have done for me." He stared down at her for a moment, then gently pressed his lips to hers and was gone.

Chapter 20

Helen lifted her hand to her lips as she sank back into her chair. If her knees had been weak after her confrontation with Basil, they offered no support at all now. She could not recall when, if ever, she had actually been kissed on the lips. Her rapist had barely touched her, except to force her over a desk, pull up her skirts and thrust her legs apart, and Samuel? Well, Samuel had wanted someone to listen, understand, and appreciate him more than anything else. But having someone else's lips touch hers so softly and lovingly was a novel sensation. She was overwhelmed with an aching tenderness . . . and something else, something that felt like being hungry. Usually Helen's body never spoke to her. This was a new and rather disturbing sensation. Thank goodness Julian had been called to the bar. He would now be too busy as a practicing barrister to have any time for Helen Gerrard which meant that her body would not likely experience such an unsettling sensation again. She should have been relieved by this; instead, the thought of never looking again into those dark blue eyes, at that lean tanned face, left her feeling hollow rather than gratified.

Helen was correct, Julian was plunging into work, but it was not the sort of legal work she was picturing.

He had left St James' Square filled with a burning desire to avenge her, to protect her from every threat that might possibly come near her, and the best way to do that was to discover more about the freehold to which the despicable Basil had alluded, and the mysterious L Askew who apparently owned it, which Julian very much doubted. Unknown commoners were hardly likely to own the freehold on such an important property in such an excellent location, and he suspected that L. Askew was a convenient straw man for the true owner who, for some reason, did not wish to be known. The best way to find out more about that was to discover what he could from the solicitor who had sent the threatening letter to Helen that was so easily disposed of by *the offer of a little extra blunt*, as Dora had so pithily summed it up.

When Julian returned to chambers, he extracted the letter from his desk. It came from a Mr. Stephen Mordaunt in Chancery Lane. "Ben?"

"Yes, my lord," Julian's boy appeared in the doorway.

"I know you are a clever lad whose skills far exceed the delivery of messages."

"Yes, my lord." Ben grinned, revealing a set of remarkably white but dreadfully crooked teeth.

"Skills so overlooked that if you were to ask a few discreet questions here and there about a solicitor in Chancery Lane no one would be the wiser."

"I'm your man. Mum's the word, my lord." He was out the door and down the stairs like a fox after a rabbit.

Definitely talent that has been wasted, Julian remarked to himself as the lad sped off. *We shall have to see what we can do to change that.*

Two days later, Julian himself, after having learned, among many other things Ben had discovered, the precise time of day Mr. Mordaunt always took his meal at the Old Bell, strolled into the solicitor's office at that exact hour and presented his card to the clerk standing at a desk diligently copying a document.

"Er, he's not in, my lord. I shall tell him of your visit directly he returns. Or if there is any way I may be of assistance..."

"I am looking for a new solicitor and I understand the Earl of Harcourt retains Mr. Mordaunt's services, which is all the recommendation I need."

"That he does, my lord, but I am not sure if Mr. Mordaunt is accepting new clients, that is to say..."

"Though I gather that Mr. Askew is also a client."

"Oh no sir, that is Mr. Askew is not actually a client of Mr. Mordaunt's, just involved with the freehold is all."

"Ah, very well." Julian nodded, resigned. "I can see I shall have to look elsewhere. Thank you. Good day."

"Good day, my lord." The young man bent back over the documents he had been copying when interrupted by his unexpected visitor, and Julian, well satisfied that his hunch that had been born out both by Ben's inquiries and his own follow-up, strolled back to his chambers.

"Lord Linton to see you, ma'am," Fenwick announced somewhat later that day.

Helen was highly irritated at the spark of happiness that ran through her at her butler's announcement, telling herself it was simply the pleasure of seeing a friend and nothing more, but she knew she was lying to herself.

"I do apologize for bothering you," Julian entered her office, "but I need to ask another favor of you."

"What? Another favor?" One delicate brow rose, but the teasing note in her voice softened the skeptical expression.

"If you would be so kind, I would like to make use of Tom Sandys' services—very briefly, of course."

"Tom Sandys?"

"Yes. You mentioned that Lord Adrian had him trail the *nice spoken, middling everything* man who made use of your servant's information, to a gambling hell where he was then forced to give up the chase after arousing the suspicions of those working at the establishment.

"Yes he did."

"Well, I encountered a *nice spoken, middling everything* young man today who could possibly be our man. He is a clerk for a solicitor who dealt with L. Askew, a Mr. Mordaunt, who, my errand boy discovered from asking around, also happens to be the Earl of Harcourt's solicitor. If Sandys could identify this clerk as the *nice spoken, middling everything* young man who hired your maid that would clarify a number of things."

This time, both eyebrows rose. "You *have* been busy, my lord. I am impressed, and not a little nervous at how quickly you unravel murky problems. Fortunately, there is nothing you do not already know about me and my establishment or I would be truly worried. However, I shudder to think what would have happened had I sought to hide anything from you. Actually, now that I think of it, I was not entirely forthcoming about my identity, and you unmasked that far too quickly for comfort. You are indeed a dangerous man, which is why I am delighted to offer you Tom Sandys' services."

He grinned. "Thank you. This should not take too long. I gather Mr. Sandys' days in the Peninsula have made him into something of a scout."

"Lord Adrian vouches for him absolutely—a formidable scout and a master forager."

"Yes, my lord," Tom replied when Julian tracked him down in the front hallway, 'I did see the gentleman close enough to be able to recognize him again."

"Good. My lad, Ben, will establish what time this man goes home in the evening, and if you could arrange to be outside Mr. Mordaunt's offices and get a good look at him that would be most helpful."

Ben was able to come up with the necessary information, and two evenings later Tom watched from a nearby doorway as the clerk locked up, and then sauntered some distance behind him, looking for all the world like a down-at-heels tradesman with nothing to do but lounge around Chancery Lane.

"It were the same man," he confirmed to Julian the next day. "I followed him a bit, but he didn't go back to that hell, just headed toward Cheapside so I left off and returned to my work. Even though he is *middling everything* I would know him anywhere—has a bit of a hitch in his gait, not so's most would notice, but it's there if you're looking for it."

Thank you, Sandys. You may have been thwarted the first time in running your quarry to ground, but we have got him now, and I feel fairly certain we shall discover the answer to the question of who sent the carriage after Lady Adrian."

"That would be wonderful, my lord, and a relief to Lord Adrian. I was that mortified I could not discover the answer to that back then."

"Never fear," Julian clapped him on the shoulder, "you have this time"

Ben and Tom had done their work, now it was time for Julian to do his. Once again he appeared in Chancery Lane just minutes after Mr. Mordaunt had left.

"He's not here, my lord. You just missed him again." Despite being a *nice spoken* young man, the clerk's tone betrayed irritation at the interruption and the apparent dimwittedness of a man who could not seem to learn when the solicitor took his meal.

"Oh I am not here to see Mr. Mordaunt, I am here to see you, Mr . . ."

"Me, my lord?" he exclaimed in astonishment. "But I am.." then, remembering the question, he added, "it's Prescott, my lord, William Prescott."

"Yes, Mr. Prescott, I am here to see you." Julian disposed himself in a nearby chair. "I am curious as to the interest you evinced some years ago in a certain young woman in St. James' Square."

"I wasn't interested in her, I mean Daisy, that is, she being just a servant and all."

"It is not Daisy to whom I refer. The woman in question. I am speaking of Mademoiselle Juliette, better known now as Lady Adrian Claverton. Daisy, mere servant that she was, was just there to supply you with information on Lady Adrian's comings and goings. Now why was that?"

"It weren't me," the young man blinked rapidly, "I had no interest in her."

"But someone else did. I believe that, that someone else may have been a Harcourt, else why hire you among the hundreds of young men in the city who could do the job?"

"I . . . er . . ." William paled and swallowed several times, then squared his shoulders. "I figured the young master was taken with her and wanted to know when and where he could happen upon her, if you know what I mean. And that's all I know."

"I know what you mean," Julian's face was grim, "but I don't for a moment think that, that is all you know. You were followed, you know, right after you met the servant beneath your notice, to a rather disreputable sort of establishment, not the sort of place frequented by up and coming young men like you. I wonder who you met and why?"

If the unfortunate clerk had been pale before, he was white as a sheet now. "I . . . I canno . . . I must not . . . it's as much as my life is worth."

"Come, come now," Julian smiled reassuringly, "I am sure we can help one another out. There are other solicitors in the City, you know, who are in need of an industrious young clerk and I can put in a good word for you..."

"It's not like that, my lord... er, I mean it is, but it's worse."

Obviously the lad was in over his head. He looked like a diligent sort, head bent continuously over his work, even with his employer out and even though he stuttered and stammered, he continued to look his interlocutor straight in the eye. Julian took pity on him. "How about if I tell you what I think happened and you can correct me where I am wrong?"

William nodded, too unnerved to speak.

"I imagine that somehow the Harcourts have a hold over you or someone you love, and they have exerted that hold to force you to do things that make you most uncomfortable."

William nodded vigorously.

"I think you met someone at that questionable establishment, someone who was the sort of person who could be hired to drive a carriage dangerously through St. James' Square at the precise moment Lady Adrian would have been returning to Mrs. Gerrard's."

There was no response this time, but the lad's look of misery was all the confirmation Julian needed. "And if it had not been for Lord Adrian's quick thinking and acting, she would have been grievously injured, or, quite possibly, killed."

"I thought he was just supposed to scare her, and I was told by Lady... er, I was told to find a jarvey who wasn't too nice in the way he did things and might like to earn a bit of blunt. I didn't know a person like that, but Jim, the stableboy, knew of just such a one, and he frequented that, er, place you mentioned, so I went there to find him."

"Jim, the Harcourt's stableboy?"

Again the stricken look, followed by a barely discernible nod.

"And it is not Lady Harcourt to whom you refer," Julian was rapidly putting two and two together as a likely scenario was forming in his mind, "but Lady Lavinia."

"Yes. She is the one who runs ev... er, well..."

"A woman of iron will, Lady Lavinia, a woman who knows what she wants and gets it, I take it."

"Exactly, my lord, but now what am I to do? My life is over and my mother and sister..."

"Tell me about them," Julian directed, not unkindly.

"Well, my father was a tenant farmer for Lord Harcourt when one day he and I were coming back from the village in our wagon, and a curricle went flying by, barely missing us, but it panicked the horses who bolted. My father fell out and was dragged until he hit his head on a boulder. He was killed instantly. I managed to jump clear, but I broke my leg."

There's a hitch in his step. "Let me guess," Julian scowled, "the driver of the curricle was none other than Viscount Wormleigh."

"Yes. His lordship, the Earl, I mean, felt badly enough for us that he has let my mother and sister remain in the cottage while another farmer rents the fields. My sister works at the Park, Harcourt, that is, as an upper housemaid. My mother is too frail for work, but she does take in mending, so you see . . ." he shrugged his shoulders helplessly.

"What I see is that you have been of inestimable help to me and I shall not only find you a clerkship elsewhere, but I have a small cottage on my estate that should suit your mother and sister nicely, and Mrs. Farnham, the housekeeper there, is definitely in need of just the assistance your mother and sister can provide."

"Bless you, my lord." William's face lit up and he straightened his shoulders as though a great weight had been lifted from the.

"And one more question."

This time there was no hesitation. "Anything, my lord."

"Tell me about this L. Askew."

'He was a wealthy banker, my lord, whose wife had social aspirations, and he knew Lord Harcourt from handling the mortgages on his estate. He offered to purchase the leasehold on the St. James' Square property for a great sum of money, which his lordship was in desperate need of at the time, in return for which the Countess, Lady Harcourt that is, would introduce his wife and daughters to the *ton*."

"Of course his lordship was most reluctant, it being a blow to his pride and all, but he desperately needed the money for Lady Lavinia's Season. In fact, he was so embarrassed at having to sell the leasehold, he asked Mr. Askew to act as a straw man to cover up the true owner of the freehold, for a certain pecuniary consideration, or course."

"Of course."

"But then Mr. Askew himself needed money, him not being familiar with the exorbitant cost of launching two daughters into society, so he offered to sell the leasehold to his old friend and colleague, Mr. Ward, who then gave it to Mrs. Gerrard, with whom we have since had correspondence."

"Which was again resolved by *a certain pecuniary consideration*."

'You have it exactly, my lord."

"Thank you, William. Once again, you have been extremely helpful, not to mention illuminating. I shall let you know as soon as I have found you a position and I have assured myself that the cottage is fit for your family's arrival."

"Bless you, my lord." The young man's eyes filled with tears. "I didn't mean to... I didn't want to do anything wrong, but..."

I know, I know," Julian concluded sadly, "but you were forced to do it. That is the way the world works where the rich and powerful are concerned, at least."

Chapter 21

Julian strolled back along Chancery Lane in a fog, not because he was surprised by what he'd learned—he'd always suspected the Harcourts were somehow at the bottom of all of it— but he had not expected Lady Lavinia to be the *deus ex mechina.* A grim smile twisted his lips. This revelation made it all the more intriguing and opened up a whole new wealth of possibilities. The question at the forefront of his mind, however, was what, or how much to tell Helen. In all honesty, he wanted to rush right over to St. James' Square and share everything with her, as he was increasingly inclined to do. There was nothing as stimulating and comforting as being able to lay the facts before a mind clever enough to appreciate all the implications and give an opinion, for where Helen Gerrard was involved, there was always bound to be an opinion.

Hang it all, he *would* call on her, and now, when everything was still fresh in his mind. His mind made up, he waved down a hackney.

"It's his lordship." By this time, Julian had become *his lordship* to Fenwick who had taken quite a shine—though he would have died rather than admit it—to the gentleman who seemed determined to make Fenwick's mistress' life easier.

"What? Linton again?"

Fenwick nodded.

"Well he must have something to the point to contribute or he would not be here. The man is not given to idle chatter. Send him in." Helen could not help being as eager to hear what he had to say as her visitor was to relate it to her.

"I gather you have news, my lord."

"I do."

She could see he was bursting to tell her, and she found his eagerness rather touching. "And?"

"In a word, it's Harcourt."

"The Earl of Harcourt is mixed up with a bawdy house? But he's never darkened our door."

"No, but he owns the freehold it stands on."

"Oh." It took her a minute to absorb the information. "He is L. Askew, then?"

"No. L Askew truly was a friend of Samuel Ward's, but in exchange for the social advancement of his wife and daughters, he bought the leasehold from Harcourt and agreed to act as straw man on the title of the freehold because the Earl was too ashamed to admit he had to sell the leasehold."

"Mmm." She nodded, taking in the logic and thinking, not for the first time, that having no reputation at all, in the standard social sense of the word, was almost worth it, considering the machinations people were forced to go through to maintain one. "But what was it about Lady Adrian, or this establishment that so concerned Harcourt that . . ."

"Not Lord Harcourt, Lady Lavinia Harcourt." He watched as enlightenment dawned, thrilled that she was so quick to see it all. "Of course, Freddy!"

"Yes, Freddy. Poor Wrothingham. He kept deferring the wedding with the excuse of readying the estate for his bride, and then he met Mademoiselle Juliette . . ."

"But if Mademoiselle Juliette were no longer around, Helen picked up the thought and continued, "he would no longer be distracted and would return to the obligations from which she had distracted him . . ."

"Except that because of the delightful company, not to mention the genuine appreciation of his very real talents, he found in St. James' Square," he nodded at Helen, "he continued to patronize Mrs. Gerrard's even after Mademoiselle Juliette had married his brother. What to do?"

"Try to scare the proprietress of the establishment into abandoning the leasehold, her establishment, and . . ."

"When it didn't work and she offered him *filthy lucre* to allow the thoroughly legal leasehold to remain in place unchallenged, the only recourse was the magistrate . . ."

"Who has been so well treated by the establishment in question, and his constables so well remunerated, that he neglected a crucial piece of information from the document rendering it useless," Helen finished triumphantly.

"Precisely." Julian was thoughtful for a moment, but a look of unholy glee soon lit up his face. "Lord, I would have given a monkey to see Lady Lavinia's face when she learned how easily her father had abandoned questioning the validity of the leasehold."

"So, you think . . ."

"The clerk to Mr. Mordaunt, the Harcourt's solicitor implied, completely by accident, that it is Lady Lavinia who is the power in that household."

Helen thought for a moment, then agreed. "Lady Georgiana, her prospective sister-in-law, says the servants all call Lady Lavinia *the duchess- to- be*, so often does she rub their faces in her future position. If she tries to exert that authority in the Claverton household, one can only imagine what she does in her own. Poor Freddy, no wonder he keeps delaying the inevitable with one renovation after another."

"Perhaps not inevitable." Julian's eyes narrowed in thought, then he rose. "At any rate, that is what I have uncovered so far, and I shall keep you abreast of any developments, should they occur." *And they will occur*, he promised himself.

Helen rose too, and this time it was she who held out her hand. "Thank you, not only for doing all this, but for sharing it with me."

She looked so beautiful standing there with the sunlight glinting on her hair, making a halo of red that set off the vivid green of her eyes and the emeralds twinkling in her ears, that he wanted to kiss her again, to tell her that he did not want to be her friend; he wanted something so much more. Reason prevailed, however, and he bowed over her hand and kissed that instead.

Julian returned to chambers in Essex Court and remained there deep in thought, going through the notes he had amassed and the documents Helen had shared with him. The time had come for him to confront the Harcourts. He sent a note around to Brook Street requesting a meeting with Lord Harcourt concerning the leasehold in St. James' Square. That was bound to catch that man's interest enough to make him agree to a meeting, and if Lady Lavinia were as involved in it to the degree that Julian suspected she was, she was bound to be nearby when the discussion took place.

The response came as quickly as Julian could have hoped, and three days later, he was ushered into the dim, dark-paneled library at the back of the Harcourt's slim house in Brook Street by a butler so ancient that he looked as though one foot was already in the grave and the other poised on the brink.

The man who rose to greet him was as dull and unprepossessing as the room, with thin, sandy hair, pale blue eyes, and not a distinguishing feature in his face. His manner was no livelier than his appearance as he gestured listlessly to a chair on one side of the empty fireplace and sank into the one opposite. "Linton," he acknowledged Julian, "you said you had some concerns about a leasehold and a freehold in St. James' Square, but I have no idea why you have come to me."

Because I knew you own the freehold on this property.

The man's eyes shifted uneasily as he reiterated, "I have no idea why you should come to me."

"I am a barrister, my lord," Julian couldn't help feeling a spurt of pride as he uttered the words, "and I know how to discover these things despite Mr. Askew's acting as your straw man."

The uneasiness grew into dismay as the Earl muttered, "But, but . . ."

"Never fear, I have not come to expose you, I have come to purchase it from you."

"You what?" The Earl sputtered. "Why it's been the family for centuries; I could not possibly entertain such a notion!"

"Nevertheless, I think you will," Julian continued smoothly. "You have already admitted to the ownership of the property, and I know it was your solicitor who wrote a fraudulent letter to the owner of the leasehold, claiming utterly false concerns over its legality. Then there was the letter from the magistrate accusing the owner of the leasehold of running a *disorderly house*."

The blank look on the Earl's face was proof enough that he was not the mastermind behind any of this. "Ah, that also must have been your daughter's idea, as was the runaway carriage."

"How dare you!" The Earl mustered enough energy to rise out of his chair, "How dare you bring my daughter into this? How dare you mention her name?"

Julian hadn't actually mentioned her name, but he let this minor detail slide. "Because I have proof that she hired a jarvey of exceedingly questionable character to run down Lady Adrian Claverton who was Mademoiselle Juliette at the time, an arrangement concluded by your solicitor's clerk, Mr. William Prescott."

"Mr. Prescott is a rather weak young man with an overactive imagination, and how dare you threaten my father," a voice so cold it could shatter glass spoke from the doorway as Lady Lavinia Harcourt swept into the room, disdain written on every feature of her countenance, from the beady, close-set eyes glinting angrily, to the high bridged nose that quivered with disgust.

"I am not threatening your father," Julian responded calmly, "I am offering him an excellent price for a piece of property he can so ill afford he has already sold the leasehold."

"How dare you, you impertinent . . ."

"But I *will* threaten both of you if you continue to act unreasonably. Now, as I was telling your father, I know about the threatening letter over the leasehold which he happily abandoned when presented with a pecuniary incentive to do so."

"I *told* you . . ." Lady Lavinia rounded on her father, then, remembering her audience, drew a sharp breath and froze into icy dignity again. "Nonsense, utter nonsense."

"Then there was the warrant against the leasehold for having a *disorderly house* that the magistrate unfortunately neglected to fill out properly, leaving it null and void." Again Julian saw the furiously accusing look his daughter darted at the unfortunate Earl.

"Again, utter rubbish."

"No, it is not utter rubbish. As I told your father, I am a barrister, I have read the law, and know whereof I speak. I also know that it is not only frowned upon, but it is actually illegal to plot another's death."

"What? The indignant red spots on her ladyship's cheek were replaced by a waxen pallor. Now it was her father's turn to look accusing, but he remained silent.

"And yes, I do have witnesses, so I suggest you consider my proposal. First, this is what I am prepared to offer for the freehold." He handed a paper to the Earl who took it with trembling hands. "Second, if Lady Lavinia calls off her engagement with the Marquess of Wrothingham, the entire sordid affair will be forgotten. But," he held up a hand as Lavinia opened her mouth to snap out a scathing reply, "If you do not agree, then I shall be forced to see that justice is done. Now what the courts will decide to do with someone who tried to engineer an innocent woman's, a prospective sister-in-law's death is not necessarily certain, but what the *ton* will do is absolutely certain. Do you truly believe the Clavertons would countenance a connection, no matter how longstanding, with someone who tried to murder a family member who is currently the mother of the only Claverton heir?"

This time it was the Earl who took charge while his daughter sputtered with rage. "I shall inform the Duke that my daughter, after much consideration, cannot find it within herself to continue with this protracted engagement and has decided that they will not suit one another after all."

Julian rose. "Very good, my lord. I shall have my solicitor draw up the papers, and upon your signature and that of Mr. Askew, he will present you with a draft on my bank." Bowing, to both the Earl and his daughter, he left, forcing himself to descend the stairs with measured dignity instead of taking them two at a time the way he wished to.

"You spineless fool!" Lavinia hissed.

The Earl rose to his full height which, admittedly, was not great, his usually pallid complexion crimson with frustration. "And you are a reckless, interfering female whose meddling accomplished nothing except this."

"*Someone* had to do *something*, and it is certain that you never would."

"Yes, *someone* had to do *something*. All *someone* had to do was control her managing ways long enough to bring her fiancée from birth up to scratch, but no, you were constantly demonstrating to him what living under the cat's paw would be like, poor fellow. No wonder he was not eager to set a date."

"Now we are ruined!"

"No, we are not ruined. We are quite plump in the pocket again after spending the entire sum from the leasehold on your come-out, not to mention settling your feckless brother's gambling debts. You can find yourself a rich husband, and he a rich wife, but I am no longer dancing to either of your tunes." The Earl stomped out, leaving his daughter open-mouthed in the middle of the library, and the maid, who had been dusting the pictures outside in the hallway agog with the anticipation of regaling her fellow servants with it all over supper.

Chapter 22

"Come upstairs, I have news!" Lady Georgiana Claverton breezed into the back room at Maison Juliette where her sister-in-law, Lady Adrian, was bending over a sketchbook designing a carriage dress for Lady Serena Cholmondely while two-year-old Auguste sat on the floor surrounded by blocks and a wooden farmyard set.

"Oh?" Juliette looked up from her work, her fair hair slipping out of the ribbon she'd tied it with to hold it back.

"Freddy is free, free, free from Medusa!"

"Who? Lavinia?" No one in the Claverton household called Freddy's fiancée by her proper name, Lady Lavinia Harcourt never having bothered to cultivate the good opinion of anyone in Claverton House, from its owners down to the servants. "Surely that is a rather drastic appellation for the unfortunate woman."

"Unfortunate? Lavinia?" Georgie was indignant. "She sucks the joy out of any gathering and turns Freddy, poor dear, absolutely stone cold with trepidation whenever her critical gaze falls upon him."

"Good heavens, this is quite a development. I am glad I left Claverton House early enough this morning to miss it." Lord Adrian and his family had come to town on one of their frequent forays, Adrian to see one of his prize thoroughbreds auctioned at Tattersall's, and Juliette to stop in and make sure Alice and everyone in the shop were doing well, and Auguste to be played with and doted upon by both sets of grandparents, the Duke and Duchess of Roxburgh and the Comte and Comtesse de Flournoy.

"Yes, I gather it was quite a thing. The Earl of Harcourt called on Papa this morning to inform him that his daughter had decided they would not suit. Can you credit that after all the years of her duchess-to-be-ing all over Claverton House?"

"No." Juliette laid down her pad and pencil. "I cannot. From all I heard from Grace, who encountered her on Brook Street when she taught music to the Countess of Edgefield's daughters, and from the way Freddy always seems to be where Lady Lavinia is not, I would have thought she was so determined to be Duchess of Roxburgh that a mere difference in personality would be of no importance at all. I wonder . . ." Juliette's voice trailed off as she considered the astounding revelation.

"So, do I. Something, or someone must have made her change her mind, which is a very good thing because she would have made us all miserable. Besides, Freddy needs someone kind and shy and artistic like he is and Lady Verena Carstairs, with her passion for gardening, is perfect. He would be perfect for her too—give her the town bronze and the confidence she needs."

"Georgiana!"

Georgie grinned. "I know, I know. I would hate it if someone meddled like that in my life. I promise I will simply be helpful. But if someone or something caused this delightful state of affairs, who do you think it is, or what do you think it is?"

"I don't know, but I'll ask Helen. She knows everything about everyone."

Georgie could well believe it. She'd only seen the formidably elegant Mrs. Gerrard at Juliette's wedding, but she looked like a lady capable of anything, and Freddy, John, and Adrian spoke of her with awe as though she were some sort of oracle or something.

Juliette did just as she suggested when Helen and Dora stopped in the very next day to look over materials and trimmings for carriage dresses. This time there were no blocks or farmyard animals on the floor, Auguste having gone for a walk in the park with his father. Juliette greeted them with the latest development. "Georgiana dropped in yesterday, so full of news she could not wait until I returned to Claverton House later in the afternoon. Apparently the longstanding engagement between Freddy and Lady Lavinia is over. The earl himself called on the duke to say that Lavinia had decided she and Freddy would not suit—not that they ever suited," she mused, then fixed Helen with a look. "What do you know about that?"

"Why would I know?" Helen protested. "Oh very well, I do not know, but I can guess."

The dreamy smile that followed was so unlike Helen that Juliette and Dora stared at one another in surprise. "And?" Juliette prompted.

"Well Lord Linton, who has just been called to the bar, and who is very grateful for my confirming his fears that Basil Harcourt is a thorough blackguard, and for identifying where he might have taken Lord Linton's niece,"

Juliette and Dora gasped, "became most suspicious about the letter concerning the leasehold that we received and dealt with last year, and then a visit not long ago from Constable Peabody with a badly executed warrant from the magistrate accusing me of running a disorderly house, both actions which threatened the establishment. He did some research into the solicitor involved with the letter and found it implicated the Harcourts so he reached the conclusion that it was all designed to keep Freddy from the dangerous lure of our drawing room by destroying Mrs. Gerrard's. He also discovered proof that Lady Lavinia was behind Juliette's near fatal accident with the runaway carriage, so I imagine, like the kindhearted gentleman he is, he threatened to expose her unless she cried off."

There was an audible gasp from Juliette who paled and clutched her throat with one shaking hand.

" But the main thing," Helen continued, "is that Freddy is free of that woman's clutches."

"To think of Freddy in the toils of . . . of a murderess," Juliette's voice quivered with outrage. "I was always sad that duty was forcing him into marriage with someone who clearly made him uneasy, but this! This! How could a woman, any woman, be so dead to human feelings as to . . . and not even to have the decency to voice her concerns to her fiancee. Thank God Lord Linton has saved him, and all the Clavertons, from the machinations of such a truly evil person. We all owe Lord Linton a great deal."No one deserves a loving, supportive wife more than dear, kind Freddy, and Georgiana is determined to find him one."

Dora snorted, "As will be every matchmaking mama in the *ton*. His life will be hell."

"I don't know. I put my money on Georgie. She is very practical, and a force to be reckoned with. She will protect him and help him find the right person." Juliette rose and gathered her things. "But now I must go. Adrian and Auguste will be returning to Claverton House and expecting me to be there. It is just a short walk and I need the fresh air. Tilly can accompany me."

After bidding her a fond farewell, Dora and Helen looked over the materials and the trimmings they'd come to see, chatted with Alice, and then they too availed themselves of the fresh air as they walked back to St. James' Square.

"I had no idea you had been of such service to Lord Linton," Dora shot her companion a sly look.

"You would not have me leave some poor girl to suffer her fate with Basil, would you? Surely not!" Helen's logical response may have been designed to prove that she would not be baited into incriminating herself, but Dora, familiar with her employer's every look and tone, was not fooled. She saw the conscious flush tinge Helen's cheeks and drew her own conclusions. It was obvious Helen was much taken with Julian Bracebridge, Earl of Linton, and he must be equally taken with her, for what man ever consulted a woman about anything, much less a problem, unless he was thoroughly besotted or in awe of her cleverness, or both? The situation certainly bore watching. Dora wanted to hug herself with delight.

Dora would have been even more delighted, and more certain of her conclusions if she had been near enough Helen's office to witness the encounter the next day.

"His lordship, ma'am," Fenwick announced.

Helen laid down her pen and rose to greet him, refusing to acknowledge how a visit from Julian could turn a dull day into one full of promise. Whatever one might say of the man, and she could not think of anything that was not to his credit, he never called without a mostly compelling and always interesting reason.

"I have come to repay my debts," Julian smiled down at her in a way that made her heart, which, until now, Helen had considered a non-existent organ, hammer in her chest, "and to give you this." He held out an official looking document.

"Helen took it and opened it. "But it looks like a . . ." She began to study it with rising incredulity, ". . . a deed, . . . the freehold . . . with my name!" She sank into the chair in front of her desk, too amazed to speak.

"Yes." He grinned, literally, from ear to ear. "I had a most productive conversation with the Harcourts—the earl and his daughter, who, as you said, is the true head of that household—and they agreed to sell me the freehold and . . . er, call off the engagement with Wrothingham. The last," his face hardened, "was in exchange for my promise not to reveal the true circumstances of Lady Adrian's near accident. So all's well that ends well."

Helen had recovered her wits enough to look up at him and shake her head in disbelief. "There was no need. You owe me nothing. I consider it a privilege to save someone from the clutches of a blackguard like Basil Harcourt, and a pleasure to do what I can to stick a spoke in that man's wheel."

Julian sank down on his knees before her, taking her hands in his and gazing into her eyes with an intent, but unreadable expression in his. "But I wanted to do it. I wanted to give you something that could truly make your life better. I know, you are so incredibly resourceful and brilliant that, thanks to your tireless work and boundless energy there is nothing you cannot accomplish, and very little anyone can give you that you have not already won for yourself, but I do know, "his mouth quirked into a teasing smile, "you like control, and this will give you complete control over Mrs. Gerrard's." There was dead silence. "Helen, my love, what have I said?" He scanned her face and tried to pull her into his arms as she withdrew her hands to cover her face and burst into sobs.

"Nothing. I don't know." She could not gather her riot of overwhelming thoughts and emotions enough to say anything more so she collapsed against him and gave herself up to the heaven of a broad chest to lean on and strong arms to hold her when she was utterly at sea.

At long last, she raised a tear-drenched face, looking so hesitant and unlike his cool, collected, sardonic Helen that Julian's heart was wrenched all over again. "I don't deserve it," she whispered.

"Do you mean you don't deserve it, or you don't like feeling beholden to someone even though his niece owes her life to you? Even though he loves you."

"What?"

That got her attention, and Julian didn't know whether to laugh or cry at her look of alarm, or was it horror? Well, in for a penny, in for a pound, he told himself. He hadn't meant to blurt it out like that, but what could he do? It was the truth, even if more baldly put than he would have liked, and even though he had only just realized it himself.

He drew a deep breath. "Yes, Helen, I love you. I know that you do not believe in such a thing as love, and I would die rather than make you uncomfortable, but there it is. I didn't believe in it either until I met someone I could admire with all my soul, someone who challenges me constantly to be a better person, and someone who inspires me with her drive and her compassion. So, I put it to you, how could I help it?" If he had hoped to win a smile from her, he failed utterly.

"But this is serious. I do not know if I can return . . . I only want the best for you, but I cannot . . ."

He cupped her chin with one hand and tilted it up to look into her eyes which were deep and dark with warring emotions. "Do not distress yourself, my love. I am just happy being able to love someone. I want nothing from you except to make you the complete mistress of your own life and, if possible, make you happy." He wiped away a tear that would escape and roll down her cheek, despite her best efforts to stop it.

"Th..thank you," she gulped. "You understand me so well." She scrubbed away another tear and smiled shakily at him. "It's nice to have a friend like you who knows who and what I am, yet remains my friend, no matter what. I think?" She cocked her head with a bit of her old spirit and he chuckled. "Yes, always your friend, no matter what."

That was enough for today. He'd taken her by surprise in more ways than one. She needed time to recover her equilibrium after the emotional onslaught. But he couldn't help himself, her lips were parted irresistibly, and he had to show her what she meant to him; there were no words special enough to convey it. Slowly he lowered his mouth to hers, tilting her face to his with gentle hands to press his lips against hers. Heaven! He poured his whole soul into that kiss, then, grasping her shoulders, set her away from him.

"Do not fret. I took myself by surprise as much as I did you. A wise man would have remained silent, but I had to be honest with you. You deserve nothing less." And with that he was gone, leaving her staring after him.

Chapter 23

In love with her! Was he mad? Probably he was, Helen chuckled grimly to herself, but he had been so forthright about it and so concerned that she not be made uneasy by his revelation. It was so, so Julian—not at all flirtatious, aware of all the possible implications of his admission, and determined to be open, to have no secrets between them, trusting in their friendship to sustain them. His concern for her feelings was the mark of a true friend. That was all she wanted, a true friend. But did she? Or did she secretly want something more? Was she being completely honest with herself? Helen wanted to tear her hair with the frustration of it all, of not knowing herself when she was usually was so certain.

The heaven of having him hold her and comfort her spoke to a need deep inside of her, a need she hadn't known she'd possessed until now, for more than a friend. It was a longing for something like a defender, or protector... a soulmate. The glow in his eyes when he spoke of how she had helped save his niece told Helen that she offered the same to him: defender, protector, soulmate.

Then there was that kiss. Who could not be moved by it? His lips, so warm, so firm, were so right, so perfect that hers had responded before she could even think about it, as though they were made for one another. It was a generous kiss—one that shared his entire being—not a selfish kiss born out of lust or the seeking of purely physical gratification. *Oh Helen, Helen,* she asked herself, *whatever are you going to do?*

The old Helen would have immediately stopped having anything to do with him, resolutely putting as much distance as possible between her and someone who spoke words of love, but Julian was not that sort of man, and she didn't want distance between them. In fact, the more time she was in his company, the more time she wanted to spend in it. Perhaps *she* was the one who was mad.

"Are you ready?" Dora appeared in the doorway attired in a carriage dress of jaconet muslin over a peach-colored sarsnet slip and covered by a white lutestring spencer that showed off her dark curls and glowing complexion to perfection. A wide-brimmed Leghorn hat dangled on peach satin ribbons from one hand.

"Ready?" Mired in her swirling emotions, Helen stared blankly at her prospective companion.

"For a turn around the park." Dora scrutinized her. Such vagueness was not like her employer. Something was definitely occupying her mind and it wasn't Mrs. Gerrard's select establishment. Dora had her suspicions as to who was so distracting, well-founded suspicions, which Helen confirmed by silently handing her the deed to the freehold.

"Good Heavens! He did this? For you?" She came to a full stop as she was heading out the door. "I mean, of course it's for you. No one deserves it more, but . . . well, it is very generous," she concluded lamely.

"But surprising."

"Not exactly surprising when you consider his lordship," Dora grinned. "Now there's a man who can drive a hard bargain. I'd give a monkey to have seen the Earl of Harcourt's face when he was, er, *convinced* to sell his freehold. No English lord wants to give up an inch of his property, even if it is mortgaged to the hilt. Too much stain on the family honor and all. Lady Lavinia must be mortified. How delightful! On the other hand, I imagine she found it a cross to bear that the den of iniquity where Freddy was enjoying himself too much to become leg-shackled to her was on Harcourt property. It's too delicious for words. We owe Lord Linton a debt of gratitude—all of us."

"We certainly do," Helen replied softly, a strange look on her face.

Now we are in the basket! Dora fiddled with the ribbons to her bonnet before donning it and tying them briskly into an enormous bow. "All the more reason to enjoy a carriage ride. Come, put on your bonnet and pelisse. There's nothing like fresh air to clear the mind." At least Dora hoped it would. They all needed Helen to have a clear head and sharp mind at all times. She knew Helen, and she knew that happy as she would be with the security of owning both the freehold and the leasehold, she did not like to be under obligation to anyone. It spoke volumes about what Julian meant to her that she had allowed herself to accept such a gift from him.

The drive in the park did help. The day was glorious, the air fresh after a recent rain, and the parade of magnificent equipages, with their exquisitely turned out occupants a distraction in itself. And no one was more exquisitely turned out than the ladies of Mrs. Gerrard's in the latest fashions from Maison

Juliette and their own establishment's splendid barouche built by Sharp and Bland. Dora marveled at it all. Here she was, a country innkeeper's daughter casting much of the *ton* in the shade at the most fashionable place and the most fashionable hour in the city, and she had Helen to thank for it, that, and for inspiring her to save and invest and trust in her natural instinct for business.

Of course, Lord Maximilian Hawkesbury who, at Grace's urging had come to teach them all about insurance and annuities, had also encouraged Dora with gifts of books on commerce, but it was Helen's belief in her own capabilities and those of her ladies that had made it happen. Dora wished she knew how to repay Helen for saving all their lives. Perhaps the best thing she could do was encourage her employer, friend, and mentor to recognize and follow her heart. After all, Juliette had her shop, her Adrian, and her Auguste; Grace had her singing, a life in Italy, home of the opera she loved, and her Max. Maybe, just maybe, Dora could help Helen find the same thing, but first she resolved to make sure Helen knew how grateful she was.

Another person also poured out her gratitude; when they returned from the park a letter from Annie Bentley was waiting for them. It was full of enthusiastic detail: the lovely fresh air, the majesty of the ocean, the servants she had hired and was training. She was operating under the same principle that his lordship's beloved mother had followed which was to identify some poor unfortunate like the redoubtable Betty, who had become a staunch ally and friend, and train them to provide the best of service, no matter what the task.

She was also extremely busy cutting silhouettes for clients of all kinds. Betty had friends among the tradesmen who were delighted to capture the likenesses of loved ones for such a reasonable price, and his lordship's *aunt*, Lady Sstandiford, made certain that it was known among her friends that Annie Bentley was a superior talent where silhouette likenesses were concerned. All in all, she had never been so happy, and she had Helen and Lord Linton to thank for it. Not only was she safe among friends, doing good works, but she was being paid a most generous salary, and, best of all, her husband had agreed to a separation, thanks to his lordship and his lordship's solicitor. Of course, when she sent her regular reports to his lordship, she always made sure to express her gratitude, but she hoped that the next time Helen saw him, she would also convey Annie's heartfelt thanks.

Helen smiled as she laid down the letter. Yes, she would convey Annie's thanks. *His lordship* was a good man and deserved to know it. Annie seemed fairly certain of the probability of their seeing one another on a regular basis, but was Helen ready to risk it? She did not want to hurt the man who deserved so much of her own gratitude, but she was afraid that if she did not stop seeing him, he might begin to hope for more than she could ever give . . . to anyone—her independence, her freedom, and her control over her own destiny.

The thought of losing any of these precious, hard-won things turned her quite cold with fear and sent her knocking on the door of the only other woman who could treasure these things the way Helen did, Olivia Childs.

The actress welcomed her with open arms. "How delightful to have one of my favorite visitors on one of the few days that I am not at the theater. Do join me in a cup of tea and tell me everything. How are Maison Juliette and Lady Adrian and her family doing, and what news from Italy? I trust Grace is winning singing roles as she continues her studies with Signor Banderali." The actress tilted her head, eyeing her guest curiously. "You should be bursting with pride over what you have done for those two women, but instead you look a little *distrait*."

"I do?" Helen straightened, rearranging her features into calm assurance. "But you deserve as much credit as I. After all, it was you who rescued them and brought them to me; I just gave them a home."

"And financial security, emotional support, and the example of what a woman can accomplish when she follows her dreams. Well, they followed their dreams and look what they have done, but perhaps you have not followed yours, despite your incredible achievements."

"I had no dreams. I was too young, really, to have dreams when Papa died. But after my, er, *unfortunate experience*, I did have the dream of rescuing women from impossible situations like mine and making men pay for what they usually take from us, and take for granted. Once I did that," she smiled grimly, "I became more ambitious and I wanted to help them learn skills and establish financial stability and be independent."

"And so you did, but what brings you here today?"

"I came to share another success story of ours, Annie Bentley." Helen held out the letter.

Olivia read it. "And this time you have not only found her a home and financial stability, but you've provided her with a powerful protector who fought and beat the man who hurt her. Lord Linton is a new weapon added to your arsenal for defending and protecting women who have suffered at the hands of men, someone who can punish those men." Olivia nodded approvingly, but that did not mean she hadn't seen and wondered at the blush that rose to Helen's cheeks or the conscious look in Helen's eyes at the mention of Lord Linton.

Knowing her friend's determined self-sufficiency, she declined to comment, remarking instead that it was a happy circumstance that had brought Helen to her doorstep today. "I have been thinking that I too need to take advantage of the economic and investment counsel you have been giving the residents of your establishment, for I am thinking of retiring."

"Retiring?" Helen was shocked. "But you are at the height of your popularity."

"Precisely the time to leave," came the wry response, "while audiences still remember one kindly."

"And you are younger than Mrs. Siddons when she retired."

"Precisely. I am not Mrs. Siddons, and there are fewer and fewer roles for females of a certain age."

"But what will you do? I do not picture you as a lady of leisure."

"Nor am I. For one, I would like to attend the meetings of the female friendly society you have started, if you do not mind, that is. I need to learn more about that sort of thing, and I know that Lord Maximilian Hawkesbury taught you all a great deal before he returned to the diplomatic service. Perhaps I shall even become an investor in some theatrical endeavor, that is, if I can convince the other investors to take a female seriously."

"Being taken seriously, the eternal problem," Helen agreed.

"And I shall continue identifying and rescuing unfortunate women in dire circumstances," the actress' lush lips pressed together with determination. "One would not necessarily call that a dream of mine, but it is definitely an ambition."

"A good thing it is for all of us." On that note, Helen rose and bade her hostess good day, feeling her confusion fade as, inspired by her friend, her energy and resolve returned.

Chapter 24

Helen recalled the conversation a few days later as, again seeking distraction from her own confused thoughts, she perused the shelves at Hatchard's where her eye was caught by a slender young lady whose pallor and thin face aroused suspicions, heightened by years of rescuing women in distress. Helen edged closer, trying to get a look at the book absorbing the woman's attention—*Seneca's Morals by Way of Abstract.* Not the usual sort of book to attract a young woman's interest. She was fashionably, if plainly, dressed in a white cambric walking dress with a Pomona green Cossack mantle over it. The Cossack mantle had been out of fashion this age, as had the poke bonnet of yellow satin, but despite their age, their excellent quality and condition betrayed the care that had been lavished on them. This was a young woman who had seen better days. Then she looked up, caught Helen's glance, and blushed the deep blush of someone who had suffered a disastrous change in fortune.

That did it. Helen stepped closer, blocking both sight and sound from other customers. "Do not be alarmed. I don't wish to intrude, but I sense you find yourself in distressing circumstances, and . . ."

A look of alarm, hastily banished, flashed across the woman's face. "I . . ." her shoulders slumped, "how did you know? Is it that plain for all to see?"

"No, no." Helen smiled reassuringly. "The signs are obvious only to someone else who has found herself there."

"You?" The woman took in Helen's own walking dress with its embroidered flounce, and the dark blue Gros de Naples spencer, which was the *dernier cri* of fashion, and shook her head in an incredulity that said more than words.

"Yes, I, and now I make it my mission to do what I can to help other women like me." Helen dug in her reticule and handed the young woman a card.

"London can be a dangerous place, and you would be right to be cautious, but coaching inns, rather than bookshops are the usual places young women are preyed upon. You can trust me. Here is my name and direction. Feel free to call on me any time, or feel free to forget we even met; whatever is best for you." Then, her mind so preoccupied by the young woman's possible story that she forgot she'd come to look for books—and distraction—Helen, having found the distraction, headed back to St. James' Square to await developments, developments which soon appeared from another quarter as Tom Sandys handed her a letter when she returned to St. James' Square.

My dear Mrs. Gerrard, the letter began, *or should I call you Miss Falkland?*

Helen gasped and dropped it, and, taking herself to task for being a spineless ninnyhammer, glanced quickly to the signature at the bottom, *Honoria, Lady Standiford.* She drew a deep breath, sat down and read the rest of the missive which was brief and to the point: having heard from her *nephew,* Julian, Lord Linton, that he had apparently discovered Lady Standiford's long-lost relative, Lady Standiford was now anxious to meet the long-lost relative herself and invited Helen to visit her at Standiford Hall at her earliest convenience.

Helen sat for some time with the letter in her lap, staring out the window of her office. Was she ready for this? Did she even want this? For so many years after her mother had died she had longed for family, but her father, when she had asked about them, had been so vague and uninterested that she assumed them all to be dead. When her father had died, Helen had been struck with longing for some place to flee, where she could belong, possibly even be loved.

Then Lord Broughton had happened and she had been glad she had no family to suffer the shame with her. That relief, if she had thought about it at all, had only deepened as she had made her way in the world in the only manner she could. It had been lonely, but with it had come a certain freedom from obligation. Now she would lose that. But what would she gain? Had Julian told Lady Standiford who and what she was? He must have related some part of her story if Lady Standiford knew her direction. Julian would never allow his *Aunt Honoria* to assume, mistakenly, that Helen was as fine and respectable a lady as her St. James' Square direction implied; he was far too forthright and honest to do that.

In fact, at that moment, Julian was regretting this forthrightness and honesty and was about to call on Helen to make amends for them.

After blurting out his feelings for her in what he could only label as the selfish awkwardness of a callow youth utterly lacking in discretion or self-control, he had been crucifying himself for being such a bore. He had undoubtedly sounded like hundreds of her other admirers who had only wanted one thing from Helen Gerrard, but Julian wanted more—so much more, and he was going to ask for it right now.

Taking his hat and gloves from Griggs, whom he barely acknowledged, he strode out the door, down Piccadilly to Duke Street to St. James' Square where he gave the briefest of nods to Fenwick who only had time to respond in the affirmative as to Mrs. Gerrard's presence, and then he was up the marble staircase, two steps at a time.

"Oh!" Helen, still clutching the letter, rose as he burst unceremoniously through the door. "My lord, this is . . ."

"A surprise? I know, and I apologize for intruding on you like this, but I suddenly realized what a dunderhead I had been."

Dunderhead? Julian Bracebridge, barrister, businessman, and Earl of Linton? Not likely. She regarded him curiously.

"Helen, I apologize. I was the most callow of fools when I said I loved you."

So he realized how misguided, and yes, foolish, he had been.

"What I meant to say to you is that yes, I do love you, but it's not like that . . ."

Of course it wasn't, because what man in his right mind would love the owner of a seraglio, even if it were the most exclusive seraglio in London?

"I want to marry you."

"You what?" Now he *did* have her full attention. "Are you mad?"

He laughed, an eager, awkward laugh that was annoyingly endearing, then he drew a breath and gathered his wits about him, regaining some of his usual air of assurance. "What I meant is that the kind of love I have for you is the kind that wants to share my life with you, our lives. You give me inspiration and strength and belief in all the things I want to do, and ever since I met you, I have treasured you and our friendship as a rare and wonderful thing, and I want it to last forever."

Good lord, the man was serious! Whatever was she to do? Helen saw his heart in his eyes as he laid it at her feet, but she could not take it. What would happen to her, Helen Gerrard, mistress of her own destiny, if she did?

He saw the struggle on her face, bless him, and she could see him absorbing and understanding all the conflict within her. "I . . . I know I have no right to ask, and it is utterly gauche and insensitive of me to keep springing such things on you, but I didn't want to leave you with the impression that my feelings toward you aren't everything that is honorable."

Lord, Julian cursed himself, he sounded like the verist coxcomb and a prig of a coxcomb at that, but she smiled at him, thank heavens.

"You are very kind, and I do appreciate it, I truly do." Now Helen sounded just as stilted and awkward to herself as he had. They were both sophisticated, worldly adults; what was wrong with them? "I know you mean to be kind. You have always been kind to me, witness the letter I received today from Lady Standiford."

"Aunt Honoria?"

She nodded, noting his surprise. So he had not put his Aunt Honoria up to this. That was encouraging, in one way at least; it meant that Lady Standiford was acting of her own accord, acting on her own wishes. "I gather you mentioned me to her."

He heard her question, unstated though it was. "Yes, I did tell her about you." He looked straight into her eyes. "Everything."

"Everything?"

"Yes. I know her for the strong, caring person she is, the woman whose spirit kept my mother's alive. I told her about your experience as a governess, the dreadful thing that happened to you, and your dedication to helping women the only way you could. She understood. She understands that women like my mother, who were married to the highest bidder, are no different from the women at Mrs. Gerrard's, except that they now have control over their own lives, respectability, yes, control, independence, happiness, no. She recognizes that if a woman like you had saved my mother, she would still be alive today." He paused, swallowing hard, "That's what she knows about you."

Helen's eyes misted. He had told his Aunt Honoria all that. How dear of him. She could not bear the thought of hurting such a man, but she could not bear the thought of giving up her independence or risking making herself vulnerable to . . . no, it was too much. No matter how much she admired him, or how fond she was of him, it was too much.

Julian smiled, a sad, but utterly understanding smile. "I realize that this is a shock, but . . ."

Helen held up her hand as she struggled to keep her voice steady, "I am honored . . . no, I am touched and unbelievably honored by all that you have said. I do not deserve such a thing from a man like you who . . ." tears clogged her voice, "but I cannot. I cannot leave all of this," she glanced around, "my ladies . . . it just isn't possible, but," she looked at him with a hesitancy he had never seen in his proud Helen before, "but if we could still be friends," she whispered, "I would like that very much."

His heart broke, not so much for himself, but for the agony he saw in her eyes. "Of course," he clasped her hands, "always friends." He tilted his head, summoning up a teasing smile, "And perhaps. even if you cannot love me or marry me, you could come see me argue my first case in court."

He saw the relief flow through her as some of her old spirit return. She gave him a watery smile. "Of course."

Julian would have to be content with that . . . for now.

Chapter 25

Some days later found Helen and Dora seated in the gallery of the Old Bailey surveying the courtroom below. "Not our customary outing," Dora whispered, "thank heavens. Think of the poor wretches who have passed through these doors."

"Let us hope that the poor wretch his lordship is defending is one of those who never has to see this place again; he's a captain accused of negligence that caused the loss of his ship and its cargo. Neither Lloyds nor the Board of Trade is very happy with him, which is why Mr. Maule suggested Lord Linton defend him. No one could be more sympathetic or more critical where the loss of goods and a ship is concerned. If his lordship believes in the captain enough to defend him, then he is indeed innocent. He just has to convince the jury of that."

"I am sure he will. As I have said before, Lord Linton is . . ."

"Very clever. I know. But is he convincing and can he win the hearts and minds of a jury?"

Helen could not remember ever watching anything—play, opera, procession, or sermon—as intently and with such trepidation. This was what Julian wanted to do with his life, his energies, his passion. She wanted desperately for him to succeed. No, she wanted more than success for him; she wanted him to cover himself with glory. But she cared enough to study his performance as critically and dispassionately as any disinterested onlooker. She chewed her lip when she saw that his question, subtle the point though it made, was too subtle for the jury. She sighed in relief when, recognizing that, he asked it in another way, and in a way that obviously engaged their interest and their sympathy. He painted a clear picture of the defendant as an honest, loyal, dedicated mariner, beset by bad weather and worse luck.

"In the end, I thought he did quite well," she remarked to Dora as the carriage made its way along Fleet Street toward the Strand and home.

"Quite well?" Dora was indignant. "He was brilliant! He was so forceful, so commanding. He is a natural-born defender. If I were ever in need of defending, he is the one I would want at my side."

Privately, Helen agreed wholeheartedly, but she had been too afraid to trust her own judgment. She would do Julian no good if her fondness for him colored her opinion of his capabilities. He was counting on her for her critical abilities and her honest opinion. Her fondness for him? Where had that come from? Yes, she admitted, she *was* fond of him, fond of the way he cared about right and wrong, the way he wanted to help people, just the way she did. She was also fond of his ability to see the humor in a situation, to tease her despite his very serious outlook on life.

In fact, she was so fond of him that, that afternoon she wanted to order her carriage back down the Strand toward Essex Court and his chambers on the slim chance that he might be there. She told herself that she actually wished he would be out so that she could direct her congratulations to Mr. Maule or Ben and depart without having to see Julian, but, truth be told, she did want to see him, to let him know she was proud of him, though why he should care about the opinion of someone who ran a bawdy house and knew nothing of the law—though a great deal about mathematics—she did not know.

Fortunately, before she could give herself up to such shameful self-indulgence, Fenwick appeared to announce a visitor. "It's a Miss Elizabeth Mountjoy," he said somewhat apologetically not having recognized her as a regular who could expect to be welcomed into his mistress' inner sanctum, "but she did give me your card and said you had asked her to call on you."

Helen rose. "Yes, I did. Thank you Fenwick. I appreciate your being so protective of my time and my privacy."

Fenwick's face remained as impassive as ever, but Helen could see from the straightening of his shoulders that she had relieved him of worry. Dear Fenwick, how fortunate she had been to have encountered him that day in Gin Lane after he had been brutally and unfairly dismissed from the nameless family he had loyally served for so many years.

"I beg your pardon for intruding on you, but you did tell me to call if . . . if," Miss Elizabeth Mountjoy's voice trailed off as she took in the room's damask covered walls, elegant rosewood desk, and the floor-to-ceiling bookcase where her gaze lingered longingly.

Helen saw the look, and smiled. If anything, the poor girl looked paler and frailer than when she'd last seen her in Hatchard's, so she gave the bell-pull a vigorous tug, instructing Mary, who appeared almost immediately, to bring tea and cakes. "Yes, I did tell you to come see me because, as I indicated to you when we met, I am willing to hazard a guess you have suffered some untoward event, and now find yourself in unfortunate circumstances and unfamiliar surroundings. Am I correct?"

The young woman's blue eyes filled with tears as she nodded.

"You will tell me all about it in a moment, but first I must be utterly straightforward with you about this, er, this establishment. Not to wrap it up in fine linen, this place, Mrs. Gerrard's as it is known to the gentlemen of the *ton*, is a seraglio."

Elizabeth Mountjoy's eyes widened.

"The most exclusive seraglio in all of London. To put it bluntly, we provide *companionship* to gentlemen of the first stare, the most well-bred, most sophisticated, and the wealthiest men of the Upper Ten Thousand, but we are paid for that companionship, handsomely paid. We earn, individually, more than most prosperous merchants and tradesmen, and we invest our earnings in a variety of interest-earning enterprises. We have created our own female friendly society and a beneficent society to provide income for us in our old age, and in case of accident, disease or disaster. Yes, we sell our bodies to men, but how many women do not, though it is legitimized by the benefit of a clergyman and a religious ceremony. Now," she fixed Elizabeth with a compelling, but not unkind look, "I gather from the unease I saw in your eyes whenever a gentleman entered Hatchard's the other day and the way you flinched when they passed too close, that someone has already taken advantage of your unwilling body. Why not exact your revenge by taking advantage of men's desires and their pocketbooks? Now I will let you absorb all this while you tell me your story. But first let me assure you that, no matter how bad it is, it is probably very similar to the stories of those of us here—a vicar's daughter brutally raped when forced to become a governess, the daughter of a well-born musician, fallen on hard times, who had to give herself to the theater owner in order to save her father's job, the daughter of French nobility raped by the husband of a customer of the modiste where she struggled to earn a living. Do these sound familiar?"

Elizabeth gulped and nodded. "My father, Lord Mountoy, and my mother were both classical scholars of note, and when the continent was freed from Napoleon, we hastened to Rome so they could resume their studies, but not long after we arrived, they both contracted a putrid fever and died soon after. I was forced to make my way home to Kent where my brother was now in charge of the estate."

She paused, gazing blankly at the bookshelves as she pushed aside memories and collected her thoughts. Lawrence, my brother, was always a wayward child, never listening to any adults, not that my parents, devoted as they were to one another and their studies, paid much attention to him or tried to curb his headstrong ways. They left that to the tutors and servants and masters at one school after another where he was the despair of one and all. From a wayward boy, he turned into a wild young man whose impulses were never checked, so when Papa and Mama died, he pursued a ruinous course of dissipation, inviting his friends to the estate for weeks of carousing, drinking, cards, women . . . .and eventually, me." She bowed her head, her hands twisting in her lap. "Most of the time they were so befuddled I could escape with a grope or a kiss, but some of them became angry and they hurt me, well not intentionally, but then I resisted, and, well, then there were too many of them." She paused and drew a deep breath. "So I sold what clothes and jewelry I had and came to London, hoping that with my education I might become a governess."

Helen nodded and patted her hand. "No need to go on. I apologize for making you re-live such shocking, horrible, degrading acts. You should never have suffered; we, all of us, should never have suffered, but yours is the worst I've heard."

Helen rose, walked over to her visitor, gently tilting up her chin to look into her eyes. "I promise you I will do all that I can to give you back at least something of what you have lost. At the moment, you know what I have to offer. I imagine that you are low on resources."

Elizabeth nodded.

"Then I offer you lodging here. It is only a maid's room, but it is clean and safe. You are among friends here. If you wish to learn more about us, you may play the maid in the evenings and observe us in the drawing room and, during the day, get to know those of us who live here. If it is not to your liking, I will see what I can do to help." Helen lifted her own chin proudly. 'I am not without resources. I may be able to help you in other ways. Who can say?"

And that, Helen thought with a surge of happiness, gave her the perfect excuse to call on Julian and compliment him on his courtroom performance. She would consult with him about Elizabeth's plight and ask if there were any legal recourse for demanding some sort of support from her brother, enough for her to live comfortably, if modestly, on her own. But the next day was Sunday so she would have to contain herself until the beginning of the week. Since when did Helen Gerrard have to contain her eagerness, or anything else, for that matter, she asked herself in disgust. The answer? Never, not before she met Julian, was the all-too-discouraging answer. Had this one man caused her to change so much? Surely not. Surely she was being overly sensitive. Surely no one else would think she had changed.

Helen had reckoned without the observant eyes of the Reverend Lord John Claverton who could recognize the slightest difference in a parishioner's bearing from the exalted distance of the pulpit, and very often guess the reason behind it as well. He had already sensed an air of abstraction in Helen during their last few card games. In anyone else, it would have seemed normal attention to one's hand of cards, but in Helen, whose intense focus was carefully masked by a rigidly neutral expression, the lessening of alertness, to her observant partner's eye, was significant. Even more significant was the connection between the lessening of alertness and the presence of Lord Linton. Highly intrigued, John had waited patiently for the opportunity to learn more. Today, as he took a chair in her office after celebrating Sunday services, he pulled a book out of his pocket. "I know your passion is Algebra, but I have brought you *The Key to Mr. Reynar's Geometria Legitima* to expand your horizons."

Helen laughed. "Always encouraging me to grow, be it intellectually or spiritually."

He grinned in return. "I can't help it; it's my nature. It is also in my nature to be curious. Tell me, are you behind this sudden decision on Lady Lavinia's part to set my brother free? If you are, by the way, I am eternally grateful, as we all are."

"My lord, how could you think that I, a simple female . . ."

"Cut line, Mrs. Gerrard. You are the most dangerous person I know. Who else would be capable of such insight and finesse?"

"I am flattered, but no, it was not I. I do know, however, who is responsible, Lord Linton."

Oho, what have we here? John watched the faintest color appear in her cheeks. How interesting, most interesting indeed. "And how did that come about?"

"Well, Lord Linton, whose sister-in-law and niece met Basil at Lady Cholmondeley's ball . . ."

"Thanks to your asking Freddy to do what he could to ease the niece's introduction to the *ton*."

"Er yes, but anyway, his lordship, being a man who is awake on all suits, sensed something havey-cavey about Basil and came to ask me . . ."

"Source of all knowledge of the *ton* . . ."

"Came to ask me what sort of fellow he was. I told him about Dora and about Adrian's suspicions over Juliette's accident, and the threatening letter from the owner of our freehold. At any rate, after we rescued Linton's niece from Basil's clutches . . ."

"You what?"

She waved a hand, "More on that later, but the point of the story is he followed up on his suspicions, did some digging, and found not only who was the true owner of the freehold, Lord Harcourt, but that Lady Lavinia was behind Juliette's near miss with the carriage."

"Lavinia? I knew she was a very determined woman, but I had no idea."

"So Lord Linton threatened Lady Lavinia with exposure unless she broke the engagement, and he ensured Lord Harcourt's agreement and silence by making a very attractive offer to purchase the freehold of this, too attractive to resist."

"The Claverton family owes that man a debt of gratitude," John declared with reverent conviction, "and Freddy must never know the truth of this. He would be too horrified at the depths of depravity to which someone he had been ready to marry for the family honor, no matter what it cost him, would stoop. He has suffered enough, my brother. We must spare him this."

John recalled the dazed look on Freddy's face as he had emerged from his father's library after the Earl of Harcourt's visit.

"It's Lavinia," he had responded to John's inquiry. "She . . . she doesn't think we would suit. I . . ." Freddy's eyes had filled with tears as, dropping his head in his hands, he had sunk into a convenient chair in the hallway outside the library door;

John laid a comforting hand on his brother's shaking shoulders. "She is right, you two do not suit; you never have and you never will."

The two had remained in silence for a while, taking in the momentous implications of it all, then Freddy raised his head and John realized that the tears he had seen had been tears of exhausted relief. Now Freddy's eyes were shining, not with tears, but with joy. He rose to his feet. "I am free."

"You are free," John agreed, flinging his arm around his brother's shoulder to pull him into a fierce hug.

"And now Linton owns the freehold to the property for which you own the leasehold."

Helen's delicate blush deepened into such a dark shade of rose it could almost be called red. Helen Gerrard never blushed.

"No, actually, I now own the freehold.

John leaned forward, his eyes intent. "You!"

"Yes, he gave it to me. I . . ." Helen's hands twisted in her lap. "I don't deserve it of course, but, well, there you are."

John reached forward to quiet the hands twisting in her lap with his own. "Of course you deserve it. You have done so much for so many, it is time someone did something for you for a change." He paused, reflecting for a moment on his next words, then took the plunge. "I think you mean a great deal to Lord Linton."

She stared down at her hands. "He says he loves me." It was the barest of whispers.

"And?"

"And, and I . . ." At last she looked up, the green eyes dark with agony. "I cannot after . . . and then he asked me to marry him, and I cannot . . ."

"Cannot love him or cannot marry him?"

"Both."

"Cannot or will not?"

She shrugged helplessly, glancing around her. "I am responsible for all of this. I cannot simply abandon it to marry someone, and . . ."

"But you could love someone and still manage all of this. Why the agony?"

"Because I cannot. We are just friends. That is all he is to me, and I do not want to hurt him. He is so good and kind. He should have someone to love who loves him in return."

"And you do not? You are just friends? Are you certain of that?"

"Yes, just friends, good friends, but just friends."

'Helen, look at me." He stared into her eyes, his own kind, but uncompromising. "We are friends, you and I, are we not?"

She nodded.

"One might even say we are good friends."

She nodded again.

"Then do you feel towards me what you feel towards him?"

The arrested look in her eyes said it all.

"I thought so. I do play, cards with you, you know; I know all of your tells. So now, explain to me again why you cannot . . . er . . . will not love this man who loves you. Why you will not, even considering that this man wants to spend the rest of his life with you."

"Because I cannot be a wife to him," she burst out. "He should have a wife who can give him children, who wants to have children with him, and to give herself to him and . . ."

"That's it, isn't it, Helen?"

It was quietly asked, but she could see he understood. Dear John who only wanted to help those in need, those in pain. "I can't, I'm too . . ." She burst into tears.

"My dear girl," he began softly as he handed her his handkerchief, "I do not know what happened to you, but I do know that when a governess is dismissed with no character and forced into the life you were forced into, the only one at fault is some brutal male in the household that employed her. I am also certain that Lord Linton, a perspicacious man if there ever was one, a man sympathetic enough to tackle Annie Bentley's predicament and solve it, understands what you have suffered and what it has likely done to you. If he knows all that and is willing to risk loving you, then you ought to be brave enough to risk loving him back, as I know you do."

He rose, laying a comforting hand on her shoulder. "I will leave you now, having made you cry like the utmost cad," he smiled ruefully, "and it is not because I do not care about your sorrow or your dilemma, but because I know you need to be alone with your thoughts." Then, pausing in the doorway, he turned back. "But I am always here for you, Helen. Day or night, if you are in distress, do not hesitate to send for me."

The door closed quietly behind him. *And there*, Helen thought, *goes a very good man and a true friend.* A true friend, not one like Julian, who, as excruciatingly observant Lord John Claverton had pointed out so very plainly, was definitely something more than a friend to her. What was that? Emotionally challenging as it would be, Helen Gerrard was going to find out.

Chapter 26

Julian sat in his chamber staring blankly at the papers in front of him, but all he saw was Helen's glorious tear-filled eyes as she had whispered *it just isn't possible*, and his heart contracted all over again. Even before he had confessed his love for her, before he'd asked her to marry him, he'd known what her answer would be. How could an independent woman with so many responsibilities give them up for love? But, his life, his feelings had been so transformed by the thought of sharing them with someone he admired, loved, and trusted that he had allowed himself to hope against all rational odds. As the Scripture said *Love bears all things, believes all things, hopes all things*, and now he would have *endure all things* without her.

Still, she had promised to remain friends. At least he had that. He remembered the rush of joy as he had glanced up into the gallery at the Old Bailey and recognized the bonnet she had worn when they had gone after Basil. Who would have thought that he, a man of business and law would recognize a bonnet? It just went to show how far gone he was over Helen Gerrard that he noticed and remembered every little detail about her. Just knowing she was watching him that day, and of course Dora too, made him feel as though he could conquer the court with his arguments. Surely her being there meant she was serious about remaining friends. He had to be content with that, and he thanked Providence he had not driven her entirely away with his rash behavior.

"A lady to see you, my lord."

Could it be? Julian tamped down on the rush of hope. But what other woman would visit him in chambers?

Helen had been cursing herself for a fool as she entered 3 Essex Court. Any reasonable person would have made an appointment, but where Julian was concerned, she was not a reasonable person. It had been an impulsive decision to consult him and she had not sent a note in advance because she'd been afraid of losing her nerve. If the truth were told, it had not been an impulsive decision; she had been looking for an excuse to see him again to tell him how impressed she had been by his defense. Then Elizabeth had arrived and provided her with the perfect excuse.

"Mrs. Gerrard," he rose to usher her in, and she was struck all over again with how drawn she was to him: his commanding height, his alertness, his energy, the sense of purpose he exuded.

"My lord." She took the chair offered, wondering how to begin after their last conversation, and chastising herself for being so weak and indecisive. She drew a deep breath and plunged in. "Another poor woman in need of your counsel has turned up on my doorstep. Having seen your superb defense in court the other day, I am all the more confident you may be able to help us. No, my lord, don't dismiss my opinion with a modest shake of your head when you have so often complimented me on my critical faculties. You did an excellent job the other day and I foresee a brilliant career ahead of you."

Her approval shouldn't have meant so much to him. He knew he was good, and that was all he needed to know, for no one could be a harsher critic of himself than he was, but knowing she thought well of him meant everything in the world. "Tell me about your latest rescue."

"She is the daughter of a scholar baron and his wife who both died of a fever while studying in Italy, so she returned home where her debauched brother, having inherited the title and the estate, lives a dissipated life and has forced her to ah... *entertain* his equally debauched and dissipated friends. Unable to bear it, and being extremely well-educated, she sold her jewelry and ran away to London, hoping to find a position as a governess. Well, we know how that story goes. I found her in Hatchard's, and recognizing the hunted, hopeless look, I invited her to St. James' Square. Right now she is getting her strength back and becoming familiar with the establishment and its inhabitants before deciding if it will be her future. However," she cocked a speculative eyebrow at him, "if you know some clever way to save her from this by forcing her brother to give her an allowance so she could live on her own, she could be rescued from this."

"What? Rescued from a life of wealth and luxury at Mrs. Gerrard's?" he teased.

"Hah! You say that now, but I remember when you thought otherwise."

"Do not remind me. I still suffer from remorse."

"But, in all seriousness, for a woman, a respectable life, even in the most modest of circumstances, is more comfortable than the one we live."

Once again, he saw the pain that still lingered in her eyes, even after all she had accomplished. "If it is lived independently," he amended.

She laughed. "How well you know me. Yes, if it is a life of independence over which one has sole control."

Julian thought for a while. "It all depends on her father's will. Surely, if there were some settlement on her, the family solicitor would have told her."

"She was in Italy and stayed to arrange for her parents' burial there so news of their death preceded her, and, having heard what an utter blackguard her brother is, I wouldn't put it past him to have kept all the details from her."

"Hmm. It is to be hoped she knows the name of the family solicitor. If she does, then inquiries can be made. Where is the family from?"

"Kent, near Tunbridge Wells, I believe."

"Well then, I can send Mr. Duncombe to see what he can learn. Trust me, I will do my best to see she gets what she should."

"Oh I trust you," the emerald eyes glinted, "as a force to be reckoned with."

"I thank you. Now, if you trust me . . ."

Her chin came up and the glint became wariness. "Yesssss?"

"If you trust me, then I offer you my escort to visit Lady Standiford. I promised Annie when I took her to Brighton that I would visit her within a month's time to see how she was doing."

"What?" Helen shook her head. "Oh no, I couldn't, I can't . . ."

"Hear me out, Helen. You told me that she wrote you asking you to visit. I know you, you are cautious and, er, cynical. No, don't poker up at me, you are a cynic—deservedly so—I can see that you might not want to visit a relative you had never heard of, a relative from a family that rejected yours. It is bound to be uncomfortable, but she wants to meet you. She is getting older, has no children of her own. Lord, if she allows herself to be my *Aunt Honoria*, you know she is desperate for family. Yes, she has her brother whom she has always despised as a stiff, self-important prig. My mother was her closest friend, and she has lost her. Please consider it. If I accompany you, I can provide the distraction of other company, and it will be less taxing with me as a buffer or go-between, whatever I can do to ease the awkwardness of the first meeting."

Still she shook her head. "To what end? I see no point in pursuing a connection that very well may be disastrous to her."

"Or to you. What is this? Helen Gerrard afraid?"

"I am not!"

"You have created your life out of nothing, a feat for which I am lost in admiration, but it is a life that has protected you from a certain risk, the risk of caring too deeply for others because, even those to whom you dedicate your life, whose welfare you care about so strongly, you are determined to make so successful and independent they can leave you and follow their own dreams, make their own lives." Julian saw the hint of sadness, quickly hidden, cross her face. Yes, she did miss those who had succeeded and moved on—Lady Adrian,

Lady Maximilian, and yes, eventually Dora Barlow. "To admit to having a family, paltry though it may be, invites that possibility of closeness that can cause so much hurt, but I also believe it can bring so much joy."

He might have been talking to himself, Helen thought. There was a faraway look in his eyes that told her he had once dreamed of finding that again with his mother once he had returned triumphant from India, but he had been too late. Perhaps he needed this visit to Lady Standiford more than she, and she didn't even know whether she needed it or not. She could not do this visit for herself, but she could do it for him. "Very well, but I need some time."

He rose and, taking her hands in his, pulled her up to face him, smiling gently. "Take all the time in the world. I do not think, knowing Aunt Honoria, that you will be sorry you did it. In the meantime, I can send Duncombe to Tunbridge Wells to make his own discreet inquiries, if you can share this unfortunate woman's name, until we find out the solicitor's name, if we do find it out."

"It is Mountjoy, the Honorable Elizabeth Mountjoy. Thank you, my lord."

"'Tis nothing. Thank you! You know this is just the sort of problem I live to solve."

"That I do." She smiled, retrieved the hands that somehow still remained in his warm, firm clasp, and headed back down the stairs and out to the waiting carriage, feeling oddly lighter and more clear-thinking than when she had entered.

Elizabeth did know the name of the family solicitor, as Helen expected she would, and was not only able to provide that, but the solicitor's direction in Tunbridge Wells. "It is Somerville, Milton Somerville, with his office in the Pantiles," she responded when Helen found her in the *schoolroom* deep in conversation with Clarissa and Dora. "But why do you want to know? I never had anything to do with him."

Helen explained Julian's suspicion that perhaps not all the details of her father's will had been shared with her.

"Actually no details at all were shared with me. I just assumed Lawrence inherited everything, and control over it as well."

"From what you have told me of your brother," Dora gave her a darkling look, "I wouldn't put it past him to do his utmost to keep you enslaved and subservient, the miserable blackguard."

'Yes," Clarissa chimed in, "my father always encouraged his clients to make provisions for their daughters." She blinked rapidly, overcome by fond memories of a past ruthlessly destroyed by a conniving stepfather.

"I see Dora and Clarissa have been introducing you to our establishment." Helen smiled at them.

'Yes." Elizabeth glanced around the small sitting room which doubled as a schoolroom during the week and a chapel of sorts in Sundays. "And I am most impressed with your courses of instruction."

"In which she could assist," Clarissa broke in, "for she knows the classics far better than I. She might even be able to fill in when duties call you elsewhere."

"Which reminds me," Helen turned toward the door, "I shall be back shortly.

She reappeared some moments later with a package which she handed to Elizabeth.

"For me? But why?" Carefully she undid the string and unwrapped the paper, then gasped in utter astonishment, "Seneca's *Morals*! Then she burst into tears as Dora drew her into her arms.

"I saw you admiring it and thought it might be of some use to you."

"I told you she was that sort of person." Clarissa beamed as Dora nodded at Helen to leave.

Quietly she shut the door behind her, knowing that the comfort of the two women would do more for Elizabeth's wounded spirit than anything Helen could do. She had given the girl a safe haven for the moment and offered her a chance to support herself, such as it was. Now it was up to her, and maybe to Julian, if he could work some miracle. He had worked several already so what was one more to a man like him?

Chapter 27

Julian's miracles were the topic of conversation over tea in the morning room of Claverton House the next day. John had stopped by to pay his respects to his mother and sister, but the Duchess was out walking her spaniels in the park and likely to be gone some time, given the fineness of the day.

"I am glad I have you to myself." John took the cup of tea his sister handed him. "I think we owe a debt of gratitude to the man who has freed Freddy from a life of servitude."

"You know who it is?" Georgie's eyes were bright with curiosity.

"Yes. Lord Linton."

"Lord Linton!"

"As you know, his niece became acquainted with Basil at Lady Cholmondeley's, an unfortunate and unforeseen consequence of Freddy's wish to show his appreciation for being allowed to view Linton's cargo by introducing his niece to friends who would could make her first Season more enjoyable, but Basil, I know, inserted himself in the most pushing way."

Georgie nodded, her mouth full of cake.

"Entertaining the misgivings that any rational person meeting Basil would entertain, Lord Linton consulted that Source of All Knowledge where the *ton* is concerned, Helen Gerrard."

"She's very clever, Mrs. Gerrard, isn't she?"

"Verrry clever. At any rate, he learned more than he needed to know about Basil from someone who, apparently had her own unpleasant encounter with him." Being the soul of discretion, John avoided all mention of the mission to rescue Linton's niece from Basil's clutches. "And in the course of all this, Linton learned enough to deduce that Lord Harcourt owned the freehold on the property in St. James' Square for which Mrs. Gerrard owns the leasehold."

"London's most exclusive seraglio," his sister supplied as her brother bit back a smile. No flies on Georgie, he thought. One could count on that.

"Yes, well, at any rate, he also learned that Lavinia had been the mastermind behind the runaway carriage that nearly killed Juliette."

"No! I knew she was havey-cavey despite her high-and-mighty airs, but I had no idea."

"Nor did any of us. But having sized up poor Freddy's unfortunate situation, Lord Linton threatened her with exposure, not to mention the law, if she did not cry off."

"We do owe him a debt of gratitude for saving Freddy—no, saving us all—from that Friday-faced creature, that Medusa. Now what can we do to repay him?" Georgie plopped her chin in her hands, frowning fiercely as she considered options.

"I think the best thing we can do is to find a beau for the niece. I had thought to ask Randall."

"Not Randall. He is a dear, and she is . . . well, she is uninspiring, shall we say."

"I was about to say I was going to ask Randall if he might know anyone."

"Someone not too bright, but a decent sort, with a title, who might appreciate a sizable dowry."

"Precisely." John grinned. "You really are a clever girl, Georgie."

She stuck her tongue out at him. "Now to arrange an evening where this can occur."

"A musicale, not too taxing for Mama and not too large, say in three weeks' time," she continued. "And of course we'll need Randall's help. We'll ask him to recommend friends or colleagues to perform and he will be grateful enough to serve up a sacrificial friend."

"Georgie!"

"Well, she really is quite dull. How she came by such an interesting uncle, I'll never know."

"Fortunately for us, she did. I will speak to Randall after service as he is on the organ this Sunday.

John caught up with Randall as he rose from the organ bench and was gathering up his music.

"I expect I can find some musicians if the musicale is not on a performance night for the Philharmonic Society. I will ask Mr. Greatorex and Sir George Dance for their help too. If we were fortunate enough to get Mr. Cramer to preside at the pianoforte, that would truly be splendid," Randall suggested.

"And you will naturally be receiving an invitation." John laughed at Randall's wary expression. "You know your uncle and your parents will be most pleased to think of your attending a *ton* event."

Randall sighed. "I expect so."

"Besides, Georgie will be there. She is always excellent, if bracing, company. Bring a companion to share the social burden. Surely you know a likely lad from university."

Randall considered for a moment. "My friends are not top-of-the-trees sort of people. I like them, but most people would consider them hopelessly lacking in town bronze."

"Exce . . . er, never fear. Georgie is inviting several acquaintances who are not Incomparables either, but who are quite personable when not overwhelmed by large, brilliant gatherings."

So it was that three weeks later, John, standing with his sister, Julian, Lady Charlotte, and her mother after the musicale, beckoned to Randall and an unprepossessing young man with sandy hair who had just finished congratulating Mr. Cramer on his performance. "We are grateful to Randall who is the one responsible for this excellent program," John announced to the group. "And Randall, may I introduce you to the Countess of Linton, Lady Charlotte Bracebridge, and her uncle, Lord Linton?"

Randall knew his duty. He smiled at all and sundry, bowed and brought forth his friend. "And may I make known to you Viscount Rushbrooke, an old school friend and a fellow musical connoisseur whom I lured up from Hampshire for this evening, thanks to you, my lord, and Lady Georgiana."

"Did you not think Cramer did an excellent job?" Randall, for once not the most reticent in the group, prodded his friend.

"I did," Lord Rushbrooke blushed violently, "but then, he is always brilliant."

"Reginald, here, would not leave his estate for just any old musicale," Randall confided to Georgie, "but having performed here myself, I could assure him that the acoustics of Claverton House are exquisite, and the company even better. I do hope you agree, Lady Charlotte. Perhaps you play the pianoforte yourself?"

Oh well done, lad. Who guessed you had it in you? John remarked to himself, swelling with almost fatherly pride.

"I confess to being something of a country bumpkin," Reginald admitted shyly after receiving a nudge from his friend that was so subtle only John observed it, "but I do appreciate good music. I hope you enjoyed it as well." He turned to Charlotte with such a sweet, self-deprecating smile that she could not help taking pity on him.

"Yes I did, but tell me, Lord Rushbrooke, what do you find so compelling about Hampshire?"

"My estate," he responded with simple pride. "It has been in the family since before the Conquest so I feel I owe it my life's blood. Most recently, I have been introducing some modern agricultural practices that are improving crop production significantly."

"Since the Conqueror! Good heavens, that is a responsibility," Charlotte's mother broke in. "You are from a very ancient lineage, I take it."

"Yes, none of those Norman ways of doing things for the Rushbrookes," he admitted with a rueful glance at Charlotte, "more of a country bumpkin than you could have imagined."

"Nonsense, there is nothing wrong with good old solid Saxon ways, is there Charlotte?"

"No Mama."

John could tell that Mama approved highly of the young man, even if her daughter were less forthcoming. It was then he happened to look up to see Lord Linton observing the entire conversation with an arrested expression in his eyes and just the tiniest smile tugging at the corner of his mouth. He's figured it out, John thought.

"Did Helen put you up to this?" Julian murmured, edging closer to John as he took a glass of champagne being passed by a footman.

'No, actually, she did not. Georgie and I were trying to think of some way to repay you for the signal service you have rendered to our family. Freddy has never been happier, and we can all look forward to a more comfortable future. Helen confirmed our suspicions that a very deft hand and clever mind were behind the rescue of our brother, but no, Georgie and I were the ones who racked our brains for some way to express our gratitude." He glanced over at Charlotte and Reginald who seemed to be engaging in friendly conversation while Randall chatted easily with his sister. "I do hope our little stratagem succeeds."

"So do I." Julian looked unconvinced, but hopeful. "Believe me, I was happy to do what little I could, but thank you. I imagine your brother, connoisseur that he is, also appreciated the musical evening you have created. He does seem to be enjoying himself." Julian glanced across the room to where Freddy and his mother were talking animatedly with a young woman whom John recognized as Georgie's friend, Lady Verena Carstairs and a companion, presumably her mother.

Enlightenment dawned, and John turned to catch his sister's eye as he shook his head in mock dismay. Lady Charlotte was not the only one being paired off at this little soiree. Clever, clever Georgie. She had not wasted a minute in searching for a solution to her friend's, and now her brother's newly single state. He applauded her initiative; he only hoped it wasn't misguided, even if for the kindest of reasons.

Apparently it was Georgie's plot, as she acknowledged later that evening when they compared impressions after the event.

"Quite a success, I would say." Georgie looked smug.

"You never told me about your plans for Freddy."

"I figured that for a man of God, one subterfuge for the evening was enough."

"And I would say *Be fruitful and multiply.*"

"Touché, clever brother. I will say that Freddy and Verena seemed to enjoy one another. She was genuinely interested as he droned on about the furniture designs he is working on with Mr. Oakley using Lord Linton's wood. She admitted that her interest is in garden design, but asked if Freddy could give her some sketches to show her youngest brother, William, who is an architect. A most promising beginning. And Lady Charlotte? She seemed fairly engaged with Lord Rushbrooke."

"I suppose so, but her mother was more so, what with the ancient lineage and estate and all, in addition to the title."

"That is all that is needed. The girl truly doesn't have a mind of her own."

Freddy was happy and they had repaid their debt to Lord Linton. Yes, the evening had been a success.

Chapter 28

Lord John and Lady Georgiana Claverton were not the only ones noticing a change in their brother. "I must say, Freddy looks as though a great weight has been lifted off his shoulders," Dora remarked, taking a seat in Helen's office several days later. "He went on at great length last evening about his furniture designing with Mr. Oakley and a possible collaboration with the architect brother of some friend of Lady Georgiana's. An enterprise so smacking of trade would never have been contemplated under Lady Lavinia's rule." She tilted her head to examine her friend more closely. "On the other hand, I would say that the weight lifted off Freddy's shoulders seems to have landed on yours. Cut line, what's amiss? You can tell your old friend Dora."

The faint smile in response to this sally confirmed Dora's suspicions that something truly was bothering Helen. What could it possibly be? Nothing disturbed the carefully ordered universe of the unflappable Helen Gerrard.

"Nothing is amiss, really, just perplexing," Helen admitted.

"You, perplexed? Never."

"I thank you for your stout defense, but in this case, I truly do not know what to do. A second cousin has invited me to visit her."

"Second cousin? I thought you had no family"

"Apparently I do."

"But how . . . when did you find this out?"

As the color stained Helen's cheeks, Dora knew the answer.

"Er, according to reports, she looks so much like me that when he first saw me in the drawing room here, Lord Linton thought he had met me before. It was not until he went to visit his mother's best friend, his *Aunt Honoria*, outside of Brighton that he recalled his initial reaction when he first visited here.

More and more interesting. "And she knows that you . . ."

"He told her everything and she still invited me to visit."

"Again, I say that I was under the impression that you had no family."

"To all intents and purposes, that was true." Helen sighed. "And it was easier that way. It freed me to live life as I wanted to, well, the only way I could do after the Incident responsible for my dismissal. My father and mother never mentioned their families. Papa was disowned by his martinet of a father for going into the church and insisting on serving a poor parish, and Mama was cast off for marrying a poor vicar ministering to an impoverished parish. They didn't need anyone except one another. Even when Mama died, Papa mentioned no relations of hers. I knew he came from a noble family, but the few times he mentioned his childhood, he made it and his family sound so unpleasant I had no wish to know them and no indication that they would ever want to acknowledge me, much less make my acquaintance."

"But now one of them does. Is that so difficult to imagine, acceding to her wish? I should think it would be nice to be wanted," Dora said wistfully.

"It's not necessarily being wanted. Undoubtedly she is just curious."

"Curious wouldn't invite someone to her home. Besides, I don't think his lordship would have mentioned your existence or explained what you are if he thought she'd respond with vulgar curiosity. She invited you into her home after learning who and what you are."

"Perhaps you are right. Perhaps I should visit, if only to satisfy my own vulgar curiosity, eh?" Helen's smile hinted at the return of some of her usual spirit.

"I think you should go, if only to see this person who looks so much like you Lord Linton thought he's met you before."

"That's it, then, I shall take the plunge."

"It will be nice for John Coachman and the horses to get away so he can really spring 'em."

"Oh, I won't be taking our carriage. Lord Linton has offered to escort me in his. Besides, you all need ours here."

But no thought that Lord Linton's sister-in-law and niece might have need of their carriage as well? Interesting. Again, Dora noted the telltale blush and decided she was glad the way things were unfolding. She didn't know what it meant for the ladies of Mrs. Gerrard's, but she was glad for the woman who had saved them all and made them prosper.

If the Countess of Linton and her daughter objected to losing their private carriage some days later, no mention was made of it as Julian handed Helen in and she waved goodbye to Dora and Clarissa who were off to Bond Street on a shopping expedition.

"I am glad of this time together so I can give you my report." Julian climbed in and settled in the seat opposite.

"Report?"

"Yes. I was under the distinct impression you had commissioned me for a certain task, and I had a self-imposed task whose progress I also wanted to mention."

"Good heavens, I did not mean to be so demanding." Helen wasn't sure she quite liked that picture of herself. She had her standards, of course, but was she such a demanding female? Horrors.

"Not at all; it is more a matter of my wanting to gratify your every wish. My young solicitor friend has been in contact with Mr. Somerville, who acknowledged in their first exchange of letters that he did handle Lord Mountjoy's will. Now Mr. Duncombe, who has informed Mr. Somerville that he is representing Miss Mountjoy, is going down to Tunbridge Wells next week to see what, if any, provisions were made for the young lady's future. If her brother were left as sole guardian, that would make things rather difficult, but I am hoping that her parents knew their son well enough, and were enlightened enough to secure her something beyond his control."

"I hope so. I hadn't thought about the brother's unreliability as something that would be an argument against leaving him as guardian. Let's hope that it was. And the other task?"

"The other was to insure that Basil Harcourt never strayed anywhere near current and former inhabitants of Mrs. Gerrard's. I can safely assure you that he has not. Syed Muhammad has not been his constant shadow, but he has followed him enough to know that he is confining his activities to the family residence in Brook Street, his own chambers in Cavendish Square, and the gambling hells in Pall Mall and Covent Garden. The majority of the time he has followed him, Syed has stayed out of sight, but every once in a while, when the sun is just right, he will allow it to cast his shadow so that Basil, even befuddled as he usually is, can easily make out his turban and his height."

"Very clever. We are much indebted to Mr. Muhammad, but I do hope this assignment you have given him is not cutting into his work."

"No. He does his best work in the morning anyway, and Basil is never abroad until well after noon, so in the mornings Syed ensconces himself in the reading room at Montagu House with whatever work he is translating, and in the afternoons, if he is not teaching Persian to one of his students from the Company, he diverts himself by tracking Basil, which I think affords him some distraction and relief from his studies. I owe a debt to his family for allowing his younger brother to come work for me in Bombay discovering what sort of British goods are most desired. Now that I am here and practicing law at last, he will run everything there. I am extremely fortunate, now that I need to delegate the trading and shipping duties, that

I have someone I can not only rely on completely, but someone who is capable and enterprising in his own right. You have that too in Dora. People like Dora and Ahmed are rare and precious, and only a few of us are lucky enough to have them as our colleagues."

Yes, Helen thought, she was lucky to have Dora, stalwart support and friend that she had always been, not to mention, skilled businesswoman who understood both accounts and tradespeople in a way that Helen, with all of her mathematical skills, did not.

Dora, however, had, had a moment of trepidation, quickly suppressed, at the prospect of Helen's absence. "It won't be the same without you here, but," she added hastily, "we shall manage, Clarissa and the rest of us. It's just that neither she nor I have your éclat." (Dora was proud of the French she had learned from Juliette.) "But we shall manage and be glad we are giving you the opportunity to get away."

"Dora is my rock of strength," she agreed. "I hope your Ahmed is the same."

He nodded, and then they gave themselves up to the hypnotic movement of the carriage and the passing scenery on a fine summer day.

Julian watched as the aloof, composed features softened and the alert, critical expression in Helen's eyes drifted into dreamy contemplation of the rich, green fields and the flowering hedgerows. It was as though the years had fallen away from her, and he wondered what she was thinking as she sat transfixed by the countryside rolling past them.

A bump in the road and Helen looked up to find his eyes fixed on her. "I was remembering riding in the gig with my father as he made his rounds visiting the sick and the poor, which amounted to most of our village, and how he would quiz me on my Latin declensions or my Greek verbs." A fond smile softened her face. "He was a wonderful father. What other man would have been such a good friend to his daughter as to teach her cricket?"

"Cricket? You know cricket?"

"And that is more surprising than my having a better education than most men?" She shot him a challenging look.

"No, I suppose not, but lord," he grinned, I would like to see you play."

"I am a fair batter, if I do say so myself, but I will admit quite freely that I am all thumbs when it comes to bowling. I think Papa was rather disappointed I wasn't an all-rounder like he was, but he never let on, and I certainly enjoyed it more than the needlework I would have had to learn if Mama was alive. Not that Mama wasn't an excellent scholar herself, but she did do beautiful embroidery in the evenings before the fire."

"Perhaps I can round up a bat and a ball at Aunt Honoria's and we can play a game ourselves. She never had any children, but there still may be some equipment lying around from previous generations."

Julian had thought Helen was relaxed until he saw the rest of the tension drain out of her body. It seemed impossible that the coolly collected Helen Gerrard could be nervous over this meeting, but...

He leaned forward to take her hands in his. "You'll see, we shall have a good time. Aunt Honoria is a very casual hostess. We can go riding, we can visit Annie in Brighton and see how she is faring, though from all accounts, she is doing splendidly. And Aunt Honoria is bound to like you." His lips quirked. "After all I like you, and I am notoriously difficult to please."

And then they were there, driving up a long gravel drive to halt in front of a gray stone Palladian building of medium size, but elegant proportions. By the time they pulled up, servants had assembled on the steps, ready to take care of the horses, see to the luggage, and open the carriage door. As they climbed the steps, a regal-looking woman appeared and Helen, just reaching the top step, stopped dead in her tracks.

She was looking in a mirror! But the woman wasn't wearing a bonnet or a carriage dress, and Helen was. Helen stared. The woman stared back, and then they both burst out laughing.

The woman held out her hands. "Welcome to Standiford Hall, my dear. I must say, Julian is more of a slow-top than I thought if it took him so long to realize why he thought he'd met you before. Do come in and tell me about yourself."

Chapter 29

Lady Standiford led them through the black and white marble hall, past the drawing room to a comfortable library that looked out over gardens just beginning to show their summer blooms, and rang for tea.

"Now," she leaned forward, her face alight with eager interest, "tell me about your father. Of course, once my uncle, unyielding, sanctimonious prig that he was, disinherited him, no one ever dared speak of him again. And the present earl is just like his father so the rigid silence, as far as your family was concerned, continued." She dismissed such stupidity with a scornful wave of her hand.

"Your father was well rid of the lot of them, she continued. They would only have made his life a constant misery. My mother, no admirer of her brother, was a great deal younger than he so she barely remembers your father. She was so eager to get out of that household herself that she married at an early age to a nice young man who had come to visit a friend at a neighboring estate and, fortunately for her, had a lineage and fortune respectable enough to satisfy her brother. According to Julian, here, your father was something of a scholar and, I gather, much devoted to good works."

"That he was." Helen accepted the cup of tea from her hostess, took a deep breath, and began to speak of life in the vicarage in Nottinghamshire.

Lady Standiford was an excellent listener, quiet but engaged, and genuinely interested in learning more about Henry Falkland. Helen soon found herself completely at ease and confiding more about her former life than she ever had to anyone before, but this woman cared; this woman was family. It was a foreign concept after all these years, but Helen found herself warming to it.

She warmed to it even more as they talked over dinner. After tea, Lady Standiford had sent them to their bedchambers to freshen up after their journey, and then they had strolled around the gardens, admiring the informal design and wide variety of plants that had obviously been selected and cultivated with care. During dinner, it was Lady Standiford's turn to talk, and she regaled them with stories of Julian' mother as a young girl, and a few amusing incidents from the days Julian was in shortcoats, never alluding to the dark and menacing air that had hung around Julian's father, and eventually around his mother's life.

It was all so easy and so natural that Helen, heading off to bed several hours later, marveled at how quickly the time had flown. She was reminded of the comfortable conversations she and her father had enjoyed over dinner, sharing opinions, stories of the day's events, or plans for the days to come. Even Julian seemed more relaxed and at ease than she had ever seen him, as though the very air at Standiford Hall had turned him into a more lighthearted version of himself.

The lighthearted version was even more apparent the next morning when he suggested Helen join him in a ride around the estate. "There is a lovely wood and a meadow Aunt Honoria has left untilled with a brook running through it."

"But I haven't been on a horse in years," she protested, "and I have no riding habit."

"That is no excuse," Aunt Honoria spoke up from the other end of the breakfast table where she had been buried in the morning papers after greeting them both and assuring herself that they had slept well and were ready to take on any activities that might be suggested. "It should be no problem for my mirror image," she nodded at Helen, "to fit into one of mine, if she can bear not to be the picture of fashion that she is now."

As Lady Standiford had predicted, her habit not only fit Helen to perfection, but was becoming as well, the slate color highlighting the rich red of her hair. Even the matching boots were comfortable, but Helen could not help worrying about the prospect of mounting a horse after a decade."

"The skill never goes away, you'll see, Julian reassured her, though in actual fact, he had no experience whatsoever with such a situation.

However, when the horses were brought around and Helen was introduced to the docile Daisy who whuffled gently at her, and put out her nose to be patted, her hesitancy disappeared as she remembered her dear departed Minerva who had been a constant and loyal companion when Helen was growing up.

Watching her stroke Daisy's nose, Julian was struck by Helen's tender smile and the quiet dialogue between horse and woman. It was clear that she had an affinity for her fellow four-legged creatures, and the almost shy eagerness to make a friend, so unlike the worldly Helen Gerrard, told him that she had missed this elemental sort of companionship all those years she had been in London. He had to fight the urge to hare off and buy her an equine companion all of her own.

"You will see, Daisy will take care to make sure you enjoy your ride. She is a most accommodating horse." Julian held out his hands to lift her up into the saddle.

Helen's nervousness over the outing was quickly obliterated by the riot of unsettling feelings washing over her as she felt the warmth and strength of his hands on her waist. She told herself not to be a fool and look up at him, but for some inexplicable reason, she completely ignored her own very good advice and tilted her head to gaze into the eyes smiling down at her. Her heart did the strangest sort of somersault as all the breath squeezed out of her body and her knees gave way underneath her. Then he was lifting her up, still smiling at her, but his eyes were full of hope and questions she knew she could not answer.

For a moment she was overcome, and then she was in the saddle, settling into the familiar and reassuringly reminiscent feeling of being on horseback after all these years making her feel young and free again.

Fool. Julian chastised himself, treasuring the moment as he patted Daisy's withers and then mounted his own horse. How could he have allowed himself to hold her close to him for that extra second longer than he should have? But she was so exquisite and so dear as she established her friendship with Daisy. He had seen the alarm in her eyes and knew that his own eyes must have revealed more than they should have for someone who was just a friend. If he wanted to keep that friendship that was so precious to him—and growing more so all the time—he would have to exert better self-control. "Off to the wood." He urged Brutus forward and put everything else from his mind except the fineness of the day and the beauty of their surroundings.

They rode in silence until they reached the dappled shade of the wood. "How beautiful! Just like the woods in a fairy tale," she exclaimed. "But a good wood, not the sort with evil witches or slavering wolves."

"Definitely not." Julian liked seeing this side of her, fanciful and playful. Yes, he had been immediately attracted to her quick mind and her mastery over every situation that life had thrown at her, and he had thoroughly enjoyed the challenge of their conversations, but this? This was just fun.

Helen turned to him as they emerged into the fields on the other side of the wood. "And what do you hear from Ned Stornaway? How is he managing with your estate?"

"Very well, from all that I can tell. He was able to oversee some of the spring planting and, unlike my brother who wished to till every field all the time in order to extract the most profit he thought he could, Ned is letting some lie fallow to recover, and he is spreading manure to encourage it. I wish he could meet Charlotte's new admirer, Lord Rushbrooke, who is quite a proponent of new agricultural practices. You should have seen Charlotte's face when he described the advantages of planting turnips to restore the soil."

"A new admirer. That is a good sign."

"Yes, he is a friend of Lord Farnsworth who recommended the musicians for the Duchess of Roxburgh's musicale. I believe Lord John and his sister arranged the encounter. Very clever, both of them, and I am grateful, as is Charlotte's mother who has taken quite a shine to Lord Rushbrooke, or to his title and lineage at least."

Helen chuckled. "And your niece?"

"She has always followed her mother's lead—most of the time—and after the disaster with Basil, all of the time."

They continued on a leisurely circuit, chatting easily, enjoying one another's company, the fresh air, and the peacefulness of the countryside, and before they knew it, had arrived back at Standiford Hall to be greeted by their hostess who was holding a cricket bat and ball.

"Julian mentioned you played cricket so I unearthed these and Peter here," she pointed to a grinning stable boy, "has set up the wickets. You are still in sporting clothes so let us see what you can do. With only two of you there's no hope of a game, but you can show off your skills." She stepped back with a provocative smile on her lips that was so like Helen's that Julian could only shake his head in wonder.

"Very well, Miss Falkland," he took the bat and ball from his aunt, handed the bat to Helen, and walked to the other end of the pitch, "let us see what you are made of."

Helen took up her place, gripped the bat, and stared down the pitch at him, concentrating on his arm, the ball, and the pitch with every fiber of her being. She had not been this alive since she could not remember when. Thwack! She felt the strength and precision flow back into her shoulders, arms, and hands as she sent the ball flying. It was only a second as she realized it was an excellent shot, and the she was running to the opposite wicket.

"Capital shot!" Julian met her at the wicket, admiring her flushed cheeks, sparkling eyes, and flying hair as much as her prowess. "I can see you had an excellent teacher. Now let us see you bowl." He handed her the ball.

Helen, still flushed with triumph, took it and wound up her arm for the pitch which hit with a dismal thump a third of the way to the wicket.

"I see what the problem is," Julian strode over to steady her arm and Helen could only be grateful he did not laugh at her outright. "You are hanging onto it for too long. Here," he positioned himself behind her and took her wrist, holding it gently while sternly admonishing himself to forget everything else—the closeness, the scent of rosewater rising from the hair now loose from its pins and straggling down her neck, the soft slim wrist—and focus on the ball. "Now pitch."

She wound up her arm again.

"And release." He squeezed her wrist and the ball flew through the air . . . only to be snatched by a large dog of indeterminate heritage who caught it in his jaws and raced off into the fields.

"Bounder! No!" Peter came screeching to a halt as the dog disappeared. "I am sorry, my lord, my lady."

But Julian was doubled over with laughter, and Helen and Lady Standiford not far behind him, laughing heartily as the dog made off with his prize. "Well it would have been an excellent pitch," Julian gasped when he finally got hold of himself.

"I haven't laughed like that in years, "Lady Standiford said when she could finally catch her breath. Now come, children," she looked at both of them, fondness softening her features, "it is time for luncheon."

"Thank you." She caught Helen by the arm while Julian went off to see to the horses. "I haven't seen Julian so happy in years. And I have never heard him laugh out loud. You may not know it, but you are a miracle worker.

Chapter 30

And so the days passed in easy camaraderie. Helen tried hard not to think about Lady Standiford's words as they had left the cricket pitch. It was something she could not face. Being responsible for someone's welfare? She could do that; she was happy to do it; in fact she sought it out. Being responsible for someone else's happiness? It was a burden she could not bear, even for herself.

It did make her happy, however, to learn that there were other women in the world who took the welfare of their fellow creatures as seriously as she did. She had ample proof of this when she accompanied her hostess a few days later to the village school she had set up. "It is a simple establishment," Lady Standiford apologized, "with only one schoolmistress for children of all ages—anyone old enough and close enough to walk to the schoolhouse, which is really just a cottage in the village with a main room large enough to serve as a schoolroom. Some of the men in the village made benches and tables that can be pushed aside in the evening to give the schoolmistress, who lives there, a cozy sitting room. We only offer the most basic of subjects: reading, writing, arithmetic, and globes."

"And here we are," she said as the carriage pulled up in front of a neat stone cottage with roses climbing on a trellis by the door. Lady Standiford knocked, and then opened the door into a room with neatly dressed children ranging in ages from five to ten or eleven sitting on benches at long tables, each with their own slate and chalk and facing a desk where a lively young woman was saying, "Very well done, Mary."

"I beg your pardon for interrupting, Miss Worthington, but Miss Falkland is an educator herself, and I thought she should see all that you and your students are accomplishing here."

If Miss Worthington thought Miss Falkland far too fashionably dressed to have an interest in, much less a clue about education, she kept it to herself. "It is quite alright, I was just about to ask Henry to show us the countries he has learned to identify on the globe. Henry?"

"Yes Miss." A likely looking lad rose quickly, eager to demonstrate his superior knowledge to his fellow students. Like all the other boys, he was clad in a sturdy blue shirt and matching trousers, while the girls wore white smocks over dresses of the same blue cotton.

Observing Helen's scrutiny of the uniforms, Lady Standiford whispered, "These are provided so no one need feel different or embarrassed by their apparel, and because everyone can use an extra set of clothes."

She seemed to have thought of everything, and Helen was impressed with the vivacity and enthusiasm of the children. There was none of the rote repetition common in most village schools, and she remarked on it when she thanked the teacher for allowing them to interrupt her lessons.

"That is because Miss Worthington is such an excellent teacher," her guide replied with a wink at the schoolmistress as they headed toward the door. "She has the highest of standards, not to mention infinite patience, which is why she was hired."

"And how did you find her?" Helen climbed into the carriage after her hostess.

"I knew her from her charitable work in this village and the next one over where her father was the local vicar. He was a wonderful man who, like your father, insisted his daughter be as well educated as any boy. Her mother died of a fever when Selina was reaching womanhood, and her father of apoplexy not long after, which left her with no place to go and no means of support, for of course, no one would hire a governess without references. You know the story."

Helen nodded slowly.

"So, I thought, what better way to help everyone than to purchase a cottage where she could live and have a school and earn a salary?" Lady Standiford shook her head sadly and reached over to pat Helen's hand. "I only wish I could have done the same thing for you, my dear."

For a moment Helen wished so too, thinking of the pain and the humiliation she would have been spared. On the other hand, she would not have saved the women she had saved, and, in the end, she thought she preferred that.

Lady Standiford was silent for a moment before adding. "If I'd been able to do that for you, everyone would have been able to learn cricket as well and the village could have had a team."

They both laughed, as the carriage rolled on through the village and back to the Hall with Lady Standiford describing the points of interest along the way as Helen turned over in her mind the possibility of creating a similar school where Elizabeth Mountjoy could live and teach.

"And now that I have taken you on a tour of my good works, it is time for Julian to do the same for his," Lady Standiford announced at breakfast the next day. "Standiford's heir already has considerable properties of his own and has very kindly given me full responsibility for the estate and access to all its income if I will manage it for him, which means that today is the day I must spend going over estate business, It's another lovely day and perfect for a drive into Brighton to take in the sea air and visit Annie Bentley. If you don't mind driving something as lowly as a gig," she glanced at Julian, "you could take advantage of this fine weather."

It was a gorgeous, sunny day, and as they got closer to Brighton Helen could smell and taste the bracing salty tang of sea air. She inhaled deeply, letting out a sigh of pure pleasure. "Ah, I had forgotten how much I love the smell of the ocean. I confess that I have only been to the seaside once with Mama and Papa, but I adored it; I could have played in the sand and splashed in the water all day every day."

"Where did you go?"

"Skegness—not the height of fashion I am sure, but I thought it was heaven. As is this." Helen surveyed the house, presumably his mother's, where they had just pulled up which boasted a handsome bay window and a balcony on the first floor from which to enjoy the ocean view. "It is exquisite."

"Aunt Honoria said my mother was very comfortable here and Annie certainly enjoys it," he shrugged, but Helen's approval meant everything to him. At least she could see the life he had ultimately tried to give to his mother.

"Mrs. Gerrard!" A bright-eyed woman in a becoming morning dress, looking so happy and healthy Helen barely recognized the wan gaunt woman Olivia had brought to her a scant few months ago, came to greet them. "It is so lovely to see you. And this is Betty," she announced proudly as she ushered forward a capable looking young woman with a woefully sunken cheek that was oddly incongruous with her confident air.

"Pleased to meet you, ma'am," she dropped a shy curtsey.

"Heavens," Helen laughed, "I am not royalty, you know, or even someone special."

"According to Annie you are very special," Betty replied stoutly. "I hear tell you rescue poor unfortunates just like his lordship's mother did."

"Do come inside." Annie led them upstairs to the sunny, airy drawing room with a beautiful view of the ocean beyond. She rang for tea and cakes as Betty went off to attend to household tasks.

A young girl with a club foot staggered in with the tea and the most amazing cakes Helen had ever seen. "This is Pamela," Annie introduced her. The girl gave a shy bob and a smile and scuttled out of the room. "She is dreadfully shy, poor girl. Her mother was a monster who continually beat her because she thought her club foot made here stupid when really it was her mother's temper that kept her hopelessly intimidated."

"Like poor, stupid Byron." Helen's acid response made Julian cough so hard he nearly dropped the cup and saucer Annie handed him.

"Exactly." Annie grinned. "But the best news is," she pointed to the plate of cakes, "that Mrs. Soames has arrived."

Helen and Julian both looked blank.

"Our cook in Birmingham. George's dinners were the envy of his friends, but he never could treat anyone decently. Just as I predicted, she left soon after I did and tracked me down through Olivia, whom she remembered meeting years ago. She knew Olivia and I were fast friends. So here we are." Annie's face was flushed with pride. "And while I teach household management to people that most of the world would never hire, she is going to do the same with cooking—a school for domestics, if you like."

"What a splendid idea."

"Oh it's not mine, Mrs. Gerrard; it's all his doing." She nodded at Julian who was suddenly absorbed in selecting another cake from the rapidly diminishing plate.

Annie asked after Dora and the others, as well as Lady Standiford, and then she glanced toward the window. "But you two really should stroll along the Parade. Now is the best part of the day."

"Thank you, Annie. We shall be back to visit again before we return to London." Julian held out his arm as Helen retrieved her bonnet and tied the ribbons, and then they were down the stairs, out the door, and strolling leisurely along looking out over gentle waves.

Helen drew a deep, cleansing breath of salty air. "It is truly vast, isn't it? I can't imagine bobbing around on it for months on end. Even on the largest ships one must feel quite small and insignificant."

"A salutary experience for most human beings who are far too full of their own importance."

"So true. You are a wise man, my lord."

He shook his head. "Not so wise as experienced—far too experienced—in human nature."

"Then let us forget human nature as we admire true nature." Helen leaned against the railing, reveling in the vista before her, the sun peeking under the brim of her bonnet and the gentle sea breeze against her cheek.

Julian, ignoring the splendor in front of him, kept his eyes fixed on his companion. He liked her this way and relaxed, happy, letting her gaze and her mind wander. It wasn't that he didn't appreciate the Helen Gerrad gazing inscrutably over a hand of cards at the card table or, sparkling and alert as she engaged in and encouraged the conversation that wafted from one corner of her drawing room to another, but she spent too much of her time that way, watchful, calculating the odds, exerting subtle control over her surroundings. He wanted to free her of that—not all of it, but some of it—so she could follow her own inclinations, for once in her life.

She caught him watching her, shook her head and laughed. "Shameless woolgathering, I know, but somehow the endless expanse of sea and sky encourage that."

"I know, and I am glad. You deserve a moment's woolgathering every now and then."

"Ah, but if I do that, I shall turn into a hopeless degenerate." She took his arm again. "Shall we continue our stroll? There is nothing that enlivens the mind like gentle exercise."

They continued in companionable silence for a while, listening to the cries of the seagulls and the gentle lapping of the waves on the beach below as passersby came and went.

Suddenly, her hand clenched his arm in a frantic grip as though she were about to fall, but the paving stones were smooth beneath their feet. Julian glanced down to see her face, white as the clouds scudding across the sky and her eyes fixed on a burly figure bearing down on them.

On second glance, Julian realized that it had once been a burly figure, now crippled with gout, leaning heavily and angrily on a walking stick. The brutish, raddled face spoke of a formerly powerful man now laid low by the indignities of infirmity and old age.

"Lord Broughton," Helen managed to gasp in response to Julian's questioning look as she came to a dead stop in the middle of the pavement.

Her rapist! Julian wanted to stride up, grab the miserable bastard by the collar, and choke the life out of him—not quickly, but slowly and painfully. Instead, he reached over to cover the hand on his arm with his. "Keep walking, dear one, and look him straight in the eye. He is nothing to you now, no threat to you now."

Feeling the fury in the tensed muscles of his arm, Helen looked up at her companion, but despite the thinned lips and features tightened in anger, she read nothing but encouragement in his eyes. She gulped and took his advice, moving forward with determination as Lord Broughton shuffled toward the. They approached close enough for their eyes to lock, but only for a moment before he looked down and shuffled on. "He didn't recognize me."

"No, he did not, but better than that, he avoided your gaze. *You* intimidated *him,* my dear. In the end, you have triumphed and survived, nay, I would say, conquered, even."

Helen heard the pride in his voice. It washed away the trembling that had overtaken her the minute she had caught sight of the hated figure, aged though it now was, that had haunted her dreams for so many years. The pride in Julian's voice cleansed the helplessness she had suffered, the powerlessness that had made her a prisoner in her own body with no mastery over her own person, a powerlessness that had lurked in the recesses of her spirit in spite of all her wealth and her accomplishments. At last she was free, truly free, and the man next to her had made it happen. No, the man next to her had encouraged her to do it for herself.

Helen looked up at Julian, her heart too full for any words except a whispered, "Thank you."

But he understood. She could see in his eyes that he knew what it meant to her, what he had helped her win back.

They drove home in relative silence, punctuated now and then by desultory conversation and observations, and Lady Standiford, joining them in the drawing room before dinner that evening, had no inkling of the monumental transformation that had occurred. Nor was there anything in their discussion of Annie Bentley and her projects for educating superlative servants of all kinds that gave any indication that their day had been anything but a pleasant excursion to the exclusive seaside resort to visit a friend and enjoy the views for which Brighton was justly famous.

To all intents and purposes, it had been just another enjoyable outing like so many others they had shared during their stay at Standiford Hall . . . until that night.

Chapter 31

The screams woke him out of a dead sleep. Throwing a robe over his nightshirt, Julian raced down the hall to Helen's door and pushed it open, not even bothering to knock.

She was tossing back and forth on the bed, her face a mask of fury and despair, eyes closed. How was he to wake her without making things worse? "Helen," he spoke her name as calmly and reassuringly as possible. "You are safe. You are safe. You are loved. You are safe. Helen. Helen. Helen."

The arms that had been raised defensively over her head slowly sank to her sides, and he very gently took one hand, slowly stroking it once he saw that she was not panicked by his touch. "Helen, Helen, my love, it is a dream, just a dream." He repeated it over and over again, watching as her breathing slowed, his heart breaking as he thought of the terror she was re-living, and he wanted to hunt that miserable bastard down and thrash him within an inch of his life—no, not an inch, but until the death that Broughton had visited upon Helen when he raped her, the death of all her hopes and dreams, the death of her soul.

Helen gasped, shook herself, sat upright, and stared straight ahead.

"Helen, my love, it is over. You are awake now. He is gone. He is done. You won."

She stared at him unseeing. Slowly he lifted his hand so she could see it and stroked her cheek. The eyes focused, filled with tears, then she buried her face in her hands. "I'm sorry."

It was a whisper he barely heard. "*You* are sorry? No, mankind, men, are sorry creatures for what they have made you and so many like you suffer. My poor girl." And when she looked at him at last with recognition in her eyes, he sank onto the bed beside her and pulled her into his arms.

She collapsed against him, sobbing into his shoulder, and Julian held her with all the love and anger and strength he had, willing it into her so she could know she was protected and defended until his dying breath. At last, the sobs subsided, and she leaned, exhausted, against him, then looked up with a bit of her old spirit glinting in her eyes.

"I had no idea I could be such a watering pot. I cannot recall crying after the age of ten, and I do apologize for waking you, my lord."

"Nonsense, Helen." He was having none of her gallant fobbing off. "You were brutalized. If you had been a man, you could have challenged him to a duel, revealed him for the nasty bully he was, and honor would have been satisfied. You would have been satisfied and you could have lived with yourself. As it was, you had to suffer for years, enduring what you saw as your weakness. Do you hear me, Helen? It was not your weakness, and, at any rate, you made him bow in weakness before you today."

That brought a fresh bout of tears. "Yes. Yes I did," she finally choked out, "thanks to you." She gazed up, eyes shining with gratitude, and his heart turned over in his chest as he bent to press his lips against her brow.

He truly had only meant to kiss her forehead, but at the last minute, she had moved to look at him more closely and his lips met hers instead. Afraid that she might feel he was taking advantage of the situation, Julian was about to pull away when the soft lips beneath his parted and, with a sigh, she gave herself up to his kiss. Softly, slowly, he reveled in her mouth's silky warmness as his hands gently caressed her shoulders, soothing, calming, hoping desperately that something that felt so right for him felt just as right for her.

Helen's mind and emotions were in such a tangle she could not do anything except feel the warmth and reassurance of Julian's lips and hands. She had awakened in sheer terror and then, seeing him there, solid and comforting when she needed him most, she'd collapsed in a puddle of absolutely desperate weakness and such helplessness that she didn't even recognize herself. The world had turned upside down and Julian had righted it for her twice that day. All she could do was cling to him and absorb his strength, much like clutching a branch to save herself from being carried away in a flood.

His arms felt so strong, and when she looked up, his eyes were so full of tenderness, she just melted into him. He felt so good, so safe. And then his lips came down on hers and a wave of tenderness and belonging and need washed over her. After so many years of standing alone against the world, she craved connection, and this was connection at its most elemental, skin against skin, warmth against warmth. The hollowness she didn't even know she carried inside her receded with every stroke of his hands along her back, every movement of his lips on hers. But instead of ebbing away with every caress, the need grew and grew as if it would never be satisfied.

"Show me," she whispered.

"Show you what?"

"The way it should be."

Julian held her away from him, studying her intently. "Are you sure? Are you very, very sure?"

She nodded, her eyes locked on his. "I am sure."

"Oh my love" He pulled her to him, holding her close for a moment, then lowered his head to kiss her slowly, gently, but this time, the kisses were languorous rather than comforting, and a different sort of warmth flowed through her, the warmth of longing for she knew not what, except that it was for him.

His lips trailed slowly down her neck, pausing at a particularly sensitive spot behind her ear as he sank down against the pillows, pulling her with him, but leaving a slight distance between them, connecting with his lips only.

Helen's eyes, traveling the length of his body, saw the hard length of him pressing against his nightshirt and loved him all over again for being the sensitive, considerate man he was, trying not to alarm her. *Loved him all over again?* Where had that come from? Yes, she admitted at last, she did love him. She had loved him for a long time, in spite of her stubborn refusal to acknowledge it.

One hand, which had been entangled in her hair, slid around to cup her chin and tilt her head to look at him. "Are you sure?"

Helen smiled. "Yes, I am sure."

The hand on her chin slid slowly down her neck and just as slowly undid the buttons of her nightdress, pushing it aside so his lips could caress her collarbone, tracing the outline of it as his hands skimmed down to her waist and then back up, the thumbs brushing the sides of her breasts and pausing there as he felt the shiver run through her. "Are you still sure?" Julian dared to hope that it was a shiver of pleasure, but he wanted to take nothing for granted, to remain sensitive to the slightest bit of hesitation.

"Yeesss." Her head fell back and he swept his thumb over the nipples that were hard against the sheer linen of the nightdress. "Aaaah." It was the softest of sights, barely discernible, but the sound slid over him, heating his skin, hardening his desire. Gently he pushed the open neck off one shoulder to reveal one pink nipple atop an alabaster breast.

Growling in his throat, he lowered his head to suck it slowly, tantalizingly, swirling his tongue around it, tasting it, devouring it. As she arched up to him, warm and wanting against his cock, Julian thought he would explode with joy . . . and other things. One hand crept down her leg to lift her nightdress and slid the silky length of her thigh which relaxed in his palm as though melting to his touch.

He paused, absorbing the heat, the desire, the anticipations throbbing through him, then raised the nightdress over her head, revealing the long slender body, the high pink-tipped breasts, small, but firm, offering themselves to his kisses, first one, then the other as she lay, eyes closed, lips parted in a dreamy smile. "I love you," he whispered against the silky skin. "I want you. I want to make you enjoy your body."

"You do?" The words were spoken so softly they floated on the air.

"Yes."

She had never known it could feel like this, to ache so desperately for him, but to be so enthralled by the feel of his hands that she was drowsy and consumed with desire at the same time. Her breasts were aching and on fire as his tongue swirled around her sensitive nipples, and she rose up against him begging for his caresses all over her body. Oh God. She had no idea she could be so completely at the mercy of her body, so needy for his touch. It should have alarmed her, but she was beyond thought now, and this was Julian, Julian who loved her, who protected her against her own fears, who made her feel safe.

His hand stroked her inner thighs, first one, then the other, until they quivered with longing, until his fingers found the moist warmth in between, slowly swirling around and around. Sparks of need devoured her as her breath quickened, and she thrust herself eagerly against those clever, tantalizing fingers, until the world exploded around her. She had never known such a feeling. How could she bear the exquisite ecstasy? It was sweet agony as it rippled through her, turning her into a madwoman, frantic with wanting.

And then it slowly ebbed like an enormous wave receding from the beach and his lips were on hers, his arms holding her tight against him. "My love, my precious love."

"Oh, oh," tears trickled out of the corners of her eyes. "I never knew such a thing . . . that it could be like that."

"It can be better than that." He smiled down at her. "It can be whatever you want or can dream of."

She was silent, still grappling with the new sensations and emotions washing over her, then her mind began functioning at last, thank God. For a moment there, she'd thought she'd lost it for good. "But you? What about you? I want you to feel that way too."

"Oh I do," he grinned, "every time I look at you I am consumed with wanting you, but this is about you."

"No, it should be about us, about sharing. You gave me back my body, helped it know what was possible, now . . ." she reached down to stroke the warm firm length of cock that was rigid and hard for her, for Helen, not just any female, but Helen. He made her feel that way, unique and precious and she knew it to be true because he had proven worthy of her trust so many times. His groan of pleasure sent shivers of desire through her again. "Now I give my body to you."

He rested his forehead against hers. "Are you sure?"

"I am sure."

Julian pulled her to him, savoring the exquisite joy of it all for a moment, and then he was kissing her hungrily, desperately, all his pent-up desire and longing for this to be perfect for her compressed into his lips as he devoured hers. And hers devoured him right back.

As he slid his hand between her thighs again, they fell apart for him. She wanted him there. He could almost taste her musky scent as he slowly replaced his hand with a cock about to explode.

"Yes! Yes!"

Fighting for control, he slid into her, gasping as the warmth closed around him, and his mind went blank, empty of everything except for her, being with her, in her, one with her. In and out, rising and falling with her in a perfect rhythm, rising and falling, until the crescendo burst over both of them, and shuddering, they collapsed against one another and fell into the pillows.

"My love, my love." He pulled her close and tucked her head against his shoulder. "Now go to sleep. You are safe, you are loved."

And Helen knew she was.

Chapter 32

Helen woke the next morning in Julian's arms to find him smiling down at her. "And now will you marry me?"

A wave of dismay swept over her. "Oh Julian, I don't see, I mean, I can't . . . not that it isn't dear of you to ask, but . . . oh," a tear rolled down her cheek, but she smiled damply. "I do love you, you know, but I don't see how it is possible." She gazed up at him, her cheeks turning pink. "It is not that I didn't enjoy myself, I did. It was . . . well I could never have imagined such a thing, such a beautiful gift you gave me, such a beautiful thing we shared. Oh," her shoulders slumped, "it's all so confusing."

"Helen," he put a finger to her lips, "Shh. We need not talk about it right now, but I want you to know that this was to show you how much I love you and need you in my life, and I have wanted that—well, not since the moment I saw you," he chuckled, "but since the moment you came to my chambers to discuss Annie Bentley. I knew then that we were soulmates, that we wanted the same thing—justice and new lives for those who had been cruelly used—and we were both prepared to fight for it. I had always thought I was destined to fight my battles alone, and I accepted that loneliness—gloried in it, even—until I discovered what it was like to have a warrior at my side, and now I want that forever. Now, I will leave you to your thoughts. " he rose and glanced at the bracket clock on the mantel, "and to prepare for breakfast."

One look at her guests' faces when they appeared in the breakfast room, and Lady Standiford knew her wish had come true: these two people, one who had always been dear to her, and one who was growing dearer by the moment, had found one another. What they did with that was another story altogether, given how busy and complicated their lives were, but for the time being, they radiated love and happiness. That was enough for her, and the most she could do to help them was to act as though absolutely nothing had happened.

"Since it is your last day here, I thought it best that you relax, walk in the garden, ride, play a little cricket," she raised a teasing eyebrow, "and generally enjoy yourself in a lazy kind of way."

They did just that, but mostly they strolled around the grounds with their hostess, posing questions about Julian's mother or Helen's family. "I wish I could tell you more about the family now," Lady Standiford apologized, "but your grandfather was such an arrogant prig my mother avoided him like the plague, and your uncle, the heir was equally insufferable. If the truth be told, I think your father was relieved to be disinherited so he felt no guilt about avoiding their company, which I would do too, if I were you, but if you like, I can put you in touch with them."

"Thank you, no," Helen laughed. "I take your word for it and consider myself forewarned. I am grateful to you for having saved me the trouble of wasting a second thought on them."

The day was over too soon for all of them, and the next morning found them bidding Lady Standiford farewell. "Visit whenever you wish, dear child, she hugged Helen tightly, "you don't need an invitation, nor do you need to wait for his escort for you are always welcome and I always look forward to having you visit."

"Thank you." A lump rose in Helen's throat as she climbed into the carriage. Who would ever have thought that this late in life she would discover family. As with so many other wonderful things, the man climbing into the carriage behind her had given it to her.

Once the carriage rolled down the drive and they had waved until Lady Standiford was no longer in sight, Julian withdrew a letter from his pocket. "This just arrived in the morning post. It is from Henry Duncombe informing me that Elizabeth Mountjoy's father did indeed leave something in trust in the consols for her, and Milton Somerville, knowing his client's poor opinion of his son and heir, eventually wrote her, informing her of the bequest, not once, but several times. Eventually he called on her at the Manor where he was informed by her brother that she had gone to stay with friends for an unspecified amount of time, but was encouraged to direct any payments from the trust to her brother who would be happy to forward them. Mr. Somerville, mistrusting the brother entirely, declined to do so and was just wondering how best to proceed when Henry contacted him."

"Somerville had known Lord Mountjoy's son to be licentious and a profligate, but he had not pegged him as an out-and-out scoundrel so he was delighted to be able to give Henry the full particulars of the trust and invite Elizabeth to send him her direction and instructions. Somerville thought she could live quite comfortably, if modestly, on what she was left. Henry, of course, did not tell him the full story, but let him continue on in the belief that she is residing with friends, which she is, friends who care a great deal for her welfare." Julian leaned forward to take Helen's hand in his and give her the smile that turned her bones to water.

Those bones had been water since the miracle of the night before. Who would have guessed that her body could give her so much pleasure, could give him so much pleasure, if the gleam in his eyes were any indication. She had lain in bed the next morning reliving every touch, every caress, every look, scarcely believing that such a miraculous thing had happened to her. Rigidly controlled Helen Gerrard, who never had a hair out of place, was lying naked, tangled in sheets, her hair spread wildly across the pillows daydreaming. She never daydreamed. And now, she could see from his quizzical look that she was daydreaming again. "Er, yes, thank you for telling me." Heat rose in her cheeks as she saw that he knew exactly what she was thinking.

"Well, as to that," he leaned forward to press a blistering kiss on her lips, "more of *that* later, but now, my love, let me say my piece, plead my case, as it were, before I lose my nerve. You are a formidable woman, you know, Helen Gerrard."

She chuckled and shook her head.

"And I know I have no right to disrupt your life, but you have disrupted mine—in the best possible way, of course. First, as to Elizabeth, she can now provide for herself, but from what you say about her, it sounds as though she will want some employment for her mind and energy. Having seen my aunt's village school, I was wondering if we might create one for Elizabeth to run."

"Precisely what I was thinking myself when I was introduced to Miss Worthington," Helen replied with a triumphant smile. "Some place in or near Kettering where Dora knows so many people..."

"...and my family, irresponsible though it has been in the recent past, has some influence."

"But speaking of Dora," his face grew serious, "Could she run Mrs. Gerrard's for you, if... if...," a tinge of red stained his cheekbones. "If we were to marry? I know it's a great deal to ask of you, and her, but I do want to share life with you, and, well..."

Helen's first thought was *No!* but as she digested it, her second was *What a dear man.* Any other man would assume, would demand that she close Mrs. Gerrard's and end it and the taint it would give to his illustrious name, but no, he was merely asking her if she could find someone to manage it so they could spend their time together. "I don't think so. Of course she is capable of managing it all, the accounts, the running of the household—she does that now—but when I asked her to oversee the drawing room while I was away visiting this week, she was decidedly nervous. Besides, her dream is to bring back her father's inn in Kettering, and having encouraged Juliette and Grace to follow their dreams, I can hardly deny Dora hers. I also have a suspicion that she and Mr. Sandys are close to reaching an understanding, which I would also be loath to disrupt."

Julian saw her point and his heart sank. Dora was charming, Dora was beautiful, Dora was ebullient, but she lacked Helen's sardonic elegance which set the tone for the entire place. As a regal hostess and businesswoman who saw everything, knew everything and everyone, Helen Gerrard was without peer. No one could replace her. "There is no one," he sighed. "I understand."

The sadness in his eyes was more than Helen could bear. "But we do have one another."

"Helen, I don't want you just to make love to you—not that I don't, all the time and forever—I want to share with you our dream of helping women, I want to live together in a house in town so I can attend to my career in law and you can continue rescuing the unfortunates who come to London thinking they can reclaim their ruined lives. And I want a villa someplace nearby—Richmond or Twickenham—where we can enjoy the delights of the countryside. Linton Hall I leave to my sister-in-law to do with as she pleases."

"But," Helen broke in, "not to put too fine a point on it, you are an earl, you know."

"Yes, to my sorrow. Life would be so much simpler if I weren't, though now that I am, I plan to use all that awe in which the rest of the world seems to hold such titles to do good. But why do you bring that up?"

"Well, you must have an heir, and to have an heir, you must have a young wife of impeccable background, young being rather more important than impeccable."

He leaned forward to clasp her hands, looking at her with an intensity that gave even fearless Helen Gerrard pause. "I do not care! I do not care about my heritage, which, as far as I have experienced it, was miserable. I only want you. As for the title and the estates, my second cousin-once-removed, Gerald is welcome to them when I stick my spoon in the wall."

"I want you and I want to start schools like my Aunt Honoria's all over the countryside together. I want Annie Bentley to keep training servants who can then work for a time for us or Aunt Honoria so they have such impressive references from Lady Standiford or the Countess of Linton that families will be clamoring for those who have worked at those exclusive impeccably run establishments, establishments that set the standards for all others."

The passion in his voice and the light in his eyes was undeniable, and oh how she wanted to share in that vision of the future, but Helen's own carefully realistic view of life kept her from dreaming that dream, in spite of her temptation to do so.

"I am running away with myself, aren't I?" He smiled ruefully, settling back against the squabs of the carriage. "But I have never felt so sure of anything, never wanted anything so much for myself, or for you, in my life. Now I have done. I have said my piece and I will stop badgering you. It is another fine day, let us admire the countryside and speak of trifling things."

She was grateful to him for refraining to press her further, for recognizing and respecting her responsibilities and her reservations, but the more Helen considered it, the more amazing it was that the only obstacles he saw were obstacles for her, the worries about her establishment and all those whose welfare depended on her, and, possibly, her unwillingness to give up her independence and control rather than the social risk he would be taking on by linking his name with that of a woman whose reputation had not only been ruined years ago, but who owned and ran a bawdy house. Even more astounding than that, he had not once so much hinted that she get rid of said bawdy house, merely hoping that she could find the right person to manage it for her. What a man he was, what a truly remarkable man, and she loved him so.

Chapter 33

That love was immediately apparent to Dora the moment she welcomed her employer back to St. James' Square. Having seen the carriage drive into the square from the drawing room where she had been listening to Clarissa practicing the latest lesson Randall had given her, Dora arranged to be in the hall with Fenwick when the carriage drew up.

Dora saw the glow in Helen's face as she smiled at Julian when she descended from the carriage. Dora also saw the tenderness in the way Julian held out his hand, helped her down, and bent over her as they climbed the steps together. *Now we are in the basket!* But Dora kept that thought to herself and smiled widely as she greeted the travelers. She would worry about the implications of it all later; for the time being, she was just happy for the two of them, and she was not about to let on that she knew what was happening. She would keep her counsel until it was requested, like the good friend she was.

The Reverend Lord John Claverton, however, was not about to be so circumspect. The minute he and Helen were alone in her office after Sunday services, he broached the subject. "I gather you have discovered the difference between your friendship with me and your friendship with Lord Linton," he began as he accepted the cup of tea she held out to him.

The color rose in her cheeks. "You are supposed to be a man of God, my lord, not the Devil Incarnate. Only someone well versed in the dark arts could have that kind of knowledge."

"Or insight. As the shepherd of my flock, I see it as my responsibility to understand the deepest hopes and fears of all my parishioners, and I see both hope and fear in your face. I also see an aura of happiness about you, so why the fear? As a minister of the faith that promotes love among mankind, I applaud the happiness. It *is* love, is it not?"

"Yes," she nodded, blushing even more furiously. "It is, but he has asked me to marry him again."

"The right and proper way of things. A good man and a good woman joined together in holy matrimony? I fail to see the difficulty." The blue eyes scanned her face. He frowned. Troubled by the anxiety and uncertainty there.

"I cannot marry. I have responsibilities here, all these people who depend on me."

"I see." He grew thoughtful. "And there is no one who can take over for you? While it is true that no one can compare to you, surely someone can . . ."

"They all have their own dreams. I cannot ask them to give them up or take them away."

"But you too have a right to your dream, a dream of sharing life with the man you love."

"That is a dream now, but I have already had my dream. This," she gestured to the room around her. "This was my dream. Mrs. Gerrard's was my dream."

"And a noble one it was. to help so many women achieve theirs." He set down his cup and rose to go. "I have sick parishioners to visit, but I will think on this. There must be a way to bring this happiness to both of you. Lord Linton is a good man; he too deserves to have you fulfill his dreams."

Helen sat staring into space a good long time after he had left. Returning to St. James' Square had not felt like the coming home it had always been before. Yes, she was among her dearest friends, but looking into their faces as they welcomed her back did not make her heart sing or her bones melt the way a special smile and tenderness lighting the eyes that focused only on her did. And when she crawled into bed at night, what had been blessed peace was now loneliness and aching desire for strong arms and lips and hands that set her body on fire.

She had grown accustomed to being with Julian all day, every day, talking, laughing, teasing, and at night . . . all night. Nothing would ever equal the joy of waking up in his arms, and the thought that she could never have that again tore her apart. This was not a love between a lover and his mistress. This was a love between a man and his wife, and if they could not have that, they would have nothing at all.

Dora watched in some concern as her friend and employer lost the rosy glow of happiness, growing quieter and more serious by the day. Helen no longer had that spark of defiance and confidence that was so inspiring to all of them. At last she could stand it no longer. "Out with it," Dora marched into Helen's office a little over a week after Helen's return. "Did you not have a good time? Was Lady Standiford not a pleasant hostess?"

"She was all that was warm and welcoming." Helen smiled at the memories. "You would not credit how much we resemble one another, practically mirror images. And we see eye-to-eye on a great many things."

"Then did you not have an enjoyable time?"

"A most enjoyable time. We did ever so many things—rode, visited her school, walked by the seashore, called on Annie Bentley, who is flourishing, by the way, and making a life out of rescuing unfortunates and training them to be superior servants."

"But?"

"But nothing."

"But Lord Linton. I saw the way he looked at you when he brought you home. He loves you, but you haven't seen him since then."

"Yes, he loves me." Helen sighed. "He loves me too much to make me uncomfortable by pressing to see me."

Dora's eyebrows rose.

"He wants to marry me."

The eyebrows rose higher. "And that does not make you happy?"

"I cannot. I cannot leave this place. You, yourself said there is no one else to run it. I know, you can run the household; you do run the household, but you know . . . be the hostess and . . ."

"And so much more, all you do to give the place its tone, it's cachet." Dora's eyes were warm with sympathy.

There was a knock on the door and Tom Sandys entered bearing a travel-stained letter on a silver salver. "It's from our Miss Grace, ma'am, er Lady Maximilian Hawkesbury, that is. I thought you would want to see it directly."

"Thank you." Helen took the letter and gestured to the chair next to Dora. "I am sure you want to hear the news as well." She unsealed it. "Oh, she has left Milan and is now living in Turin at the Residence with his lordship because . . . because she has been hired by the Teatro Regio as one of their principal opera singers!"

"Hooray!" Dora clapped and Tom beamed. "That is wonderful news."

"I must go tell Olivia immediately. She will be so pleased. No, don't bother to call the carriage," she waved Tom off as he rose to do her bidding, "I shall walk. It is a lovely day and the news gives me new energy. I shall just get my bonnet and gloves."

Olivia! Helen thought as she tied the bow on her bonnet, buttoned her pelisse, and pulled on her gloves. "Olivia!" she repeated out loud as she headed towards Piccadilly. "Yes, Olivia. Perfect." She lifted the knocker at the slim house in Golden Square.

The actress was delighted to see her, and even more delighted at Grace's good news. "What an honor, not that she does not deserve it, what with her talent and hard work, but still, for an English singer to win a position at an opera house on the Continent, an Italian opera house at that, is beyond wonderful. But do sit down. I shall ring for tea."

"Please do. We are both going to need it, for I have a proposal to make."

"A proposal?"

"Yes. You *did* mention retiring from the stage, did you not?"

"I did."

"But you would still like something useful to occupy your time, wouldn't you?"

"I would."

"Then what would you say to becoming the new mistress of Mrs. Gerrard's?"

There was a long silence, then Olivia smiled a slow, sly smile. "I take it you have received a superior offer and need someone to take your place—not that anyone ever could, but someone to carry on what you have started."

"And who better than you who rescued Juliette, Grace, and Annie and sent them to me?"

The smile grew broader. "Who indeed? I think I might enjoy that very much. And you, I take it, will be a constant visitor, but your time will be much taken up as Lady Linton?" She laughed at Helen's shock. "Come now, my dear, you are known for your omniscience, but there are others who do have eyes in their heads."

"I will have to check with Dora and the rest, you understand," Helen said some time later as she bid her hostess goodbye.

"Of course. But I am sure they will be as delighted as I that clever Helen, as always, has found a solution."

Dora nodded slowly, thoughtfully as Helen explained her idea later that afternoon. "Yes, that might work." She tilted her head, considering. "Yes, I think that will work very well." And then, rising to give Helen a quick hug, "I am so happy for you, and I hope you tell the others soon because they will be asking me what I keep smiling about."

Helen did tell the others, one by one, and though they were sad at the thought of losing her, they were glad that Olivia would be there so Helen could follow her own dream as they would follow theirs someday.

All that remained was to tell Julian. Gathering her courage the next morning, Helen called in Essex Court.

"Yes he is here, ma'am," Ben greeted her at the entrance to Julian's chambers. "I shall just let him know you are here."

"Mrs. Gerrard to see you, my lord."

Helen could see through the open door as he sat at his desk staring down at something in front of him, something that was quickly whisked into the drawer when she was announced. Hmmmm.

"Helen!" His face lit up at the sight of her, but he approached cautiously, tentatively. "I trust there is nothing amiss?"

"No, nothing amiss. At least I don't think so, that is if you have not had second thoughts about our discussion in the carriage."

"Second thoughts, third thoughts . . ."

Helen's heart fell and it must have shown in her face for he hurried around the desk to take her in his arms. "Second thoughts, third thoughts, I can think of nothing but you. Here," he leaned over the desk to reach in the partially closed drawer, "if you don't believe me . . ." he pulled out a picture, a silhouette of her. "I asked Annie Bentley to make me one so I would always have you with me, no matter what you said."

"Oh Julian!" She tipped her face up to his as he swept her into his arms and kissed her until she was breathless. "I say yes."

He let out a whoop. "You do? Are you sure? I do not want to be just another person you rescued, though you have rescued me from an empty life, purposeful, but empty until you came into it."

"I'm sure."

"Then let me show you how much I love you, my wife-to-be." And he shut the door and locked it.

Epilogue

The small chapel at Standiford Hall was full to bursting. Once again, as Olivia Childs had pointed out at Grace's wedding, a member of Mrs. Gerrard's establishment, having followed a dream of her own and launched a career, was marrying a peer. *Three peers in three years.* Olivia smiled to herself as she turned, looking over the heads of Lady Standiford and assembled Clavertons, Annie Bentley, Dora, Clarissa, and Elizabeth Mountjoy, to catch the first glimpse of the bride. And there she was, radiant, in a glamorous creation from Maison Juliette, her arm through the Marquess of Wrothingham's as she waited to walk down the aisle.

Once again Freddy was giving away one of the ladies of Mrs. Gerrard's.

"Poor Freddy, *always the bridesmaid, never the bride,*" Helen teased.

"Thanks to your husband-to-be, for which I shall be forever grateful." Freddy grinned down at her. "Dreadful as it is to say so, the Clavertons are absolutely flourishing without the Harcourts."

"You may be as dreadful as you like in my presence, you know."

He grew serious. "Yes, I know. You and everyone in Mrs. Gerrard' have not only let me be who I am, but welcomed and encouraged it. You see, it is not only your ladies who owe you a great debt of gratitude, so do I. But I believe you have someone waiting for you at the altar, Mrs. Gerrard. And so is my brother, ready to join you two in holy matrimony."

Randall, who along with Lord Rushbrooke, had accompanied the soon-to-be Dowager Countess of Linton and her daughter, pressed his hands to the keys of the ancient organ and glorious music filled the chapel as Freddy led Helen past the smiling faces of so many whose lives she had transformed. And now, a bubble of happiness rose within her as she saw Julian, standing next to the

Reverend Lord John Claverton, beaming at her, her life was about to be transformed as well.

Julian was taking her to Paris for their honeymoon and then Turin, to hear a certain singer perform while Freddy and Dora had been instructed to find the perfect house for them not more than a pleasant walk from St. James' Square, after making sure, of course, to establish the true identity of the owner of the freehold.

And as Helen walked back down the aisle on husband's arm, she caught the eye of Lady Standiford, or *Aunt Honoria,* now her own *Aunt Honoria* too, as she dabbed at happy tears with a lace handkerchief. Helen remained inordinately proud of the independence she had claimed for herself, but it did feel truly wonderful to belong.

Even before studying eighteenth-century literature in graduate school, Evelyn Richardson decided she would have preferred to have lived in England between 1775 and 1830. Now living outside of Boston, she enjoys access to the primary sources that allow her to explore the details of the period and immerse herself in the same journals her heroines enjoyed which for her, as a longtime reference librarian, is the best of all possible worlds.

www.ingramcontent.com/pod-product-compliance
Lightning Source LLC
LaVergne TN
LVHW032010070526
838202LV00059B/6372